Snowstorms in a Hot Climate

Snowstorms in a Hot Climate

Sarah Dunant

WHEELER
WINDSOR
PARAGON

This Large Print edition is published by Wheeler Publishing, Waterville, Maine USA and by BBC Audiobooks Ltd, Bath, England.

Published in 2006 in the U.S. by arrangement with Gillon Aitken Associates.

Published in 2006 in the U.K. by arrangement with Time Warner Book Group UK.

U.S.   Softcover   1-59722-245-3   (Softcover)
U.K.   Hardcover   10: 1 4056 1468 4   (Windsor Large Print)
U.K.   Hardcover   13: 978 1 405 61468 8
U.K.   Softcover   10: 1 4056 1469 2   (Paragon Large Print)
U.K.   Softcover   13: 978 1 405 61469 6

This is a work of fiction. Names, characters, places, and incidents are the products of the author's imagination or are used fictitiously. Any resemblance to actual events, locales, or persons, living or dead, is entirely coincidental.

The text of this Large Print edition is unabridged.
Other aspects of the book may vary from the original edition.

Set in 16 pt. Plantin by Al Chase.

Printed in the United States on permanent paper.

British Library Cataloguing-in-Publication Data available

Library of Congress Cataloging-in-Publication Data

Dunant, Sarah.
    Snowstorms in a hot climate / by Sarah Dunant.
      p. cm.
    ISBN 1-59722-245-3 (lg. print : sc : alk. paper)
    1. Women college teachers — Fiction.   2. Smuggling — Colombia — Fiction.   3. Psychological fiction.   4. Large type books.   I. Title.
PR6054.U45756S66 2006
    823'.914—dc22   2006005749

For Margot

PART ONE

the truth . . .

One

London 1985

I was happy that day because I was leaving and I like departures. I understand why some people find them untidy, emotional affairs, but I have always had a hankering after them. That is one thing Elly and I have in common. I find airports the best places to leave from. Of course they have none of the romance of railway stations — no clinging good-byes framed in billowing steam, no last-minute touches through half-opened windows, no nineteenth-century echoes to gild the going. No, airports are altogether more anesthetized points of dispatch, conceived and constructed for efficiency, not grace. But then that is what gives them their power, what makes them so exhilarating. Because from the moment those automatic doors glide apart to welcome you inside, nothing, as far as I can see, need ever be the same again. However bad you are feeling, however caught in the quicksand of failed chances and repeating patterns, airports are the new horizon, the conveyor belt of travel, which in due course will disgorge you in some exotic location where you will be happy, fulfilled, or at the very least, different. Such were my fantasies in the departure lounge of Heathrow Airport on that last Thursday in July.

The preliminaries were over. I had arrived out of the heartland of the city alone, struggling with my own cases, anonymous. I had had my ticket torn, my baggage checked, and my name punched into the computer. I had taken the habitual last walk around the outer compound, bought a clutch of glossy magazines, and then, leaving my last handful of small change on the counter, I had sauntered through Immigration to the world beyond. In the flight departure lounge the BA 177 boarding light was already flashing, winking adventure. On the other side of the ocean Elly was waiting for me. The journey had begun.

Of course it is all fallacy, the romance just a creation of admen and soft-porn merchants. Travel changes nothing except the location. And whoever met anyone remotely interesting on a plane? There was an Egyptian woman I sat next to on a flight from Cairo to Paris once. She had silver hair and sleek features like Nefertiti. But she slept the whole way from takeoff to touchdown, and when she did finally open her magnificent almond eyes, it turned out she didn't speak a word of English. And as for the myth of erotica in the water closet — well, whoever believed that story anyway?

Not me. And certainly not now. Herded in through the giant metal tube, I discovered this particular DC-10 filled with ordinary earthbound people. I ignored them all and barricaded myself into my window seat, content to keep my own company for the next seven hours.

Outside the aircraft the tarmac shimmered in the heat daze of the engines. I pushed my nose against the reinforced glass and thought of London. Six-ten P.M. Ten million people going home. The Northern Line at rush hour: just another carcass in the truck, the smells of sweat and cheap perfume amid flapping newsprint.

At Camden Town I stand at the top of the escalator and watch myself ride up toward me, face set, shutters drawn. A dissolve to the key in the lock, followed by the unholy silence of a house where everything is exactly as I left it. The plants, perhaps, have grown imperceptibly; the flowers have drooped a fraction. I pour myself a drink and sit waiting for the tension to subside. And I congratulate myself on another day

11

beaten into submission. I consider the people I could call, except, of course, I know I never will. In the end I eat an apple, lie on the sofa, and read a book on Icelandic myths. And every day a thousand planes take off, heading in a thousand different directions. All it takes is the doing.

Back inside the bird I caught a glimpse of a man making his way down the aisle. Something to look at. Tall, slender body; a storm of fair hair and chiseled features; the kind of bone structure that turns women into willing wives and men into homosexuals. My eyes flickered and passed on. Such gourmet dishes are not for me. They are too rich, and I do not have the table manners. Anyway, on the evolutionary scale I have always found handsome princes too close to frogs for comfort. The fairy tale brought Elly to my mind; small, sparkling Elly, whose face had almost become a blur in my memory. And I wondered for the umpteenth time since her letter dropped onto my stairwell whether we would actually recognize each other over the airport barrier, or if somehow two years and transatlantic separation would have changed the contours of us both. Parrot fashion I recalled the words of her leaving: Elly curled in a wicker chair, frowning across at me on that day she bought her ticket for Mexico.

"I didn't want to tell you until I had decided. You mustn't be upset, all right? I'll miss you, you know that, but I just have to get out for a while. Be a stranger, unconnected. It's not permanent. Just a trip — a short walk in the Americas. Six months, a year at most, and I'll be home . . ."

And then I remembered the shadows in her letter, the small cramped writing, as if someone had pushed her into a corner and was blocking her way to the door. And as the engines of the DC-10 roared skyward, I wondered about the time in between.

Once we were airborne, with London miniaturizing beneath us, smart stewardesses in multicolored aprons started loading up the drinks trolleys. Once they began their trundling passage forward there would be no escape till they had passed. On the aisle seat a corn-fed American in a checked jacket was already settled into a Mickey Spillane. He grunted as I squeezed past him. A man in tune with his fiction. There would be violence before I returned. In the loo I bolted myself in and, as the light snapped on, turned to face the mirror.

Maybe now is the time for you to see what I look like. I will use only solid, simple words. That way you won't be seduced by

13

novelistic adjectives. I am tall and have big bones. I was told by my grandmother that I am the proof of the peasant stock in the family. My great-grandfather, it appears, was a delicate, slender aristocrat who was called out to India to serve the French Raj in Pondicherry and went looking for a sturdy woman who would bear heat and children with equal equanimity. He came upon a country girl from Toulouse with rippling long fair hair and big muscles. She gave him eight children in quick succession and then died of smallpox. My grandmother has a lock of her hair in a casket she keeps by her bed. I am, it seems, her physical, if not her spiritual, heir. Except for one thing. She was beautiful and I am not. I am what I think is called "heavy featured." My mouth is too large and my nose too prominent. My eyes are all right, but since they are the mirror to the soul, I have got into the habit of keeping them half closed. You can't be too careful.

On my way back to my seat I passed Mr. Magnificent. He was sitting in the first row of Club Class, long legs encased in smart soft leather boots stretched out in front of him. I followed the feet upward. Expensive trousers, tailored shirt, and the shower of golden hair over the sculptured rock of his face. Why are people so attracted to beauty?

14

There is no real reason why good-looking lovers should be any better in bed. Except perhaps that they get more practice. This particular specimen was clearly aware of his charisma. I disliked him instinctively. He was drinking a large Bloody Mary, playing carelessly with the cocktail stirrer in the glass, while flicking through a magazine on his lap. Next to him on an empty seat lay a book, cover upward. *The Meeting at Telgte* by Günter Grass. His taste surprised me.

Back with the plebeians, Mickey Spillane was making to play for real life. He had moved to the center block and was talking animatedly to the well-dressed woman sitting next to him. They both had drinks. He had already eaten his peanuts. I chased the moving trolley and came back with a plastic glass full of ice and a hoard of three bottles of Scotch. The first taste of whiskey over ice was hot and cold at the same time. It brought back images of America: dimly lit bars with country and western on the jukebox and pool tables covered in green baize under low-slung lamps.

I took another sip and settled back into my seat. Outside there was a vast skyscape, pure blue over snow-white clouds. England had gone. I invited Queen Aethelflaed, daughter of Alfred, to look over my shoulder across the ocean of cloud. She was one of the lesser-known heroines of Anglo-Saxon England; I had written my thesis on her and occasionally still kept in touch, just to see how Anglo-Saxon intelligence might respond to twentieth-century wonders. At this altitude she would probably have expected to see God. I screwed up my eyes and fantasized a host of chubby cherubim, poking their heads out of the clouds. A landscape of divinity. Do people have revelations on aircraft? And has the rate increased since the booze became free? Aethelflaed, bored by the lack of marauding armies to conquer, faded back into history. I opened my second bottle and waited for a visitation.

Later, as the sky turned crimson, the button-bright hostess brought dinner. I pushed a few carrots around the plastic plate but left the dead chicken as votive offering to Thor, just in case of thunderbolts. On the stereo I plugged into Handel's oratorio. Coffee came and went. I had a brandy and wondered if I was drunk enough to sleep. I closed my eyes, but Elly's letter was burning a hole in the bottom of my bag. The compulsion to reread what I already knew by heart was overwhelming.

Not here, not rubbing spaces with so many other people. I clambered out of my seat, realizing as I stood up that the alcohol had, after all, had some effect. In the loo my face looked significantly more yellow under the strip lighting. It seemed too early in the trip to have contracted hepatitis. It must be the booze. I sat down on the toilet seat and, from the inner recesses of my bag, dug out the crumpled airmail envelope. Elly, in trouble.

Dear Marla,

The floor is littered with paper. This is the sixth attempt. How do you start after so much silence? Especially between us? Not at the beginning, that's for sure. It would take a book. I'll go for the middle and let you do the interpreting. You always were good at that. A historian's training.

First I'll say the words. I'm sorry. There. Christ, it sounds paltry, doesn't it? But I swear it's true. We never were the greatest of letter writers, were we? But at least you made the effort. Not like me. Of course I've got excuses . . . I was never in one place long enough; too much was happening, some of which wasn't mine to tell: and then, just at the time when I thought I was settled everything started to break apart and kept on

17

breaking. Stupid I know, but that's how it was.

It wasn't that I didn't need you. I almost came to London once, just to talk to you. I even called your number one night, but you were out. Then I got cold feet. Took a plane somewhere else and talked to a mirror for four weeks instead. No substitute. Shit. I knew this letter wouldn't stay on course. I'll just get to the point, OK? I want you to come to America. For a visit. Now. This is always the time of year when you traditionally suffer the blues. Term has ended, another batch of students has left. Remember how old it used to make you feel? Wouldn't a trip to the land of milk and honey help? And I want to see you. So badly. There. It's out. I wanted to say it right at the beginning, but I was frightened it might scare you off. I need some help, Marla, and you're the only one I can ask for it. I know I don't deserve it. But I'm asking anyway.

Listen, I know this letter makes me sound like a space case. But I just want you to know that I miss you, and that I've never stopped loving you, even if I did stop showing it for a while. Remember what we always said about how

18

lovers are for sometimes, but friends are for always? Well, I think I've really learned what that means now. I don't deserve it, but if you still feel that way too, then please come. Just cable me the flight number and I'll meet the plane. Any time.

Your best friend still?

So much love.
Elly.x

P.S. Don't worry about money. You don't pay for anything. That's part of the deal.

It read like she spoke. Maybe that was what made it so raw: more than anything she said, it was the sound of her voice again after so long. I folded the letter carefully and slid it back into the envelope. Next to it sat a battered postcard. I didn't need to read that to know what it said. On the front was a picture of a sunset over a coral reef. On the back the words

San Andrés is here. Wish you were wonderful. Too much to tell and no time to tell it in. On my way to the Big Apple. Happy. Will write. Soon. Love Elly.

Soon. Since then there had been a Christmas card and a bunch of flowers three days after my birthday. No words at all. What could it be that took so long to tell? I think I knew even then it had to be a man.

Back in the cabin I found myself another seat, further away from the screen, and waited for New York and the end of the beginning.

Two

Of course I recognized her immediately. Even in the crush of the arrivals lounge her smallness stood out against the crowd. Yet if she was the same she was also changed. I knew that instantly too. Her hair was shorter, cropped and spiky with flashes of red amid the brown. But it was more than that. We stood facing each other grinning like idiots, transfixed.

"My God, it's really you," she said at last, and suddenly we were caught in a clumsy, clutching embrace. It was then I understood part of the change. She was too thin. The baggy summer trousers and loose jacket disguised the lack of flesh. It was like holding an adolescent girl. I could feel the contours of her rib cage pushing through the cotton top. She broke away from me, still smiling. I noticed the beginning of filigree line work around the eyes, and the slight bruising of shadows beneath them. I had always known she would age well, but the fragility surprised me. There was still a glow about her, but I detected a tension that had not been there before, a new way of holding her body against the air. Did she see all this when she looked in the mirror, or had it been too gradual? Maybe it was I who was overreacting. God knows what differences she saw in me.

"You look great," she said breathlessly. "Whatever you've been doing it suits you."

There was just a touch of America in her voice. I liked it, even though it reminded me of how long it had been.

"You've cut your hair," I said, because it seemed easier than anything else.

"And you've grown yours."

Another pause. She had always been better than I in social circumstances. She took me by the arm. "No more talk till we get out of here, right? The car's outside. I've left it on a quadruple yellow line, and there are armies of cops and tow trucks all around."

She reached down for my suitcase and began pulling it toward the door. I picked up the other side, and together we made a lopsided exit through the doors into a full-blown East Coast twilight.

Being outside was about as pleasant as having a sack pulled over your head. The air was so heavy that it seemed to clog up your nostrils, as if it was almost too damp to breathe. Maybe all the oxygen had already been used up by the people who had breathed it before. Summer in New York. How could anyone imagine touching in this heat, let alone being intimate? Had the birthrate been seasonal until the invention of air-conditioning? Elly seemed oblivious of the imminent suffocation.

The car turned out to be a Cadillac which would have been new around the time of *American Graffiti.* It wore its experience well, as if it were under the impression it was something of a collector's item. For all I knew about cars it could well have been. For all Elly knew either. Either she had learned or someone had done her buying for her.

Inside I pulled on my seat belt. She waited for me to finish.

"So," she said gaily, hands on the wheel. "Where do you want to go?"

"How about home?"

"Which one? I'm afraid you have a choice." She made a face. "I'm sorry. I did try to warn you in the letter, but I probably didn't put it right."

I swallowed my surprise. "What are you offering?"

"An apartment in Manhattan or a house in Westchester."

23

The mystery needed to be kept in scale. Neil Simon rather than Great Gatsby. "Manhattan, I think."

"Good. I thought you would."

From behind us, twenty yards down the concourse, came the shriek of a police whistle, followed by a bulky cop, waving his arms in exaggerated fury. Elly rolled down her window and gave him what might have passed for a West Point salute. We moved off in search of the city.

Later, on the terrace, we sat and watched the night move. I had left English time behind, blasted it away in a jet-stream shower: the power of water pressure, as American as apple pie and long-range missiles. Out of the bathroom I wrapped myself in a robe, picked up the glass of bourbon waiting for me on the bedside table, and together, the liquor and I went in search if Elly.

We found her in a large canvas chair on the terrace, an urban lookout post fringed with window boxes filled with geraniums and facing out over a dark mass of trees. Central Park and exclusive real estate. New Yorkers pay for greenery like Arabs pay for water. I wondered what the Westchester house looked like. Behind us, through tall

French windows, was a spacious sitting room lined with bookcases and the odd, exclusive Chinese print. On the floor, a huge rug on polished boards and four powerful speakers. Planned elegance. Hardly consistent with the Elly I once knew, full of chaos and good intentions.

The hum of the city moved up in hot airstreams toward us. We sat cloaked in heat, the night bringing scant relief. I poked my ice cubes down into the golden brown liquid and watched as the water and the liquor merged to form oily patterns on the surface.

I looked at her. In the darkness she was more like the Elly I remembered. Her new angularity was subdued, rubbed soft by night shadows. I stretched out my legs and felt again how large my body was in comparison with hers. The familiarity of the feeling gave me a strange pleasure. If the night had not been so charged with questions, it might almost have been two years ago. There was silence. It didn't bother me. Patience is a virtue I am familiar with. She screwed up her face into a half smile, half grimace. It was a gesture I knew very well.

"I'm not sure I know where to begin," she said at last. "It all seems so long ago."

"How about Colombia, seventeen

months ago? The last time I heard from you was a letter from an unpronounceable place somewhere near the Ecuador border. I had to look it up on a map to find it. You had just had your money and passport stolen, and you were going to Bogotá to get things sorted out."

She looked at me hopefully, as if she thought I might continue, tell it for her. What was it that could be so hard to say?

I helped. "Come on, Elly Cameron. I just mortgaged my summer vacation on the promise of a good fairy tale. If you make it riveting enough, it might even conquer my jet lag."

She stared down at her hands, then out into the night. Then she began.

Three

Well, at first I was just freaked out. I'd already spent a month in Colombia, traveling with my valuables more or less sewn to my skin. Everywhere you went you heard horror stories. It seemed the whole national economy was based on the rip-off. Looking back on it, I think I'd been in a state of perpetual tension right from the moment I'd stepped off the plane in Cartagena Airport. So, when it actually happened, when I got back to my room after the shower and found the door prized open and my money belt with passport, traveler's checks, and tickets gone, I think I was almost relieved that I didn't have to worry about the possibility anymore. Except, of course, I knew then that I would have to go to Bogotá. The armpit of the world — that's what people called it, although those who had been to Panama City would spend hours arguing the respective horrors of the two capitals. I had vowed never to go near it. Instead I'd done this amazing trip, skidding along the western edge of the country, through crumpled mountain ranges, lost valleys, and small, friendly cities. I had even got to feel quite safe by Colombian standards. Confident even. You know what they say about pride . . . well, the place I fell to was Bogotá.

Of course, there wasn't any point wingeing. I had no option. I couldn't cross borders without a passport; I couldn't eat without money; and Bogotá was the only place with a consulate and an American Express office. So I started the grinding journey back up onto the central plain — four days of mountain climbing in the back of diesel buses belching smoke and fumes. When I wasn't on the road I was sleeping. I think I sent you the postcard from Popayán. I can't remember anymore. Just like in the movies, all the towns were beginning to look the same by then.

I finally reached Bogotá late one night, after a stomach-churning eleven-hour bus ride that the ticket seller had sworn would take only eight. Even so I remember that when we actually arrived I didn't want to get out of the bus. Now I come to think about it, I can't imagine what I was frightened of. I had nothing left to lose. But that long climb down from the hills toward the carpet of lights on the valley floor had given me enough time to start worrying, regardless of reason.

When I did finally screw up my courage, haul out my rucksack, and step into the mudscape, a dozen taxi drivers instantly assaulted me. I picked the least murderous looking and gave him the name of a cheap hotel someone had recommended from the *South American Handbook.*

The city seemed to go on forever. Miles and miles of slum suburbia. Houses made up of corrugated iron and cardboard. Maybe it was simply the scale that made it so devastating. God knows, I'd seen enough poverty before, just never in such massive doses. The hotel was on the outskirts of the inner city, houses shuttered up and no streetlights. When I got there it turned out they had only a double room. I took it anyway. It was cold, and I had to go to bed with my clothes on and the blankets wrapped around me. I was too tired even to be anxious.

Next day I started reconstructing my life. The consulate was sympathetic but philosophical. It can't have been the most glamorous job in the world, making endless records of hard-luck tales. There were five other people waiting the morning I went. The rip-off stories were more or less clever, more or less painful. Some people had lost everything but the clothes they stood up in. One guy had lost even that, trusting his bag to a Colombian "friend" while he went swimming. I felt sorry for him really, but he was such a wimp. He was flying home as soon as he could arrange passage and passport.

As for me? Well, the normal wait was two, maybe three weeks. Cables had to be sent, facts checked — the usual bureaucracy. The money was easy. Just like the adverts; American Express refunded within two days, although, of course, having no passport to back up the checks caused its own hassles. Still, Bogotá coped. It was a city that had grown used to that particular problem.

Passport, money, and airline ticket inquiries took most of the first week. When I was not in smart downtown offices waiting to see someone or other, I was in the hotel. With the exception of a quick gawp at the Gold Museum, I did no joyriding. I had no wish to discover Bogotá. I remember thinking at the time that I lived rather like a small animal. I would go only where the predators were the same size as me, and I did not stray into alien territory. It wasn't just my paranoia. The first day I left the hotel the lady of the house (she was a surrogate mother to all of her "guests") made frantic signs for me to take off my watch. *"No salgas con reloj. Es Malo. Malo,"* she twittered excitedly. *"Te lo van a robar."* In the downstairs common room where the travelers congregated, the favorite topic was Bogotá horrors. One girl had her spectacles lifted off her nose as she walked down the street, while another had lost an earring. She had pierced ears and carried a bloody lobe to prove it. In the hierarchy of rip-offs, she was undisputed queen. I was insignificantly low down and determined to stay there.

Maybe my lack of courage was symptomatic. I was feeling out of joint in all kinds of ways. Maybe I'd just been on the road too long. You know what traveling is like. Your only pasts and futures are names on a map, and the theft had suddenly swept away what little sense of purpose I had. I wasn't ready to come home yet, but I didn't know where else to go. Also I was tired of being on my own. An excuse, I know, but it doesn't mean there isn't any truth in it. Latin America isn't easy for a woman traveling alone. It was my choice all right, but it took energy. Of course, there had been opportunities to change my status, and there'd been a fair number of encounters on the road

31

from Tijuana to Bogotá. I'd met a great woman in Guatemala City who I would have traveled with, but she was going up while I was going down, and no one like her came along again. As for the men, well, that had its own pattern. A week here, a week there, always easy, always defined. That old on-the-road morality; fuck who you want when you want, and then move off, leaving no regrets behind. It's amazing how your taste can be muddied by the fact that this one you won't have to meet at the launderette or someone's dinner party six months from now. In the days before AIDS and herpes descended like some plague from a revengeful God, anything and everything was easy. Even afterward we still took risks in the pursuit of pleasure. And the Bogotá hotel at that time had a constant stream of unattached traveling males, many of whom were happy to be careless with their affections.

I was quite a desired object in those days. I'd been on the road for over a year. My street credibility was high. Like everything else on the trail, there was an accepted hierarchy to mating. For example, it was always a coup to lay someone who had made it down to Chile or Bolivia, although the real star fucks came with Tierra del Fuego. Another continent scored high too. In terms of women, I was something of a catch: alone, fairly sussed, and with a clutch of passport stamps as aphrodisiacs. Just like home, really, only with the power structures based on different rules.

Anyway, by the time I got to Bogotá I had begun to tire of it all. I was lonely and felt in need of some company, but I couldn't bring myself to go through the foreplay of travel itineraries. So I opted out. Stayed in my room and read Trollope and two Jane Austens that I'd traded in my copy of *One Hundred Years of Solitude* for. I remember I got very into the eroticism of innocence. I lay curled between cold sheets and worried for Emma and Mr. Knightley. And when the Frenchman on his way north from Chile made a careless, grubby pass at me, I longed for a world where ankles glimpsed under long dresses ignited more sexual passion than naked breasts. After a while people began to leave me alone. I got that "English girl" reputation, remember? It was really quite a change for me — woman of easy virtue led to redemption and chastity through the study of nineteenth-century literature.

My isolation made those weeks a little surreal. Another excuse? Maybe, I don't know anymore. I had planned to be out of Bogotá by Easter, had banked on it. Semana Santa, with its rumors of Catholic hysteria, was not something I wanted to be caught up in. But I underestimated the disruptive power of Christ's death on a Catholic bureaucracy. Banks, airlines, offices — everywhere — simply shut down for days. My passport came through on the Thursday before Good Friday. But when I tried to buy an airline ticket out, it was like late-night shopping on Christmas Eve. I stood in a queue for two hours and then they closed early and turned everyone away. I was so angry. I remember standing outside the shop, paralyzed with fury and frustration. Useless, of course. So I decided to take it easy on myself. If I was going to be stuck here, at least I could treat myself a little. I was downtown, in the shiny expensive part of the city, where the hotels ran on credit cards and expense accounts. I marched straight into the coffee shop of one of the grander ones, sat down, and ordered a shrimp salad. It cost three times my night's rent, but I didn't care. I was suddenly tired of slumming it, and I wanted to be somewhere else. With another class of travelers. And it was there, as I eked out each mouthful for maximum pleasure, that I first saw him. Lenny. The man of my dreams. Just sitting there, about five tables away from me, a copy of the *International Herald Tribune* in his hands. What can I tell you about that moment, Marla? Maybe it was his looks, or the way he was dressed. Maybe it was because he was more interested in the news than in the cheapest way to fly to Panama. Or maybe it really was a case of star-crossed chemistry — Mills & Boon at first sight. I don't know. It hardly matters anymore. Whatever it was, I noticed him.

And he noticed me too. As he flipped back his paper to call the waiter, he looked straight at me. And kept on looking. What did he see? I remember making this cold-blooded checklist of myself. Yeah, I looked OK. I was advert thin from subsistence food; I was brown from months of beach living; and I was not unconfident. I was also ready. And being Lenny, no doubt he saw that too. Anyway, we played eyes for a while; just the basic vocabulary of interest, but with a certain ceremony. It suited me well. It had been the ceremony I had been craving. I was, I realized, looking to be wooed. By the time I got to the last shrimp, courtship was progressing nicely. I would, I decided, let him make the move. It was then he got up and left. Just like that — folded his

35

newspaper on the table, called the waiter, signed the check, and staring me full in the face, got up and walked out. It was done with such style that I couldn't help but be impressed. Maybe if I'd been older or wiser I might have read it as a warning. Some people like to control. As it was, the adrenaline was pumping. I decided to shrug it off and settle for his newspaper instead. After all, it wasn't every day an *International Herald Tribune* came my way. I walked casually over to his table, picked it up, and carried it back to my seat. No one even registered the heist. Except him. Because as I sat down to read I suddenly spotted him, out through the window, standing on the sidewalk watching me. And as he caught my eye, he nodded and smiled. I snapped the paper up in front of my face, and when I looked again he was gone. But I had this sneaky feeling that the first round had gone to him. I should have realized then. What begins as a contest always ends as one too.

Good Friday arrived very early the next morning. I couldn't sleep. A damp Colombian mist had rolled in during the night, and the cold had woken me. I was up and out of the hotel well before eight A.M., even then the day had a different feel to it. I drank sweet milky coffee at the street stall on the corner, while the owner told me how this and Christmas were always the two quietest days of the year. It was true. The place was empty. As if everyone was indoors, waiting. He asked me if I was going to watch the procession. The hotel had been buzzing for days with talk of Semana Santa. Four months ago I had seen in the New Year in Puerto Vallarta in Mexico, in a vast church crammed with people, while outside beneath the stars the village square flowed with *aquardiente*. But that had been about birth, and this was death. It would be a spectacle indeed if the same energy was poured into mourning.

The procession was scheduled to begin just after noon. It would move through part of the city, climaxing in one of the biggest and most grandiose of Bogotá's churches. I idled my way through the morning, walking out of bounds along streets made safe by their emptiness. Around noon I made my way to the city center. Here I found the people, thousands of them, all sober Sunday best in black and gray, a sea of lace mantillas on dark heads. The route of the procession was already jammed with crowds. I had come prepared. All my valuables, including my watch and my new blue passport, had been left in the safekeeping of

La Madre at the hotel. All I carried was enough money to buy a cup of coffee and my bus fare home. I remember wondering if Good Friday made honest men of Colombian thieves. I had no urge to test the theory.

I managed to squeeze myself a place in the crowd on the opposite side of the square, halfway up the steps to a large bank facing the church where the procession would end. We all stood glued together, waiting. There was a sense of excitement in the air, muted but powerful. Then, from somewhere in the distance, came this rumbling sound, low and rhythmic, like chanting out of unison. Everyone pushed forward in anticipation. The noise got louder, until from the bottom of one of the streets leading into the square I spotted this wave of people, and above them a large figure of Christ on the cross, swaying its way toward us. It was impossible to tell where the procession ended and the crowd began. Everyone seemed to be moving. The statue was huge — six, maybe seven feet high — and in the crush the men carrying it couldn't control it properly. It was lurching from side to side, and more than once it came near to falling. With each lurch the crowd would let out a kind of moan. God, it was bizarre. Like some cult reenactment of the Stations of the Cross. And Our Lord fell for the third time . . . The wave of chanting grew louder, a bed of devotion to support him on his way. The statue itself was grotesque. A typically Latin American Christ, baroque Catholic, all twisted limbs and bloodied torn flesh. Theater of the streets. The cross swayed, dangerously this time, and someone near me started to cry.

I began to feel chilled. The cross was in front of us now, beginning its drunken journey up the steps of the church. Behind it trundled the inevitable Virgin Mary, life size and dazzling in blue and white china robes, hands clasped in prayer, eyes to heaven, the perfect example of Catholic passivity. And the ultimate con job, reified and deified in one image. All I could think of was bread and circuses as I stood there crushed by the crowd. God, Marla, I wish you'd been there. I was in need of atheist companionship.

The voice came from nowhere, interrupting my heartbeat. "You look so angry. How come you're not amazed by the spectacle?"

He was standing right behind me. Funny. In the coffee shop he'd looked European rather than American. Close to, his eyes

39

were very bright; blue-gray, like a cat's. His hair was so blond it was almost white. In the middle of such Latin American darkness, he stood out like an albino. I don't remember replying to him. The only thing I can recall about that moment is the fact that I wasn't surprised to see him.

"Have you been in the cathedral yet?" He was almost shouting to make himself heard over the noise.

I shook my head. "I didn't make a reservation."

He smiled. "Everyone should see it once. Like the pyramids at full moon. They'll be following the Stations of the Cross. Christ is scheduled to die in less than an hour."

Maybe he was right. Maybe it did have to be seen. I pushed myself up on tiptoe to catch a glimpse of the vast wooden doors of the cathedral, a river of people pushing their way in. Our Lady was having trouble making it up the last few steps. "We'd never get across the square, let alone inside."

"Sure we will. Just keep your eyes on the back of my head and follow me."

He turned and broke out of the crowd, not waiting to check if I was behind him. Together we fought our way out to more open spaces, and then he plowed ahead, fast turns down small alleyways and side streets where the crush was not solid. He moved like a man who knew the city. And then around a corner at the end of a street, a side door to the cathedral. He paused to let me catch up.

"Have you got anything to cover your head?"

I hadn't. He moved over to a small stall set up by the cathedral wall, littered with devotional pictures and rosary beads. His conversation with the old woman was short and to the point. He came back with an offering of black lace. The act of putting it over my hair unlocked the whole box of Sunday morning childhood memories. It all came tumbling out; late-morning mass with my stomach weak from hunger and no hope of food until after communion. Sometimes even the incense smelled of roasting meat. I could feel the texture of the host against my tongue as I tried to peel it off the roof of my mouth. "Forgive me, Father, for I have sinned . . ." Devotion drowned by saliva. Maybe this was why I had wanted to stay lost in the crowd.

Inside the air was stiff with sweat and incense. If you looked up into the vaulted ceiling, you could see smoke hanging over the main altar, tendrils of it snaking out into the body of the church. There must have been a thousand people in there, jammed together in the semidarkness. Christ and Mary were making painful, lumbering progress down the aisle. We edged forward until we stood by the end of a crowded pew. Next to me a woman was standing, staring at the altar. I watched her lips chewing out silent prayers while her hands fingered a rosary. There was something almost nervous in her movement, as if this had more to do with anxiety than comfort. Over her head the church was dense with prayer. The weight of worship was almost tangible. My throat had gone dry, and I found it hard to breathe. The atmosphere was solid, as if some great black bird had landed on the roof of the church, and the warmth of its body and spread wings was suffocating the people below. I remember thinking what a giveaway it was that I should imagine its color to be black. Ex-Catholics have an ambivalent relationship with the Holy Spirit. I felt excluded. And oppressed. I didn't fit in and I couldn't get out. I turned and started to fight my way back toward the open door. He could stay or he could follow. For that moment I didn't care.

Outside, light and air engulfed us. I stood against the wall, feeling the stone cold through my sweater. I took in great gulps of air and began to feel better. I was looking for a way to make light of it, but he got in before my defenses were up.

"What's the problem? Claustrophobia? Or maybe a sliver of Catholic glass lodged somewhere, trying to get out?"

I shook my head. "Trying to get in, more likely," I said, folding up the lace mantilla and handing it to him. He continued to watch me, as if he knew there was more to say.

"I was a Catholic once," I murmured. "As a child. But I turned my back on it as soon as I could think for myself."

"Sure, but you know what they say about the Jesuits. This could be a rearguard action."

I laughed. "Not me, I'm clean. They never got their hands on me. It was a mixed marriage, one Catholic, one atheist. I was christened, confessed, and confirmed, but never in a convent. It was all extramural indoctrination. They never managed to instill enough guilt to keep me loyal. Anyway, how come you know so much about it?"

"These things just interest me, I guess. What makes people obey rules, what makes them keep coming back for more."

"You sound as if you admire it."

"Not admire exactly, but I'm a little impressed by its Machiavellian effects, yes. Catholicism has kept Latin America as firmly enthralled as sacrificing virgins to the sun did four centuries ago. You have to have respect for that kind of power, don't you think?"

"No, not necessarily."

We stood for a moment, looking at each other. My God, I thought, I'm having a conversation with a Westerner and we haven't yet mentioned how long we've been on the road or where we're going next. This hasn't happened to me for months. And I was feeling amazingly light and reborn, which had nothing to do with Easter.

He smiled at me, and I remember thinking he was beautiful. Or rather that I fancied him. And I wondered what should I say next to make him stay. I needn't have worried.

"I don't know about you," he said. "But I could do with a cup of coffee. Or even something a little stronger. In which case it'll have to be my hotel. There aren't a whole load of places where they let atheists celebrate on Good Friday."

I thought of the small change rattling under my left breast and the prices on the hotel drinks list. Then we both thought of a secondhand *International Herald Tribune*.

"But," he added, shaking his head, "this one has to be on me, right? After all, if I hadn't forced you in there you wouldn't need a drink. OK?"

Inside somewhere I was laughing, with an old-fashioned kind of delight. I knew it was regressive, a woman bought with chivalry and wine. But, as I said, I was looking to be wooed. Like any old-fashioned girl. And so I accepted his offer.

And as we walked back out of the path of the worshipers, it began to rain: cold, Colombian rain with a hint of the mountains in it. A clock struck three. I remember thinking that God was keeping a firm eye on the proceedings, even down to the special effects. And so we went back to his hotel.

Out on the New York balcony, Elly stopped talking and stared at her hands folded in her lap. I sat marble still. To tell stories is to relive them. And we had just got to the part which would be hardest to tell.

Time passed. I got up and went into the sitting room, collecting the bottle of bourbon from the table. I filled her glass and then my own. She looked up at me. Her foot, I remember, made a tiny nervous gesture.

"There's too much of it, Marla. Let's

leave it till tomorrow."

I sat down and crossed my arms. "In the mead halls of old England, storytellers used to recite all night. Let's tell it now."

Four

What can I say? You know what happened next. It's what comes before the "happily ever after" bit. We had coffee in the coffee shop, then a drink in the bar, then dinner in the restaurant. We drank European wine — which I had not tasted for eight months — and brandy, and then we went to bed. And I think the truth of the matter is that I "fell in love," whatever that means, that very night. Not because of the sex. No. That was the usual, messy first-night affair — strung-out desire and no finesse. No, not because of the sex. I think it was more because of the conversation.

You have to imagine how it was for me. You have to remember how starved I was for that kind of communication, that edge of sharpness, that intellect. I had got used to the meanderings of dopers, following smoke rings and getting off on diversions rather than destinations. Maybe I just wasn't as stoned as they were, but God, it had got boring. With him it was different. He was

47

bright, shiny, and very fast. He knew things. And they didn't come out of the latest *Time* magazine. Colombia wasn't just the next country on a map for him. He had studied it, knew chapter and verse of its history and people. He'd read Latin American writers I hadn't even heard of. After months of hanging out with people whose only knowledge was the relevant entry in the *South American Handbook*, he was nothing less than a miracle. I swear I was more seduced by his mind than his body. He was a challenge, a mystery. The most powerful aphrodisiac in the world.

We slept late into the next morning. Easter Saturday in Bogotá — what else is there to do between death and resurrection? When we woke we made love again, and it was better than before. And, afterward I was a little nervous, because I already understood that I did not feel entirely careless about this one.

And then, almost as if he had sensed my paranoia, something went wrong. It was as if he flicked a switch and turned off. Just like in the coffee shop. He left. Not physically, but in every other way. He suddenly became distant and chilly, treating me with a kind of patient politeness, as if he was surprised to find me still there. If he'd been English I would have just assumed emotional repression. But I'd been in the spotlight of his charm and knew that it wasn't that he couldn't give — it was more that he'd decided not to. Only this time I was prepared for it.

I took the initiative. I got up, leaving him in bed, took a long shower, then got dressed, ready to go. He could have stopped me at any point, asked me to stay, made some comment about a future — even if it was only breakfast. But he didn't say a word, just lay back on the pillows and watched me. Yet something had happened between us. Christ, Marla, you don't just imagine that. You might misjudge depths of attraction, but you can't misjudge the whole thing. But then, Lenny specializes in the unpredictable. Anyway, this one he played to the limit. He waited until I got as far as the door. I was actually walking out, but I had no intention of leaving him in total control. My anger propelled me to turn and say, "Thanks, I had a great evening. Maybe the next religious festival I can buy you for the night. See you."

I was halfway out when he called me back. "Elly, if you have no other plans, why not come tomorrow evening and we'll pick up where we left off?"

I think it was the studied lack of humility

which enraged me most. I remember thinking, Watch it, Elly, this guy is fucked up. But I didn't listen to myself. Instead of walking out I walked back in.

"Listen, I don't know about the women you usually fuck, but the silent macho approach doesn't cut it with me. I'm sorry, but I'm busy doing nothing tomorrow night. Besides, I'm leaving Bogotá on Tuesday, so there wouldn't be much in it for you."

To give him his due he didn't flinch, didn't move a muscle, just looked at me and said, "Well, I'm sorry too. I'll miss you."

"Yeah, well you know how it is on the road."

And then he did just what I didn't expect. Of course. He smiled and held out a hand toward me.

"I've annoyed you. Forgive me. I would like to see you again. Only I have some work that will take a few days to complete. If you felt like changing your plans and staying around, then maybe we could go to the islands, spend some real time together. I would like that."

I didn't move. I still couldn't work out the hot from the cold in him. "It wouldn't work. I couldn't afford your lifestyle. We're traveling on different budgets."

"So, travel on mine for a while."

50

I shook my head. "I don't live off men. And I don't have enough money to sit around Bogotá waiting for you." You see, I knew already that if I didn't start fighting, I wouldn't stand a chance. What I didn't realize, of course, was how much that was his style as well.

"OK. Let me lend you some. You could pay me back later. I'm not looking to compromise your independence, Elly. It's just I don't believe you're the kind of person to let money stand in your way."

He was smiling broadly now. Enjoying it much more than I. I think that unnerved me too. For maybe only the second time in my life I knew that I was standing at a crossroads, I could still turn and walk away without contracting a fatal disease; I still had the power of choice. And do you know what, Marla? I couldn't move. My brain had decided. It told my legs to start walking. They simply refused. Emotional mutiny. And, of course, he sensed it.

"Elly, I like you very much. Why run away?"

And I could have said, "Because I think I know what it is you do, and I don't want to get involved." Or, "Because I suspect at some level that I won't ever be able to trust you, and who needs it?" Both of those

51

things were true. I didn't say either of them. Instead I closed the door, walked back across to the bed, sat down, and looked at him.

"OK. I'll wait for you. But I'll do it from my hotel. Now you can decide whether or not you want to tell me what you do."

There are, you see, not a lot of things that a well-dressed young American could be doing in Colombia, short of spending his father's fortune. It's not a rich country: industry and export are important, and there are small fortunes to be made on the right deals, but it takes time and patience and playing the bureaucratic game, and it's too much like hard work for most people. Certainly for Lenny. That was not his style. The reason I had not asked him what he did for a living was that I already knew. You get very adept at spotting coke smugglers when you're on the road. Sometimes they try to blend in with the plebeian travelers, but more often the big fishes swim in the pools on the fancier side of town. Of course, lots of travelers do coca in the poorer hotels. Even on a small budget it's hard to resist just a taste. And some of them play with the possibility of taking enough home to finance their next trip. Most of them don't do it because they're frightened of getting caught.

Some do it and get caught. A few get away with it. But the real businessmen don't operate in that way. They act more like the establishment — they are the merchant bankers of crime. They look clean — they stay at the best hotels; and they live on the right side of the law in the sunny side of society, until they take that one step which puts them in the twilight zone. Lenny had to be moving coke. He was too smart to be doing anything else.

And there was another reason. He had to be moving it because he had told me he wasn't. When the talk had turned to professions, he had described with some enthusiasm buying merchandise for a chain of shops back in the States. We both knew he wasn't telling the truth. There may have been shops — there were as it turned out — but that wasn't what he was doing. He knew I knew. But he offered no clues. His secrecy was part of my proof.

So, you see, when I began to walk out of the door, he had a decision to make. He had to decide whether or not he could trust me with the knowledge. If he gave me that, he gave me everything. Lenny doesn't usually trust people. In general, good coke men don't. But I'd called him. He didn't have a lot of options. I wasn't interested in the casual fuck. Maybe he wasn't either. And you can't really carry on a proper affair with a coke man and not know what he's doing. In effect I did have some power. I knew when he had made that remark about work that he was giving away more than he needed to. On the other hand, I was still careful to leave him with a let-out.

His answer was to lean over to the drawer next to the bed and take out a small leather case. From his neck he slipped a key off a chain and fitted it to the lock. Inside was a glass container, the size of a marmalade jar, filled to the top with white crystalline powder. No one can tell good coke from bad just by looking at it. But you can tell volume. There must have been a good half pound in there. And that would be just the sample.

I looked at it for a moment, then took the jar from his hand, unscrewed the lid, and put a fingertip into the powder. It came out coated white. I rubbed the finger slowly along my gums, top and bottom. I could feel a slight numbing sensation immediately. I put the lid back on the jar and put the jar back inside the leather case. Then I kissed him. His tongue ran around the edge of my gums. Another kind of lust. Freemasons. There is a lot of ritual attached to cocaine. It was as well to indulge in it early. The ceremony ended, we moved apart and I said, "I want you to know I'm less interested in what you do than in who you are." And I swear if it was a lie, then I didn't know it at the time.

He was looking at me closely. "I wonder," he said. "You may find they're not so different. Let's go eat breakfast and I'll tell you some of the things you don't need to know."

And that is how the whole sordid tale began — how young, relatively innocent Elly Cameron joined the twilight world of the cocaine transport trade. And that goes some way to explaining why I couldn't tell you. One of the things he made me promise that day was silence. Another part of the ritual. But one that makes sense. The fewer people who know, the fewer people can talk. At the time I gave the promise easily. Later I understood how much it isolated me, how much it left him in control.

He didn't tell me a great deal more that morning, which was fine by me. Knowledge is responsibility, and I didn't want to know. Ask no questions and you might be told no lies. After all, it was him I wanted, not the cocaine.

After breakfast I went back to my hotel, and he went out to see a man about a drug. He would be busy for the next few days. I did not want to be around. Before I left, he handed me a small vial of cocaine. I was already a kept woman, you see. Someone else was paying for my drugs.

Back in my room, I sat on the bed and tried to read the end of *Northanger Abbey*. But Jane's world was too slow for me now. I was engulfed in my own fantasies. I took out the coke and laid out a couple of lines on the cover of the book. I would hardly call myself an expert, but even I could tell it was high grade. By the time it reached the noses of record producers on the coast, it would have been cut four, maybe five times and would be then — with luck — forty percent pure. But in that cold grimy bedroom in the slums of Bogotá it was nearer to ninety percent. I didn't stop zinging for hours. I couldn't sit still. In the end I went out onto the streets to watch the world go by. It's a funny thing about coke. You feel so alert, so fast, so clean, but in fact you're moving in a different orbit altogether. When the Indians in the Andes chew coca leaves, they do it in order to alter their consciousness. Even after all the refining and processing that turns it into street snow, the effect is still the same. Coke doesn't help you with the world — it puts you outside it.

My thinking relationship with Colombia

ended that morning. In the ten days that followed, we did a lot of cocaine. And noticed very little of what was going on.

When I saw Lenny two days later, he was high and busy. We spent another night together, making love and snorting in equal doses. I was dancing five miles high. Neither of us was ourself, but at least we were equidistant from reality. The sex was great, but then so was the cocaine. That's another of the rituals. I think now that maybe it's all a huge hype. A figment of one's stoned imagination. But I think differently about a lot of things now.

Then came a few days when he was away all the time. The shipment was already in. It had walked its way over the mountains of the Ecuadorian border in the saddlebags of half a dozen Indians, to be met on the other side by the first of an army of middlemen who would take a slice of the pie and start pushing up the price, until finally it reached its status as one of the most expensive drugs in the world. It had been refined and processed in a rural laboratory somewhere in the south of Colombia, and now all that remained was to divide it up, pack it down, and move it out. But how? That was my only prevailing curiosity. What scam could be safe enough to slide it under the nose of

U.S. Customs officials?

On the sixth night Lenny came home to the hotel, wild-eyed and ragged with lack of sleep. I was already in bed. He came and sat next to me. I woke and reached over to touch him.

"Hi, babe." I could tell from his voice that he was stoned, still "up" despite however many hours without sleep. "I brought you a present."

I sat up, rubbing the sleep from my brain. "Don't tell me. A jar full of snowflakes."

He shook his head. "Nope. Something much more valuable."

From his jacket pocket he pulled out a package, wrapped in tissue paper and about ten inches long. I took it. It was quite heavy, as if made of pottery or maybe a dense wood. I unrolled the tissue paper carefully, and out onto the bed in front of me tumbled a china statue of the Virgin Mary, blue and white robes and golden halo; the Semana Santa Mother of God, hands joined in supplication, eyes lifted to heaven. I looked up at him in surprise.

"Isn't she lovely?" he said, picking her up and holding her in front of him. He ran a finger down the line of her body, as if he could feel the flesh under the china. "Look at her. So refined, so pure, and so full of goodness."

"Lenny. Just how stoned are you?" I asked, half laughing.

He looked at me and smiled. "Oh, I would say very stoned. But you did mention that you were curious. So, here she is. Lenny's latest deliverer. The safest, most pious carrier in the world."

With a renewed sense of ceremony, I put out my hand and received Our Lady back into my palm. I held her, tested the weight. It seemed right. Not too heavy. I looked for the joins. I could see none. It was a professional job. Lenny enjoyed my appreciation.

"One tightly packed half pound in each statue. A shipment of a thousand of them. From one of the most respectable religious paraphernalia businesses in South America. A family firm. Generations of devotion. Half the shipment is clean, the other half filled with the cocaine. Our Good Lady is taking a hundred kilos of pure grade through the U.S. Customs for us. Traveling with God's blessing."

"Where does it go?"

"Half of them end up in the homes of some of our less fortunate citizens — our Puerto Rican and Italian neighbors — into whose lives they will no doubt bring a little light and love. The other half are picked up, taken apart, and distributed among the more wealthy WASP sections of the population."

I shook my head in amazement. "And how do you know which are which?"

"Aaah. Examine carefully, *señorita,* the hands of the Madonna," he said in the voice of an eager tourist guide. "You will notice, I think, a particularly attractive little detail on the fingers of the left hand. A wedding ring. See. Not strictly as Our Lady might have worn it in Galilee two thousand years ago, but nevertheless an appropriate reminder that she is indeed the Bride of Christ. Touching, I'm sure you'll agree. Those with the rings are pregnant with treasure. Those without have not been so blessed."

"My God." I whistled admiringly. "It's brilliant. Where did you get the idea?"

"You are sleepy. Where do you think? Now you understand why I go on annual pilgrimage to the cathedral during Semana Santa."

I studied her halo. "Is she safe?"

He shrugged, putting his hands together in mock supplication, appealing to his benefactress. "Nothing is 'safe.' That's part of the game. When the increased demand for the Virgin first arose, there was, no doubt, some curiosity in government agencies. They opened the first few shipments. I knew

60

they would. That's why they were clean. It won't happen again. Especially as there are now a couple of customs officials who have been blessed by Our Lady. Wealth as well as grace. It's not worth their while to disturb her progress. And if by chance something does go wrong and the wind whistles trouble . . . well, then we just don't pick them up."

"And what about the delivery point?"

He put a finger across the Virgin's lips. "That's for her to know and you not to ask. But put it this way. A small shop owner in Little Italy wouldn't have any trouble explaining with credible astonishment (should he need to) how on the very day that his Virgins arrived, some crazy came in and bought hundreds of them. But only the ones with the wedding rings. What does he know? He has the sales slip to show for it. He's just grateful for such a miraculous example of the Lord's generosity."

"So when do they arrive?" Just for that moment I wanted to know all of it. To live it through him.

"A while. Long enough for you and me to use the time in between to go to the Caribbean, pick up a little sunshine, a few more passport stamps, and then head for home."

I lay back on the pillow, still cradling the

Virgin in my hands. She looked up at me, promising intercession and forgiveness for all good Catholic girls. *Hail Mary, full of grace . . .*

"And what about her?"

"Her we take with us and break open the sacred heart on the islands."

I watched him. His eyes were shining. It wasn't just the coke that was making him high. I think it was the happiest, certainly the most unguarded, I had ever seen him. He was a man in love. I ought to have learned then.

"Is this the best bit?" I asked softly, putting my hand up against his cheek.

He smiled, the smile on the face of the tiger. "Yeah. It's one of the best bits. Living on the fault line. How do you like it, my Little English rose? Breaking the law?"

I stared at him. Half his soul was somewhere else entirely. "I dunno," I whispered. "I'm a little frightened, I suppose. But I also like the taste of it all." The words came out without my thinking about them. They were probably as near to the truth as I knew how to get.

He lay back heavily on the bed, not bothering to take off his clothes. He curled his body away from me and closed his eyes. I wanted to make love, to bring him back into my orbit, but I didn't know how to ask. I leaned over and touched his forehead lightly with my fingers.

"Yeah," he said with a sigh, the word slurring slightly. "You're right. It is a good taste. Welcome to the club, Elly."

He was asleep immediately. I lifted the figurine off the bed and put her on the side table. Then I curled my body around his and closed my eyes. Our Lady — "blessed is the fruit of thy womb" — kept vigil over us.

The day after we left for San Andrés; and then, two weeks and two islands later, baked brown and lulled by images of blue-green coral seas, we arrived back at JFK Airport, the last of Our Lady's bountiful harvest washed down the loo and our luggage and persons as clean as clean could be. It didn't matter. They didn't touch us. We felt blessed, walking through Customs hand in hand like a golden couple on honeymoon. Even the immigration officer had been kind — maybe he could see the stars in my eyes — I got a six months' stay. I had no future other than a ride to an apartment I had never seen and where I was now to live. I was an accessory to a crime which could have put me inside an American jail for a decade. And frankly, my dear, I didn't give a damn.

Love, Marla. It's a worse addiction than cocaine. But they do go together well, and I was hooked on both from the start. Some of it I'm not very proud of. But I'll tell it anyway. I know, for instance, that somewhere I was getting a real sexual buzz from the fact that Lenny was smuggling. It made him a kind of outlaw, and I got off on that. It was all part of the glamour. Coke, you see, is such a glamorous drug. The thoroughbred of narcotics. Nothing else can touch it. Grass is too plebeian, opium too passive, heroin too destructive. But not coke. Coke has style, wit, and the aura of excitement. I sometimes think that's why people pay so much for it. It can't be for the high. You can stay up longer with a handful of good old-fashioned uppers sold by the tubful in high school playgrounds.

But coke is high society, an entrance to the elite. The law forbids you to take it. It's like disobeying your parents. Everyone wants to be a rebel sometimes.

And that's what spiced my love for Lenny. He touched one of the oldest female fantasies in the book: the man outside the law, steely, confident, untouchable. I swear, Marla, my feminism went out of the window. If you'd given me a James Bond book to read during those first few months,

I would have been hard-pressed not to identify with the women. I was so hungry for him it makes me ashamed now. You know, the kind of desire that comes at the beginning of an affair, when you want to possess the other person entirely, crawl inside their brain and see the world through their eyes, colonize them, take over their pasts and become their futures. I don't care what feminism tells you you should or shouldn't do. When everything is Technicolor you don't think straight.

That's why I never wrote, never told you. What could I say? You would have thought I had betrayed you. I had. I knew it even then, you see. I knew it would lead to trouble. That I had given up something of myself and there would come a time when I would regret it. But you have to remember it had never happened to me before. I had never fallen so hard for a man. I was thirty years old and I had never been in love like that. I wanted to be engulfed. I know this is painful for you to hear, but I can't lie to you. It was like being caught up in a tornado. And by the time the storm had passed, all that was left was the debris. For me that is. For him it was different. There were bits of him that were nailed down. Maybe he had a more clearly defined sense of survival. Or maybe

65

he'd just been at it longer. It was his life-style. He had warned me. He was not dishonest. He told me right from the beginning. He had also warned me about the coke. And I had listened. I just didn't hear.

It was just before we left San Andrés, early evening at the end of another scorching day. We had baked ourselves stupid on the beach and spent hours snorkeling, an exhaustion of pleasure. Back at the hotel we began the twilight ritual. A shower, a drink, and a couple of lines to set us up for the evening. I was enjoying it. I had, I suppose, developed a taste for it.

He was sitting out on the balcony. I was inside the room at the table by the bed, chopping the coca. I remember that he was watching me. After a while I looked up and smiled. He didn't smile back.

"It's a great drug, isn't it, Elly?" He put it very casually, but there was something in his tone that set me on my guard. I carried on chopping, watching the crystals fluff up beneath the razor blade.

"Yeah, it's a great drug. Although I'm not sure if I'd pay American street prices for it."

There was a pause. "How much coca have you done, Elly? Before you met me, I mean."

"Oh . . . some. A bit. Nothing like this quantity," I said, still not looking at him.

"Have you ever been around unlimited supplies of it before?"

I stopped chopping and began running the blade along the mound, stringing it out into thick white lines. I glanced up. "No, you know I haven't. Why? What are you worried about, Lenny? That I'll get to like it too much? It's supposed to be a female drug, isn't it? Isn't that the mythology about it? You tell me. Do women have a lower tolerance than men, or is that just in-house coke talk?"

It had been a glorious day. And it had been a long time since he had "switched off." I was feeling secure. His folklore on coke had already become an in-joke between us, something I could tease him about. Although even then I think the reason I teased was that at some level I resented his sense of superiority, his possessiveness toward the drug. In all other things we thought and argued equally.

"The women I've been around usually get to like it a lot. Maybe more than the men. Yes."

"Are you warning me?"

"No. I was just thinking out loud, that's all."

He got up and came over to the table. I pushed the mirror toward him. He sat down and plucked a note from his wallet, rolling it carefully into a funnel. Holy communion. Getting ready for the host. I watched in silence. Then he put out a finger and rubbed a little of the powder on his gums.

"The first guy I ever scored from in Colombia had been doing coke for fifty years. He was a walking history book. He'd lived through civil wars, revolutions, you name it. He had a face like the north side of the Eiger, and he dressed like a fashion plate. He was right out of Carlos Castaneda, a mix of streetwise and mystic. I never really figured him out. But he never fucked me over, and he taught me a lot about cocaine. He had a particular attitude to it. Very Latin American. You won't like it. He saw it as a power relationship. He used to say that coca was like a certain kind of woman, the sort who isn't satisfied until she takes over a man. Once you understood that, you could resist her, and if you resisted her then she would love you even more and the affair would go on forever. But once you let her in, let her take you over, she'd suck you dry."

He was right, I didn't like it. "He may have felt like Castaneda, but he sounds more like Norman Mailer to me."

He shook his head impatiently. "Sure. I know it's a stereotype, but don't jump on it just because you don't like the analogy. Get behind it. What he was saying is true. If you get involved with coke, you have to work out a philosophy, some ground rules. And his advice is as good as any. Use it, but always make sure it's that way around."

I felt like a child who'd been caught playing adult games, trying too hard to be grown-up. I didn't like feeling so young to his age.

"Thanks for the lecture, Lenny. Don't worry. I think I've done enough to understand a little."

"And how much is enough, Elly?" he said softly. "If you stay around me, you're going to be swimming in it. So much you could drown. All I'm saying is don't go out of your depth. Because I won't come out and save you. The reason I'm good at what I do is that I never go that far in. We're good together. I want it to stay that way. But I won't break my rules for anyone. Not even you."

There was no reply. The words were hard and cold and deliberate. I couldn't shrug them off. It was a declaration of intent, a kind of prenuptial settlement, and I didn't want to sign. He watched me while I tried to disguise my discomfort. Then he handed me the rolled note and pushed the mirror toward me. I shook my head, got up, and went into the bedroom, closing the door behind me. He didn't follow.

I had been warned, Marla. He'd said it. On a straight fight between me and the coke, he would protect her first. I couldn't say I hadn't been told.

Of course, in the beginning none of it mattered, not for the first few months. When we got back to New York he made a couple of calls from the airport, put me in a cab to the apartment, and went off to move the coke. He didn't tell me where and he didn't tell me how long he'd be away. He was gone three days. During that time he picked it up, cut it, subdivided it, and moved it on. The shorter the time he held it, the less the risk. And it was all big deals, that was the other trick. Lenny dealt only in kilos upward, and he sold only to a few chosen people. They in turn would recut it into smaller amounts, and others would cut it again into grams. By the time it hit the streets, you'd be paying maybe one hundred dollars for a gram which contained nowhere near that amount of cocaine. Lenny told me once that he moved the equivalent of about ninety thousand grams, pure. Even with a four to five hundred percent markup, by the time it reached the punter he was making one hell of a lot of money. I didn't ask how much, and he never volunteered the information.

Enough, anyway, not even to think about working for a long time to come. Spring was exploding when we got back. We used to spend the weeks in New York and the weekends at Westchester. God, I loved Manhattan. It was like a giant toy box, and I played all day long. Movies and galleries, shops and shows. And the days danced by without my noticing.

With the summer swelter we took off, spent six weeks in California by the ocean, in this amazing house that a friend of Lenny's had built. We were living on the pleasure principle. It wasn't even to do with coke. When he arrived back from his "office," he had brought a stash home — "There it is, Elly. Shavings of profit." But he didn't touch it, at least not when I was around, and hearing the island conversation in my head, I too withdrew my patronage. Once I'd made the decision, it wasn't that hard. There was a week or so when I found myself yearning, when I seemed a little edgy and irritable. But it passed. And the world was too full to miss it.

Maybe it was California where things first

started to go wrong. I don't remember clearly anymore. But I do know that when I got back and the autumn began to roll in, I made an attempt to organize my life. I was lucky. There was work to be done in the shop. Yes, the shop. It — or rather they — really did exist. Three of them: Chicago, San Francisco, and New York. Like all careful coke men, Lenny had developed certain legit fronts. Panache was one of them. Of course, he had very little to do with it. He did the buying, in a haphazard kind of way, and left the selling to others. Boy, was it a mess. A funky little place back from Washington Square, crammed with Colombian jewelery, sweaters, and leather goods; about as much sense of design as a Liverpool junk shop. It was perfect for me. I redesigned, redecorated, and reopened it. It was something to do, something that I was good at. A kind of independence. Also a way of getting a green card. *Design Consultant.* Lenny's lawyers started the wheels grinding. If I was going to stay in New York, it was either that or marriage. And neither of us wanted marriage. Even then. Maybe we could already see the rocks in the distance.

Certainly by the autumn it was clear that something was poisoning the water. He had changed. There had been so much life to him, vitality as well as charm. Not just with me but with the rest of the world. Gradually that began to evaporate. When I look back on it, I suspect it had begun almost as soon as we got home, as if once the coke had been shifted, once the job was done, his whole metabolism started to change. He became stiller, more contained, and finally withdrawn. Of course there had always been that element in him, the sudden switch-off. But this was different. This was calculated distance, a kind of emotional paralysis almost. It wasn't that he was lazy. My God, far from it. He would spend whole days in his study or out at the library reading. And not just anything. Very particular books. Check out the bookshelves and you'll see. I tell you, Marla, you'd have a lot in common. He would have these academic obsessions. History, politics, even literature. There would be weeks when all he'd read or talk about would be the medieval church in Europe, the campaigns of Napoleon, or the work of Carlos Fuentes. And all with such discipline. He'd get all the right books — he even has an account with Blackwell's in Oxford — he'd take notes and then hold seminars in his head, or with me over the dinner table. And he was good. But there was such iron in his method, like an athlete in continual training, as if he was always trying to prove something. But what? I asked him once why he hadn't become an academic. But by that time he'd stopped volunteering information about himself. God, when I think about it now I realize how little I still know about him. A New England boy from a rich family who dropped out of college rather than follow in his father's footsteps, squandered a fortune from his grandfather's legacy, and then used the last $100,000 to finance his first shipment. The rest is mystery. At first I saw his secrecy as a challenge. By late autumn I knew it was simply the shape of things to come. I suppose that's when I started to get scared, and begin to wonder whether all this study wasn't just a substitute for something missing.

Then, out of the blue one morning, he announced that he was going to do another run. I knew then I was losing. It wasn't the money. There was still plenty of that. He just wanted to plug in again. Not to the coke — he could have done that anytime — but to the fault line, the excitement. That was what mattered to him. That, not the coke, was the drug, and it worked by long-term release. Now it was wearing off, it was time for another shot. I had a choice. To go with him or stay behind.

I went. My visa was about to expire, and I needed an extension till my green card came through. The New York store needed more merchandise, and I wanted to bring in some new ideas, build on the success. Excuses. I went because I was terrified of being left behind. It was a disaster. We spent four weeks in Bogotá, trampling underfoot the memories of the time before. I hated that city the second time around. Coming straight out of the American dream, its poverty was obscene, especially as we were there to make money — and a grotesque amount of it.

When I tried to explain my disgust to Lenny, he told me it wasn't the time or the place. I started to do coke again, just to get me through. Lenny was doing it too. Yet another part of the ritual. Love the drug and she will love you: made in her image you can do anything. Except it wasn't like that for me. Not this time. This time all she gave me was paranoia. Lenny was high. I was freaked. We grew further and further apart. And this time all the sunshine on the islands could do nothing to melt the ice.

Back in New York the reentry was even worse. Lenny went off to the office, and I stayed home and snorted my way through a couple of grams waiting for him to come back. Communication had broken down entirely. On the islands I had wanted to talk about what was happening to us. He, still "doing the business," did not. When he finally arrived home four days later, he was too tired and I was too stoned to say anything. When he got up the next day, he acted exactly according to custom. He put a bag of white profit in the drawer, never touched it again, and went back to his books. In both of his love affairs he had gained control. In both of mine I was going under.

Cocaine. The most addictive nonaddictive drug in the world. It's clever though. Its hold is more subtle than most. All the time you're taking it, it whispers in your ear that you're doing fine, coping well. That's what I believed. That I was in control, that I had the whole thing down and there was nothing to worry about. It was just that New York was such a fast city, and in order to hustle with it you needed to get up your own speed. And I had the excuse of the shop. Busy girl, busy life. Of course I needed a little extra energy. So there would be a line or two before I went out in the morning. Then another line or three to get me through the day. And a few more to speed up the evening; to make me sparkle, make me shine, make me able to ignore what was going on.

And, of course, at some level I knew what I was doing. I knew it was a symbol of things destroyed. But while I took it, the coke made me feel as strong as Lenny. And I needed that. The times spent together became a complete nightmare. At the beginning there was still the occasional abstract conversation about this or that, but often I'd be too coked to listen. I would begrudge the pauses and the time it took him to make his point. My attention span was nil, and we lost patience with each other. He "left" completely. Sometimes literally — he would take off for Westchester without telling me, come back a week later. The more he withdrew the more I snorted, to block out his contempt for my weakness. Within a month of coming back I must have been getting through a couple of grams a day. Why not? It was always there. He made sure of that. And, after all, it was my profit too. I had aided and abetted its safe passage. I ran his legitimate business for him. I warmed his sheets. It was mine as well as his. And all the time he just sat and watched, as if I were some kind of controlled experiment. And, of course, I knew that it was all a test that I was being put through. And that I was failing.

It was a kind of suicide. In my more lucid moments I understood that it wasn't just about Lenny either. Everything always connects finally, doesn't it? Family patterns — how many years of my life did I waste trying to get my father to notice me? I suppose in a way I was bidding for both of them. Except I was hardly in the greatest of shapes for a contest. The coke was taking its toll. My nerves were closer to the surface. I couldn't handle people. Even the simplest of human contacts left me impatient. I was like a walking emery board. I stopped listening, even to myself. I got scratchy and tight and frightened, and I wouldn't let anyone in. Not that anyone tried, I had no friends, Marla. That was one of the prices I'd paid for Lenny. I'm not making excuses. It was my fault. I was in orbit, all contact with ground control lost. But it was his fault too. He could have helped. And he didn't.

In the end, I stopped myself. I got pregnant. Accidentally, but no doubt on some level on purpose. Unlike Our Lady's, it was not an immaculate conception. By that time we had almost stopped fucking. But one night I was particularly out of it and more or less pushed him into making love to me, although love is hardly the word for it. For

78

both of us I think it was more an act of anger. Anyway, I had forgotten to take the pill, and by the time I remembered four days later it was too late. I realized almost immediately. Then had to wait four weeks for some smart uptown gynecologist to tell me what I already knew and to offer guarded congratulations. That night I told Lenny. It was February 14, Valentine's Day. The perfect irony. I asked him to take me out to dinner because there was something I wanted to say to him. We went to some fancy place on Columbus, all palm trees and salads. I remember I even put on a new dress for the occasion, although by that time it was like dressing a wraith, I was so thin. The thinnest pregnant woman in the world. A good joke, I thought at the time.

And so I told him. I don't know what I had expected. Maybe I'd had some romantic notion that it would bring us together, that he'd take me in his arms, stroke my hair, and say, like in the movies, "It's OK, Elly. I know things have been bad, but I love you and together we'll work it out." I wasn't thinking very straight by then. Anyway, his screenplay was a little more realistic. He looked at me over the white tablecloth and said, "Is it mine?" which even in the circumstances I found a little cruel.

And when I assured him that it was, he replied, "Well, I think you'd better get rid of it." Just like that. And then I began to cry — or maybe sob would be a more accurate description. Six months of tears. When people started staring at us from the other tables, he paid the bill and took me home. Then he went out for the rest of the night.

The next morning he came into the bedroom and told me he was going away for a while. He suggested I do the same. He had put eight thousand dollars in my checking account for me to use in any way I wanted. It was my decision, but he wasn't ready to have a kid, and in his opinion neither was I.

It was just like that first morning in Bogotá. The same dreadful coldness. The memory of it gave me courage, stirred me into fighting back. Fighting ice with fire. I exploded, told him he was as responsible as I was, for all of it, the whole fucking mess, and that he had no right to walk out on me. His answer was to deliver a speech. At least that was what it felt like. It was so rehearsed and so bloodless that I couldn't help wondering if he hadn't used it before.

"Elly, you know as well as I do what's happened between us. You walked into this with your eyes open, and now you're going to have to walk out of it the same way."

"Without any help from you, of course. Because to show some understanding would be admitting weakness, wouldn't it?" I tried to keep my voice steady, to meet fact with fact, but I couldn't do it. Instead I said what I meant. "You are a bastard."

It didn't penetrate. "This won't help us, Elly. I told you right from the beginning. I said it as clearly as I knew how because you were important and I wanted you to understand. It was your choice. You had everything you wanted, and you screwed it up. If you can't play the game you shouldn't join in. You make my life dangerous when you're like this —"

"And you can't have that, can you, Lenny?" I smashed back. "Because it's as cold and clear-cut as that, isn't it? My God, for a man who's so smart you are so dumb. What do you think this is all about, eh? Me having a good time? Christ, didn't it ever occur to you that the coke was just a substitute? That the reason I took it was because it gave me something you couldn't?"

That pricked him. Despite himself, he was interested. "A substitute for what?"

"Attention." The word shot like a missile across the room. "Yeah, attention. For the short amount of time when we got on together, the coke gave me its full attention. It made me feel important. Wanted. Needed. And it gave me something else. Something that no lover of yours should ever be without. It gave me self-containment. It made me as impenetrable as you. And that's what made your absence bearable. Of course, *you* can do without it. You don't need help to grow cold. You are already. That's why your precious white mistress doesn't dominate you. I took coke to be like you. To make living with you less painful. But unfortunately I couldn't mold myself in your image. However many ounces I shoved up my nose, I still needed. And I still loved. More fool me."

I hadn't meant to say so much. The effort exhausted me. Too many tears and too little sleep. And no drug to numb the pain. I remember that I turned over in the bed, away from him, and lay with my eyes closed, waiting for him to leave. I heard the floor creak, then felt the weight of his body as he sat down beside me on the bed. I kept my eyes tightly shut. He put a hand on my shoulder. Not a sustained touch, but a real one. More real than for a long time. I didn't move. I didn't want to cry in front of him, to give him the pleasure of my weakness. Not again.

When he spoke I could almost have believed I was hearing the man I had once
loved on an island. There was something
close to tenderness in his voice. "Elly,
you're not telling either of us anything we
didn't already know. You always knew there
would be limitations, priorities. No, I don't
need people in the same way. I never have.
That's just how I am. But that doesn't mean
I don't care for you. I've stayed with you
longer than I've stayed with any other
woman because you seemed to understand
that instinctively. But I can't change for
you. Yeah, I know I've given you a rough
time. But you pushed me and you knew the
score. I'm not the one who has changed."

I wondered if that were true, if I had once
found easy something that I could now no
longer bear. It didn't matter anymore. The
air was full of splintered glass, and there
seemed nowhere to tread where we
wouldn't draw blood. I didn't trust myself
to speak. After a while I felt him stand up
and walk away.

Then I heard him say: "It's your decision,
Elly. All of it. I met a woman in Bogotá ten
months ago. She was bright and clean and
independent. If you come across her again,
tell her I would like her back. I'll be gone for
a while. Maybe she'll be here when I return."

And so he left. And I didn't see him again for two months. I called you that day, February 15. But you were out, and somehow I didn't have the courage to pick up the phone again. That evening I hired a car and drove to Vermont. It was a hard winter. Everything was ice and snow. I booked myself into this beautiful old hotel, all open fires and brass bedsteads with mounds of quilted covers. That night I flushed ten grams of cocaine down the washbasin, dosed myself with Valium, and stuck it out. At the end of the week I called my fancy gynecologist and set up an abortion. I paid a share of Lenny's profits for a high-class vacuuming of my womb and then squandered a little more on a plane ticket to Hawaii. I spent six weeks lying out in tropical sunshine doing nothing but trying to work out why the fuck I still loved him. I wrote to you a couple of times, but the letters never got posted. I guess I didn't want to hear what you would have to say. I slept with a few men and instantly forgot them. He did bestride my narrow world like a Colossus, and I could find no place where his shadow didn't touch me. I thought about it until I knew the thoughts by heart. And then I made one final attempt to sort it out. I flew back to America. I went to the only person who I knew had been closer to Lenny than I had. To J.T., Lenny's ex-partner, the guy whose house we had stayed in the summer before. It was a long shot. He's not exactly the world's most outgoing person — you'll see when you meet him — but he'd known Lenny for years — lived with him, scammed with him, traveled with him, seen him, presumably, with other women. He was the nearest, in fact, that Lenny had ever got to a friend. And although we hadn't exactly become close that summer, he'd been OK with me — even Lenny had been impressed. It was J.T. or no one. And I needed advice.

If he was surprised he didn't show it. Just picked me up at the airport and drove me back to the guesthouse, no questions asked. For two days I sat watching the ocean, remembering the times Lenny and I had spent there until it hurt too much to think about. Then I plucked up the courage to talk. I told J.T. something of what had been going on; the rest I think he guessed. I waited for his comments. He said very little. And, of course, what he did say I already knew. That there had been other women, and that the affairs had never outlasted the marriage. That Lenny loved me in his fashion, but that his fashion would not — could not — change, and that if I couldn't live with that,

85

then I should leave. It was my decision. But if I decided to stay, then he would advise me to say nothing of this visit. Lenny, he implied, would see it as a betrayal. Their friendship, it seemed, did not include emotional confidences.

There was nothing more to say. He took me to the airport, and I bought a ticket for London but at the last minute took a plane to New York instead. When we left the ground I was sure I was going to leave him, but somewhere over the continent I became haunted by memories and a kind of Dory Previn stubbornness that finally I alone could "cater to his passion and his pride." Romantic shit, I know, but still powerful. By the time we touched down, I had decided to give it one more try. I took a taxi into town and walked back into the apartment, brown, clean, and bright, but not, I know now, independent. I was asking him to take me back.

He had been home a couple of weeks and was still riding high from a scam well done. He looked gorgeous, so defined, so sure of who he was. And I knew it was stupid, but I wanted him. And more important, I wanted him to want me. Enough to make it happen. We talked for a while, prowled around each other, and then went to bed. In the morning

I made my pitch. I told him that I would stay and play by the rules, but that I couldn't live that way forever. That if there was to be a future, he would have to think about his loyalties and finally decide between us. Her and me. And he listened and nodded and said he understood. Said that he too had done some thinking and that yes, for a while at least, he would give her up and see how it affected us. I was amazed, entranced, suspicious. I both believed and did not believe him. And so we began again.

And since that day I have not done a line of coke. You probably find it hard to believe from looking at me, but I am fatter than I was. My body is healthy again, I have a purpose to life. I work a couple of days at the store. I am employed. I even employ others under me. I hold a green card, which gives me an identity separate from Lenny. I am legal, justified. And on the days when I am not working I draw, take Spanish lessons, learn the flute, and wander the city. I fill my time. I am busy. As busy as Lenny.

And Lenny? Well, he has both changed and remained the same. He is still the amateur academic, but only for some of the time. For the rest he is away. On trips. Business. The shops. Or so he says. I don't know. I don't want to know. If I asked, he might tell me the truth, and then I would have to face facts. I don't mean to be unfair. It's not that he hasn't tried. He has. He still does. Gives me what he can. Sometimes I think he has almost forgiven me my weakness. But deep down I don't trust him. And, when I'm feeling really paranoid, I think he doesn't trust me either.

It's crazy, because in some ways we get on even better than before. In bed, for instance. The sex is great. My desire for him increases. As if I take from sex what I can't get elsewhere. And *take* is the right word. I'm grabby and selfish. We both are. It's good. I like it. It touches something in me, makes me powerful. But it never lasts past the orgasm. And he never says he loves me, because, of course, he doesn't. And the lack of it sometimes drives me distraught with pain.

Hard to believe, isn't it, Marla? Me, Elly Cameron, life and soul of the party, old before my time. I mean it. It's as if he's taken away my youth. When things were really bad, do you know what I used to do? Go and sit for hours in coffee shops watching other women, wondering how they did it. I was fascinated by the ones younger than me. I don't think I'd ever noticed them before. Suddenly they were everywhere. I used to marvel at their skin, the softness of their flesh, the confidence of it. And I would so envy them their possibilities. I knew I was being absurd. That it's as easy to be fucked over at twenty as it is at thirty. Only it didn't feel like that. Not anymore. I had been young in the world for so long that I had grown to assume that was how it would always be. But, of course, it isn't. I know that now. There's less room for mistakes now. That's what being with Lenny has taught me.

And if I'm being truthful, I think that I'm in too far ever to get free, that when they sucked out my womb, they took half of my will as well. He's like a disease inside me, Marla. But one that I don't want to recover from. Of course I say nothing. I keep to my side of the bargain, demand no more than he feels able to give. And meanwhile his other affair he conducts in greater and greater secrecy. And some nights, after we've screwed and he's fallen asleep, or more likely gone out on the balcony to read a tome or two, some nights I wonder if it means that I am becoming just like him. Or if I have simply become accustomed to being a victim.

I should know the signs. Women who are victims always throw themselves in the path of the oncoming truck and then complain when it runs over them. Remember those people? We used to know a lot at one time. And we were so scathing about them. Well, sometimes I think I'm one of them now.

And the terrible thing is, Marla, you'll see nothing of this. When you meet him he'll be charming. He'll smile and shine and talk and listen, and you'll believe it's all there for the taking. But it won't really be him — any more than the person he had made me is really me. Or at least not the me you once knew.

Which is where this all began . . . and which is why I asked you to come. You're my last hope, Marla. I can't do it alone. I want to leave him, but I don't know how. It feels as if it's not allowed, like a rule which can't be broken. I want you to help me break it. Please.

Five

So ended Elly's tale. Outside, even the city seemed stilled for a moment. She sat huddled in her chair, her body awkward and taut, as if a kind of rigor mortis had set in.

I went over and put my arms around her. She did not respond. I held her tight, willing her to relax. "Listen, look on the bright side. It's fortunate I didn't bother to unpack. This way we can be on the first flight home."

But she missed or decided to ignore the irony in my voice and pulled away from me, brittle again. "It's not that simple," she said angrily. "Don't you understand, I can't leave. That's just the point."

I watched her carefully, as one might watch a child whose tantrums might lead her to inflict some damage on herself. It was a long time since Elly Cameron had so lost her sense of humor.

"Come on, Elly. This is me, Marla, remember? We're the ones who used to hit each other's shins with hockey sticks to

91

avoid having to play games in winter. Comrades in adversity. Nothing's changed. It's all right. I understood what you said."

Now, at last, her body loosened, and she let out a noisy sigh, caught midway between tears and laughter. "Oh. Marla, what a mess, eh? How the hell did I get into this? Does it really make any sense?"

"Of course." I was only half lying. It could never have been my story because I would have lacked the original courage to get that involved. Because Elly had always taken life in such huge gulps, it was inevitable that sooner or later she would ingest something that would disagree with her. But people seldom die of food poisoning, and Lenny, potent though he may have been, did not strike me as a lethal dose. At least not for the Elly I once knew.

"Listen, you know the legend as well as I do. All you have to do is slay the Minotaur, then start winding back the thread until you reach the entrance, which will also be the exit."

This time she grinned. "Trust in the gods, eh? Oh, Marla, I'm so glad you're here. Don't you wish you'd taken a package to Majorca instead?"

"Perish the thought. Haven't you heard? They're blowing up English tourists out there. Anyway, you know me. Why lead my own life when I can live through someone else's? Why do you think I've been so disturbed by your silence? I always knew there had to be a good story behind it."

Talk of our separation brought us back to time present. She looked at her watch in a kind of disbelief. "Christ, Marla, we've been sitting here for hours. You must be shattered. It's already morning in England."

And did I miss it? Not a jot. I could have stayed up till lunchtime. But she was in more need of sleep than I. Now it was told, the energy had seeped away and she looked gray with a tiredness worse than jet lag. I stood up.

"One question. How long before he gets back?"

She made a face. "Your guess is as good as mine. He left last Thursday. Said he'd be away for ten days. But he's always unpredictable. In my more paranoid moments, I think he does it deliberately, just to check up on me. Let's just say he could walk in at any time."

"Good," I said with a firmness designed to impress.

"You sound like you really want to meet him."

"After that buildup? I wouldn't miss it for the world. I'm even looking forward to it."

Boasting, of course, is a kind of hubris. In the still of the night such things are heard and visited upon you. Four in the morning. Almost two hours had passed since our good nights. My body was grumbling at me to sleep, but my mind was running the show. Elly's story was everywhere. There was no place where I didn't crash into it; a feeling, a fear. Twenty-four hours ago I had been obsessed by other things, expending energy sewing up the few loose ends of my life. None of it was there anymore. Elly had whitewashed it out.

I was fighting two quite separate emotions. The first was exhilaration at being plucked so suddenly out of my deliberate, controlled existence into the maelstrom of her life. That much was positive, full of warmth and color. The second emotion was fear, fear that I would not be strong enough to defeat him — or rather the him in her, because, of course, in every dragon myth half the problem is the princess. I knew her. I did not know him. Still, after all those words, he remained incomplete. Her emotions garbled him, minced him into a strange hybrid of villain and hero, explained nothing. A man who wielded the weapon of self-containment. If that really was his secret, then he and had something in common besides Elly. Would he recognize it? Had she?

In the eighteen years we had known each other, Elly and I had always operated differently. I turned somersaults in my head, walked across beds of nails, and spent too many years listening to my own heartbeat. I did not engage with the world. It was not my style. My act was perfected early, and it worked. People stayed clear of me. Even my parents had accepted the stranger in me. But not Elly. Elly had stayed. Right from the first moment outside the staff room, when I was the new girl, brainy and aloof, and she was the blithe spirit of the class, dropping a pile of textbooks in the path of the assistant headmistress and forcing me to laugh as she clowned about, trying to pick them up. I had expected to be lonely as an adolescent, had accepted it as my fate. Elly had marched straight through the Do Not Disturb signs and refused to go away when I tried to freeze her out. She had known that I needed someone. And she had decided that someone would be her.

We had things in common, had even shared a certain attitude to the world. Maybe it came from the fact that each of us was an only child and used to our own company. My mother had always been terrified of procreation, afraid she wouldn't know how to cope. She was right. She didn't. She was too much of a child herself. Since she needed a father more than I, and since there was not room enough for two children in the family, I became the adult. It suited me fine. The only person who took any interest in me was my grandmother, but she lived in Paris, so her parenting was reserved for holidays. As for Elly, well, she always said she had been conceived in an absence of mind, which was not quite the same thing as an absence of contraception. Her father had wanted a son and had lost interest immediately. Elly had spent much of her childhood trying to win him back. A course of action which had, no doubt, alienated her mother. Certainly, by the time we met, the Cameron household was a battlefield, and Elly had started to enjoy the war. Finding me provided another outlet for her emotional energies, this time a positive one.

Her sense of fun brought another dimension to those early teenage years, and I owed her for times which would otherwise have been dismal. Aggressive timidity is hardly a social asset, particularly during the first mating seasons. Whereas school dances and dates tempted others into alternative forms of learning, I went underground. Boys did not interest me. Or that was my story. So, I cut my long blond hair and became a scholar. But Elly never stopped pestering me. And her methods were robust. Once, when the blackness was particularly dense, she marched into my room and announced that according to a book she had just read I was either gay or intellectually overdeveloped. Did I fancy any of the fourth-formers? If not, I would just have to sit it out and wait for my body to catch up with my mind. We found it very funny at the time, although looking back, I see she wasn't so far from the truth. Certainly things got worse before they got better. And even if she couldn't always help, she knew how to handle me. There are some things you can't repay. Now, thanks to her and the occasional man persistent enough to brave the scorn, I have come through. True, I still enjoy work more than sex. But then how much pleasure does Kim Basinger get from reading Anglo-Saxon poetry? I am not so much strange as unfashionable. Yes, I have found a way through. And now I would help Elly to do the same.

I must have slept, because the next thing I remember was opening my eyes on a room more defined by light. I was covered in sweat and in need of a drink. I unglued my eyes and pulled myself out of bed, my cotton nightdress sticking to my skin. Outside in the corridor I was halfway to the kitchen when something made me stop.

Across the hall, through a half-open door, I glimpsed the living room, where a grainy dawn was creeping its way across the wood floor. At the other end of the room, one of the balcony doors was open. I remembered with an absolute clarity that the last thing Elly and I had done was to lock them, because it had occasioned a crack about New York paranoia reaching eight stories high. My stomach turned over. Don't be foolish, Marla. There must be an explanation. Probably Elly, unable to sleep. I stepped forward with silent footfalls. On a chair I spotted a jacket, pale cotton, and a briefcase. Next to the briefcase a book, with half its cover showing. I registered a bold, black-and-white ink drawing of a hand holding a quill pen: firm powerful stroke like a Dürer woodcut. Stupid the details one's brain records when it is concentrating hard on something else. Except that something rang a bell. I couldn't connect what. One thing was clear. This was no burglar. In which case there was only one explanation. Lenny was home.

My curiosity was enormous. To see him without being seen, watch him in his lair. I edged across the room, bare feet on rug. The floorboards did not give me away. When the balcony was in sight, I stopped. The man sitting out there was in oblique profile to me. He was tall, slender, and very fair, with long legs splayed out in front of him. He was wearing smart leather boots and designer trousers. The storm of hair was almost white. His face, had he turned fully, would have been clean and chiseled and beautiful. Mr. Magnificence himself. There was no doubt about it. The man on the balcony was the man on the plane.

I stood transfixed, my heart beating so loudly that I was surprised it didn't disturb him. When I felt more in control, I turned and glided from the room. I needed no second glance at the book cover. I already knew that the artist was not Dürer but a fellow countryman who, centuries later, dabbled in the same art. The book was Günter Grass's *Meeting at Telgte*, the novel he had been reading on the plane. What current obsession did this reflect? It took a sturdy mind indeed to find pleasures in the maze of the Thirty Years' War.

I sacrificed the glass of water to the cause of security. Back inside my room, I lay awake for what seemed like a small eternity, hearing Elly's voice in my head. "His other affair he conducts in greater and greater secrecy." Chicago on shop business? Among his many sins, Lenny was also a liar. What should I tell Elly? Or him for that matter? Maybe I should wait until I met him face-to-face. I felt a certain confidence that I, in my role as St. George, should have been granted such an early advantage. It would be a pity if lack of sleep undermined it. I recited a few pages of Bede and felt better. New York was stirring as I fell asleep.

I woke buried in hot sand. The sheet was over my head, a torture presumably self-inflicted to protect me from the light, which was streaming in through half-closed blinds. The morning might have been the afternoon. There was no way of telling since my watch had stopped at 6:43 A.M. I made a run for the bathroom, where I showered and dressed. I had no intention of risking formal introductions in a bathrobe. I needn't have worried. The flat felt empty. In the living room the balcony doors were closed; both Lenny and Günter Grass had gone. Along the corridor their bedroom door was ajar. I tiptoed in. The bed was unmade, and the room was decorated with a pleasingly familiar hurricane of Elly's clothes. But with no sign of tailored jacket or Gucci boots. I was heading for the kitchen, nursing the suspicion that maybe I had dreamt it all, when the phone rang somewhere near the bed. It took me a while to find it, and when I did I couldn't remember the number. Elly's laughter danced over the wires.

"God, you'd make a lousy maid. Well, I needn't ask how you slept."

"Where are you?"

"At the store. Crisis management. The girl who works here woke to find a gas leak in her apartment. She's watching the repairman while I'm waiting for a delivery. Didn't you get my note? It was under the orange juice."

"I haven't made it as far as the kitchen. What time is it?"

"Put it this way, you've missed two meals already. It's after three." The sleep of the dead. Except for the interruption. "And guess what?"

"What?"

"Lenny's home. Came in at dawn. What did I tell you? Perfect timing. As always."

"Where is he now?" I said at exactly the same instant as my eyes registered the door across the room leading to the en suite bathroom.

"Don't panic. You're safe. He was up and out early. Business, no doubt. I didn't catch the details. I arranged for us all to meet for dinner this evening. That is unless you want to change your mind and go to California today?"

Not for the world. I wanted to see the expression on his face when we met. "It can wait."

"That's what I hoped you'd say. Great. Why don't you get dressed and meet me downtown? . . ."

In the underworld no one moved more than was absolutely necessary. The air, baked in the folds of the tunnels, was stale and unprofitable, and the train when it arrived, roaring and screeching its way out of the darkness, was like the set of a Roger Corman movie, tacky and menacing.

I climbed in and sat down. New York. There is a different balance between madness and sanity in this city. Maybe that's why so many gravitate here. More room for deviancy. But you have to have the stomach for it. I remember my first visit, when I had taken the subway late at night, riding a compartment that was totally empty. I had spent four stops staring at the thick black graffiti which saturated the ceiling, seats, and walls.

I could almost see the madness seeping out of the spray paint, and crawling its way toward me. It was hard to know whose violence I was feeling, theirs or mine. In the end I got out of the train and took a taxi. Of course, I was younger then and my psyche a little less resilient. Graffiti is just graffiti now. Even in Manhattan.

Aboveground it was raging sunshine. Following instructions, I crossed into Washington Square. The place was swarming with people, sitting, striding, watching, playing. Two black kids body-popped to the roar of a ghetto blaster, while a small crowd gathered for the show. On the grass people were stretched out in the sun, and a middle-aged man was roller-skating along the paths.

I stood by an ice-cream stall and watched him. It was hard to know whether or not he was enjoying himself. There was something manic in his concentration, and after a while he made me uneasy. I left him traveling in circles.

From the square it was a five-minute walk to the store. Once you hit the right street you couldn't miss it. HERMOSA, as it was now called, in bold gold lettering across the window, was altogether a fancier piece of work than I had anticipated. The front was all glass, dark and smoky, giving the bags and garments displayed a kind of instant exclusivity. In one respect at least it was Elly who had taken Lenny upmarket, trading on memories of Biba mixed with Bauhaus.

Inside it was cool and luscious: summer shoppers must buy just to get away from the heat. No Elly. Instead, at the sales desk — a kind of mirrored altar — sat a High Priestess, dark and statuesque, eyes buried inch-deep in mascara. The man who had come to repair her gas leak must have thought he had been called out to visit Theda Bara. She was talking on the telephone but slid her hand over the mouthpiece as soon as she saw me come in.

"Hi there. Can I be of any assistance?"

She had one of those drawling voices which implies brain damage. I knew better than to be fooled by appearances: such lazy somnolence can hide unexpected sharpness. On the other hand, there was no immediate evidence to suggest that this girl was the Truman Capote of the rag trade. She seemed so languid that I feared the effort of raising her head in my direction might prove fatal. I had to admit it, though, she did suit the store. They might almost have been designed together.

"I'm just looking, thanks," I said, loitering over some leather, pretending to browse.

"Sure thing." She went back to the receiver. I fingered a few pieces and registered their price tags on the Richter scale. The stuff was a long way from the usual traveler's magpie hoard. The sweaters, the rugs — even the leatherwork — looked more Manhattan than Bogotá. Elly had undersold herself. A lot of energy had gone into these four walls, and a good deal of commercial imagination. There was only one thing wrong with it. It didn't feel like Elly.

"You know I will, I told you." Her voice was breathy, for his ears only, but I happened to be en route to the jewelry, passing close by the desk. Maybe all salesgirls call their lovers when the store is empty. "Yeah, of course I'm sure. Listen, there are some things she doesn't — Hey, look, I have someone in the store. I'll catch you later. I promise."

Behind me the telephone tringed. This time the voice reached out to caress me. "Oh, that is just beautiful, isn't it? You know, it's the last one in the store. Perfect for day or evening wear."

Perfect yes, for someone else. I laid the necklace back down on its black velvet.

"We have other kinds in stock if you'd like . . ."

"No. No thanks." This time our eyes met. It seemed churlish to pretend any longer. She would only resent it later. Anyway. I had a curiosity about her, this languid lady whom Elly had not seen fit to mention.

"I'm a friend of Elly's. From England. I arranged to meet her here."

"Oh, you must be Marla." She became almost flustered. A hand, which I now saw carried deep mauve fingernails, fluttered up from the counter in a gesture of recognition. Was she worried about her phone call? Surely not. "Elly's just out at the bank. She'll be back any minute. She asked me to look after you. Oh, I'm Indigo, by the way."

It wasn't that I disbelieved her. But let's just say I had a nagging suspicion this was probably not the name she had been born with. Surely her parents had nurtured a different vision for her future, one more befitting a Sandra or even a Tracy. Indigo must have been a more recent baptism, perhaps marking her arrival in a New York where Andy Warhol legends still promised fame for fifteen minutes — especially for those with names like Indigo. Evidently things had not worked out quite as planned. But then the world is full of people who didn't, after all, become famous. She seemed like the kind of person who could look after herself.

"How's the gas leak?" I said to make conversation.

"The gas leak? Oh, oh, it came from the apartment upstairs. Some ditz had put a chisel through the pipe. Hey, imagine you knowing about that."

Pause. Both of us spoke at once. After the clash I let her continue.

"This is your first visit to the store, right? It's pretty neat, don't you think? All thanks to Elly."

"What was it like before?"

"Oh, I don't know really. I wasn't here then. But I've seen a couple of pictures. It was kind of hokey. Lots of money but not a whole lot of taste."

"How long have you been here?" And who were you talking to on the phone? Be quiet, Marla, you always have had a suspicious nature.

"Four, five months, I guess. I came when Elly was . . . er . . . sick. Just to help out. And then I kinda stayed on."

"And did you know her and Lenny before then?"

She shook her head, and a wave of dark hair shimmered over her shoulders. In the light, without the coal deposits around her eyes, she might well have been a pretty girl.

107

As pretty as Elly. "No. No. I met Lenny at a friend's house — just before Christmas. I was looking for a job, and he took my number. A couple of months later he called me up. And here I am. When Elly got back, she liked what I'd done and they asked me to stay. Of course, you know, this isn't my real profession."

There was something about the simplicity of her innocence that troubled me. I knew she was about to tell me that she was really an actress or a dancer, and that this was just temporary employment, filling in between engagements.

"Actually, I'm an actress." She smiled coyly. "But well, you know how it is. It's nice to have something to do when you're resting."

I didn't ask how long it had been since her last exertion. "Were you born in New York?"

"Oh, my God, no. No one is born in this city. I come from the Midwest. Iowa City. It's in Iowa. A real good place to leave, believe me. I should never have been born there, of course. It was a complete mistake. We were gonna live in Chicago, but then my grandfather died and my dad had to take over the family business."

She paused, presumably for breath. I was

fascinated by this sudden garrulousness, so out of place beside the more assured, glamorous appearance. But then people who tell their life stories so readily to strangers always intrigue me. Does that mean they have another life tucked away for more intimate occasions, or is it the same shop-soiled one in private as well as in public? On the other hand, she was a performer. I had the impression she was trying for Dolly Parton. But all I was getting was Ruth Gordon in *Rosemary's Baby*. Absurd but true. It all went to support my thesis that she was not as birdbrained as she might have liked to appear.

Behind us the shop bell rang. I turned, anticipating Elly. Instead there was a well-dressed woman, immaculate in spite of the heat and with a haircut you could have hung in the Guggenheim. She glided over to the rails and fingered her way delicately through some cotton shifts. Over my head Indigo's voice wafted, lush and persuasive.

"Lovely, aren't they? And of course, all our own designs."

The woman scooped up a small handful of clothes and disappeared behind the curtain, presumably in an attempt to get away from the voice.

The shop bell rang again. This time it was Elly. She was dressed all in white. I looked at her in the chic surroundings she had created. There was still an edge of tension about her, an energy gone sour. She came to us grinning.

"Hi. Did you two introduce yourselves? You haven't bought anything yet? Indigo, you must be slipping."

Indigo smiled serenely and put a finger to her lips, indicating the curtain concealing a wallet of credit cards. The woman emerged, cool and clean in silky cotton. The dress was well cut. She stood in front of the full-length mirror and sucked in her cheeks in that way all women do when presented with themselves as models. She went over to the jewelery section and began picking out necklaces to put against the dress. She was the right shape for them. Indigo, smelling blood, melted off her stool and re-formed herself next to the woman. It was like watching mercury move. Elly watched me watching her and smiled, pulling me toward the back of the store. Out through heavy velvet curtains there was a storeroom, mercifully more scruffy, and piled high with crates and boxes.

"We should leave her to it. She's very good. I've seen her send people home with

110

whole wardrobes they didn't think they needed."

I nodded. "Is she as dumb as she makes out?"

Elly laughed. "Not quite, I think. We don't really have that much to do with one another. Her staying on was one of the decisions Lenny made when we got back together again. I'm grateful really. It gives me more time to do the buying — the day-to-dayness used to bore me stupid. She doesn't seem to mind. And there's no doubt that when she puts her mind to it, she's shit-hot. Look at her now. I couldn't do that."

Outside Indigo was leading the woman gently toward the cash desk, necklace and earrings in hand, ring in her nose. "Maybe it's the performer in her," added Elly.

"Maybe. How much does she know?"

"About what lies behind the business? Nothing. It was all set up long before she came along."

"So where does she think Lenny got his money from?"

"She believes what he told her. What he tells everyone. That his rich, indulgent father squandered some of the family fortune on his wayward son. It's not so far from the truth. Well . . . what do you think of it?"

111

I searched for the right word. "It's very exclusive."

"You betcha. And the higher we write the price tags, the more people buy. You don't approve?"

"I don't know. It doesn't feel like you."

She looked at me for a second, then frowned. "Well, perhaps I've changed." She stood up abruptly. "This place gives me the creeps. I'm always waiting for tarantulas to crawl out of the crates. Let's get out of here. Celebrate our last few hours of freedom."

It was the kind of cocktail bar that could have doubled for an album cover, all pink and white with a shimmer of chrome around the edges and a background of jungle potted palms. Everything in the place was shiny, including the waiter. It was 6:15 P.M. Smart New Yorkers were beginning to trickle in for the first alcohol of the evening. We sat at the bar facing fractured images of ourselves in mosaic mirrors, happy-hour concoctions with cherries and Japanese umbrellas in front of us. We were, as they say, in a countdown situation — Lenny was due to meet us in just under an hour. One hour. I was impatient to get him center stage and throw some light on this character actor, while I, the inquisitor, lurked in the shadows. He had prowled around the edges for too long.

We had tried talking of other things. But I had no story to put against Elly's, just a lot of day-to-dayness with the odd question mark, not the kind of thing to go with multicolored cocktails and pistachio nuts. So I dodged the inquiries, and somehow in the silence that followed all roads led back to Lenny. But still I said nothing of my sleep-walking visitation. Why not? The subconscious, they say, is a many-splendored thing. Sometimes you should trust it. Sometimes.

"So, what does he know about me?"

"I'm not sure. In the beginning I told him quite a lot. Recently I've kept you to myself. But he has a good memory."

"Does he know why I'm here?"

A nervous shrug of the shoulders. "What Lenny knows and doesn't know is a continual mystery to me. When he got home last night, I told him you were here. I said I had called you on the spur of the moment and that on the spur of the moment you had agreed to come. It was near enough to the truth. He was very interested. Asked a lot of questions, paid me a lot of attention. Very Lenny. He does that sometimes — switches on as well as off. And just as there is a sense of his absence, so there's also a sense of his being there. You'll see. It's almost tangible. Like being caught under an ultraviolet light. You can almost feel the plants grow. Last night it kind of spooked me. I kept wondering if maybe he hadn't been there all along, hiding out somewhere on the balcony, listening to our conversation."

"Houdini he may be, God he isn't," I said lightly, but she didn't seem to hear.

In the prism behind the bar, the door had opened. Elly glanced up, and I saw the spark in her eyes. The barman snapped into attention. Trumpets blared and angels sang. I, however, refused to be rushed. I turned slowly and began with the feet. Maybe it was the white shoes which gave him away, such a delicious contrast with the wild pink of the carpet.

Traveling upward, it was all a similar hymn to good taste. Ours were not the only heads that turned. Unpredictable as ever, Lenny was early.

He came toward us, a high-voltage smile cracking the air. It pains me to say this, because it is not in my nature to believe in charisma, but Lenny was special. I had hoped that my airline memories might have blown him out of proportion; that he was really just another good-looking guy with more than his fair share of confidence. But it was more than that. Confidence, vanity, energy — call it what you will — Lenny came into one's life like a prizefighter, dancing on his toes, watchful, wonderful, and unable to contemplate the possibility of defeat.

At the bar he bent to kiss Elly lightly on the head, then, stationing himself behind her, turned the spotlight on to me. You will, I think, believe me when I tell you that he knew me. And that he knew I knew him. Not that there was any outward sign of recognition; no flickcring glance, no half frown or split-second hesitation. But it was there all the same. Something crossed between us. Maybe it was simply the warmth of ultraviolet, who knows.

"Hello there, Marla." The voice was dark, melodious even, but hardly the kind of song to draw sailors off course. "I've heard so much about you I feel as if we've already met."

"We have," I said, with less music but more force. "It's just we haven't been formally introduced." And I smiled.

He smiled back and laid a hand on Elly's shoulder. I looked at them. Yes, they went well together. Her small dark head beneath his fair one. A couple to sell engagement rings. There was a hint of implied ownership in his stance. I found myself thinking of the times they must have made love together, taken each other for granted in all kinds of ways. And I felt suddenly as if I was watching two people in a foreign film with the subtitles erased. I began to feel like a voyeur, and a familiar shiver crept over me. For that moment I wished I wasn't in New York at all, but back within my own four walls, in an environment controlled by me, as bland and safe as I chose to make it.

I caught Elly looking at me. I had forgotten how much she noticed. It used to be one of her specialities, leading me back out of exile. She picked up her drink and handed it to Lenny.

"Here, you finish this. I'm going to the washroom. Why don't you find a table? We can't talk at the bar."

He chose a corner, framed by palm trees. Over on the other side of the room, a man in a gray velvet suit settled himself at the piano. I brought my gaze back to Lenny. He was sitting watching me, smiling. In the background, Mr. Music sent out a ripple of notes. *Unforgettable, that's what you are* . . . Lenny took it as his cue.

"Well, who would have believed it? Of all the flights, in all the cities of the world, fate has to off-load me onto your plane. Obviously, Marla, you're here to be my un-doing."

New England formality, coated in Casablanca charm. There was nothing to say.

"You know, of course, that I wasn't meant to be in England at all. That Elly thought I was in Chicago, and if she were to find out the truth . . . Well, put it this way, my surprise would no longer be a surprise, would it?"

I was beginning to see how it worked. He made you assume there was a conversation in progress, even though he was the only one talking. "I'm afraid I don't understand." My voice sounded promisingly cool, Bette Davis faced with blackmail in a cocktail lounge.

"Of course you don't. And as soon as I start explaining, Elly will walk back in and we'll have to change the subject. Still, that's a risk I'm going to have to take." He left another, apparently deliberate pause, during which I did nothing to reassure him. His left hand was cupped around the stem of his glass. I noticed veins running under brown skin, sculptured fingers that were strong and slender at the same time. Damn the man, even his hands were beautiful. Across the room a bridge of chords joined Irving Berlin to George Gershwin. The pianist began to build a stairway to Paradise while Lenny made his bid for entrance through the pearly gates.

"Elly and I have had some trouble. No doubt you know that. Both of our faults, I think, but the damage is done. Damage from which she is not yet recovered. Perhaps you know that also. I think part of the problem is New York. I think she's homesick. Homesick for people, but also for England. But she's scared to admit it because she thinks it would be admitting failure. So I figured I might help her along. Arrange a trip without telling her — a kind of magical mystery tour — and spring it on her at the last minute. Maybe then she'd agree. I went to Britain to fix it up. I even thought of calling you when I was in London, but I didn't have your number. And I wasn't sure you would want to become accessory to the fact . . . Well, I needn't have worried. It seems you are anyway." He paused. "Unless, of course, you're planning to give me away."

His eyes shone, blue-gray diamonds, the very stuff of romantic fiction. I blinked to cut out the glare. Elly had been a long time in the washroom. Obviously she wanted us to get acquainted. I considered his proposition. Should I believe him? What was there to disbelieve? Either it was the truth or it wasn't. There was even, I had to admit, a kind of perverse logic to it. Maybe Elly was homesick. Certainly she was afraid to go home. She had left England on impulse; maybe that was also the way she would return. I had come to help her. Indeed I had come to take her home. Only he didn't know that.

Over his shoulder, the door to the powder room swung open, and a small dark figure emerged. He registered my glance but didn't take his eyes off me. I had to hand it to him. He had strong nerves.

"All right," I said, when she was almost upon us. "You have my silence."

"Terrific." He made his voice public with a laugh, turning to greet her with impeccable timing.

"What's terrific?" She was looking at me rather than him.

"Oh, we've just been discovering areas of common interest," he said, glancing up at her. "You got to remember, I don't get to meet too many professional historians these days."

"Oh no, you're not going to talk shop." She groaned, but you could tell she was pleased.

"Uh-uh. We've finished our revision of

the past, haven't we, Marla? Now I suggest we get on with the present. Champagne I think. To celebrate the reunion."

And so mine host took charge, and under the grow lamp of his attention, small shoots of conversation began to appear. The champagne was accompanied by questions: my impressions of New York, the changes I found, my work, the trials and tribulations of teaching. Unspectacular subject matter but impressively handled. He appeared to find my replies riveting. He certainly listened, tossing back thoughts, playing with possibilities, picking up on my dust-dry humor, giving as good as he got. It was a game, of course, albeit consummately played. I remembered Elly's description of that first night in Bogotá, and I know I was being charmed and coaxed into complicity. But then, what option did I have? After all, wasn't this just a social occasion? The meeting of Elly's friends. No, I had wanted to see Lenny in action. Now was my chance. And all the time Elly sat and watched us spar until, gradually, as the illusion of relaxation grew, her apprehension faded and she too began to join in.

Three minds with but a single thought — to avoid confrontation and observe the protocol of pleasure. And thus, against all odds, the evening began to blossom. After the second bottle of champagne — the credit should be shared — we floated on to the streets and hailed a taxi, cruising our way through the crimson New York twilight to an expensive, exclusive Japanese restaurant, where everything was opaque and cool, and where we sat on tatami and played at being Oriental, bowing our heads at silken, smiling waitresses and eating our way through an endless art exhibit of tastes, while gently but surely crippling ourselves on a warm stream of sake.

And here it was that Lenny really came into his own, telling witty tales of his travels in Japan, mixing fact with fiction, the sacred with the profane. And because I am susceptible to intelligence, I allowed myself, temporarily at least, to be seduced by him. He, in turn, did not become complacent. Indeed, he never once forgot the complex energies of the evening. Thus he kept me in close contact while always being alert to Elly's needs: a hand on the back of her chair, the odd touch, a way of recalling incidents shared which gave them an intimacy without excluding me. And she accepted his ministrations gracefully, unable to resist the temptation of pleasure from having us both — her lover and her best friend — so close.

And as for him? Well, it was a virtuoso performance, and obscured for those few hours all shadows of the other Lennys, the cold, the cruel, the distant ones. And so I learned a lesson for times to come. That my battle was not so much with a dragon breathing fire as with Proteus changing shapes, and that whatever magic was woven around me, I should always be on my guard.

Finally we picked up our pampered bodies and carried them home to the apartment in the sky, where all that remained to do was to sit out in the night air and sip bourbon. And it was there, on the balcony, that the spell wore off, and the ghosts of last night's conversation came back to haunt our newfound bonhomie. And so I got up, excused myself, and retired to bed.

After a while they too made their way to the bedroom. I heard footsteps and whispered voices. Then I felt my door open and caught sight of Elly's white figure hovering like some Victorian angel over my bed.

"I came to say good night," she whispered. "And to tell you how happy I am that you're here."

And I looked up at her, her face all snub and cubist in the night shadows, and said, "I think we should go to California."

To which she smiled. "Of course. Is tomorrow soon enough? All it takes is a phone call. What happened, Marla? Did you get sunburned already?"

And if I answered, I have no recollection of what I said. Indeed I remember nothing more of that night, for which I am grateful, for the walls of the apartment were thin and I had no wish to hear their lovemaking.

Six

The black guy who sold us the Greyhound tickets at San Francisco Airport looked like a baseball pro with the day off. I kept thinking he must be wearing roller skates, the way he darted around the booth checking timetables and punching tickets. His efficiency was designed to be admired. As he took our money, he flashed a smile which cracked his face from ear to ear. The teeth revealed were a monument to private dental care.

"Ladies, the bus to Santa Cruz leaves in exactly eight minutes from the stop at the end of the Arrivals concourse. Take care, have a good journey, and thank you for going Greyhound."

We all grinned, none of us believing a word of it, but all colluding in the myth. Then Elly and I picked up our suitcases and headed for the sign of the dog.

We had taken an afternoon flight from the East, sipping tea and watching the epic performance of prairies, mountains, and deserts unfold beneath us. It had not, to date, been the best of days. Morning had broken to unauthorized drilling in the back of my skull, a warning too late of the comparative strengths of English and American cocktails. Next to my bed was a scrawled note from Elly:

I thought you used to be an insomniac? I'm at the store tying up loose ends. We're booked on the 3:45 flight to San Francisco. Are you still up for it?

Clearly not. At that point it seemed inconceivable I should travel as far as the bathroom, let alone the West Coast. Think big, start small. I crept out of bed. The door to their bedroom was closed. Thank God, Lenny was still unconscious. After a few gallons of water, my vision improved, but my head still hurt. In the kitchen the orange juice was sweet and thick with pulp, but I could manage only a few gulps. I filled a mug with black coffee and made my way out onto the balcony. I was practicing focusing when I heard the front door open. Elly doesn't waste time, I thought, just before Lenny's voice tapped me on the shoulder.
"Good morning, Marla."
It was the casual look this morning. T-shirt,

designer jeans, and sneakers. Casual with a capital *C*. Funny how Lenny's clothes always drew attention to themselves — "Look at us. Look at us. We belong to Lenny." I think I muttered something in reply.

"You interested in contemporary history?" he said, pulling out *The New York Times* and burdening me with a couple of volumes of it. "More coffee?"

I shook my head. Slowly.

"You sure? You look like you need it. Got a hangover?"

"Nothing a brain transplant wouldn't cure."

He laughed. "Don't worry. I have the perfect remedy."

At least it got rid of him for a moment. I sat staring down at the front page of the paper. From the kitchen I registered the sounds of the fridge, then the blender. I was grateful the noise wasn't any closer. REAGAN URGES STRONGER PENALTIES FOR DRUG ABUSE. I read the headline twice. Lenny appeared with a tall glass of yellowish liquid.

"What is it?"

"I wouldn't ask."

I cradled it in my hands, then took a sip. It tasted rancid. He waited for me to show my disgust. I took a breath and finished it in one

126

long, foul gulp. As I put it down, I began to feel a fizzing in my stomach. Then I most definitely felt sick. Lenny had poisoned me. Of course. I had fallen straight into the trap.

"You feel sick, right?" he said, leaning against the railing, watching, amused. I decided not to risk opening my mouth. "Good. That means it's working. Give it a few minutes and you'll feel like a new woman."

To my relief the old one returned, feeling more herself than ever. For a while we sat in silence. Then he said, "So, you're a historian, Marla. That gives us something in common. I've just finished that Günter Grass novel on the Thirty Years' War, *Meeting at Telgte*. Have you read it?"

I shook my head.

"Pity. I would have been interested in your professional opinion. I think it's pretty good. Brings it alive. But then, of course, he's a novelist rather than a historian — more interested in atmosphere than in facts. You probably despise that kind of thing."

There was no doubt about it: Lenny wanted to talk.

"I'm not averse to imagination in history, if that's what you mean. Facts are just facts without interpretation."

"And history is interpretation?"

127

"Yes, something like that."

"What about when interpretation becomes distorted?"

"Then it ceases to be history." I shrugged. "Maybe that's when it becomes fiction."

"So what about Bergman's *Seventh Seal*?"

"What about it?"

"Fact or fiction?"

I was becoming aware that I was feeling distinctly less accommodating than the night before. Of course, it might just have been the ragged end of the hangover. But something told me that the feeling was mutual.

"Neither. Swedish art doesn't count."

He smiled. "How about your own period? Anglo-Saxon Britain, isn't it? Have you ever seen a movie which captured that for you?"

"Absolutely. Tony Curtis and Kirk Douglas in *The Vikings*," I said with a perfectly straight face. "A breathtaking recreation of an early medieval soap."

He raised an eyebrow. "You don't like talking about your job, is that it?"

"People don't usually ask. It's not exactly an immediately arresting period."

"Is that why you chose it?"

Ten out of ten, Lenny. "I don't know. Certainly I like the fact that it's underpopulated. By historians at least. Not like the Tudors or the Borgias. Researching them is like shopping in a supermarket on Christmas Eve: too many people squabbling over the same dead flesh. In Anglo-Saxon history you can go for years without meeting another living soul."

"And you like that?"

"Yes, I like that."

Blood out of a stone. I was weary of his concentration. There was too much of the inquisition about it.

"Elly tells me you're leaving today," he said, changing the subject as if he had read my thoughts. "It doesn't give us much time to get to know each other. I'd been looking forward to that."

"You could always come out and join us." I felt forced into being charitable. "Later."

"I'm not sure I should disturb your reunion. You two have a lot of catching up to do. Although I gather you've done some of it already."

"Yes," I said softly. So was this what it was all about? "Some of it."

"Elly assures me you're a very discreet person." He smiled. "But then I guess I had proof of that last night." Still I said nothing. "I do hope you can help her, Marla. She worries me. She doesn't seem to be able to relax anymore. There's a kind of perpetual tension about her. Maybe you've noticed?"

This time he waited, as if he seriously expected a reply. What kind of treaty did he think we'd signed last night? *Détente* does not mean disarmament. "No, I can't say I have. But then it's been a long time."

He nodded. "Anyway, I want you to know how happy I am that you're here. I know you'll do her a lot of good."

How is it that you know when someone's lying? Is it really in the eyes? Or maybe it's the voice. Or the body. Because something has to set off the alarm bells, and just at that moment I had developed a severe case of tinnitus. I decided it was my turn to change the subject. There was something I was curious about.

"I have a question."

"Be my guest."

"It's about the flight. Last night. I wondered if perhaps you'd spotted us meeting at the airport — Elly and I?"

There was just the hint of a frown.

"It was just that you didn't get home until so much later. I thought perhaps you'd seen us in the arrivals hall and decided to give us some time together."

He laughed as if the theory brought him genuine pleasure. "God, no. Nothing so ingenious. You had disappeared long before I cleared Customs. I had a slight problem. You see, I had no luggage to clear. It wasn't on the plane. I spent the best part of three hours waiting for them to track it down. They finally located it revolving around an empty conveyor belt in Miami. They flew it back first thing this morning. That's why I was up so early. I tell you, it's the first and last time I ever fly British Airways. Speaking of which, you're booked on American Airlines this afternoon. I hope that doesn't offend your patriotism. So, you know California?"

"A little," I said, admiring what Elly would have called the stage management.

"But not J.T.? I'll be interested to see what you make of him. I don't know what Elly has told you, but he's quite a character."

"You're good friends."

"Like you and Elly." He smiled. "We go back a long way."

No time to reflect on this or anything else. The front door rattled Elly's arrival, and she entered like a small whirlwind, all heat and hurry. I stashed the conversation away to be regurgitated later. We were almost late for the plane.

The Greyhound, on the other hand, was

punctual to the minute. We settled ourselves in the back seats, a small ocean of
space between us and the nearest passen-
gers. Outside, California appeared like a
movie set, sharp acrylic light on
Technicolor landscape. Santa Cruz and our
host were just an hour away over the hills
and the redwood forest. Over the rainbow
to blue skies and paradise living. And another man of mystery, this one so enigmatic
that he didn't even have a proper name. It
was time to open a file on this latest character. Beginning with his initials. What exactly did J.T. stand for?

Elly turned from the window laughing.
"Your guess is as good as mine. Why don't
you ask him? I've never had the nerve. Boy,
if you think Lenny plays his cards close to
his chest, you wait until you meet J.T. He's
a one-man secret society. What do I know
about him? Let's see . . . That he and Lenny
met in Bogotá, five — maybe six — years
ago. He was set up by then; Lenny was just
starting out. They got on, worked together
for a while — something of a legendary part-
nership I gather — then split up and went
their separate ways, east and west. But they
still keep in touch. Sit out on each other's
porches, drinking beer and reliving the good
old days."

"You sound as if you disapprove."

"*Approval* isn't the right word. I just have a little trouble with the whole 'We were there together, *amigo*' routine, that's all. It's a bit like being the girl in the Butch Cassidy legend. A lot of fun until you're the one who gets left behind."

"Aren't there any women in the business?"

"Oh sure, but you don't often find them running the show. They work on the ground, moving it on once it comes in. And there are some who bring it in: the mules, lovely *señoritas* tightrope-walking their ways through Customs. But usually in someone else's operation. For the most part it's all much like life in the fifties. The ladies stay home and spend their old men's money. I tell you, it's a very traditional business, despite all the hype and the glamour. You're looking at a kept woman."

"Come on, Elly. Profit margins like Hermosa's don't make themselves. You earn your living. You and Lenny both know that. What about J.T.? Who launders his banknotes?"

She shook her head. "No one. Or not that I've come across. Anyway, they don't need cleaning anymore. He's retired."

"What happened?"

"As usual, I don't know the details. It was a couple of years ago now, just before Lenny and I got together. J.T. used to run a big operation around the Palo Alto area. Same deal as Lenny, bringing it in and moving it on. Then, just after he'd cleared a big shipment, someone got busted and the links led directly to him. They never touched him, but he saw it as an omen. He'd made his killing anyway, plowed it all into real estate. There was so much money moving around California in those days that no one looked too closely at where it was coming from. Land was safe, small holdings led to big profits, and once you'd bought in you could push all your earnings through it. He was a rich man. He'd already bought a chunk of coastline and started putting down houses on it. He sold off a few and built one for himself. That's where he lives now, in early and comfortable retirement, although he doesn't splash it around."

"What does he do with his life?"

"Search me. He certainly hasn't reentered society, that's for sure. He's crazy about stargazing and gardening, that's all I know. Grows enough to feed a small army, and gives most of it to the chickens. He's the kind of guy who a hundred years ago would have made a great rancher. He's built like an ox, doesn't like company, and isn't really interested in the twentieth-century bits of life. One of nature's genuine eccentrics."

"But you like him?"

She smiled at herself. "Yes, I suppose I do. Although I don't quite know why. He's a hit of a misfit really, less glamorous than Lenny. Maybe I've just come to mistrust the gloss. Also, he was good to me. Helped me when I needed it."

Of course, it had been to J.T. she had come after the separation. And it had been J.T. who had advised her to leave Lenny. Although not in so many words . . .

"It was funny. He never said it directly. But I knew what he meant. Brotherly advice." She pulled a face. "Except, of course, I ignored him."

"What did he say when he found out?"

"I don't know. We never discussed it. He just left me at the airport and I flew out. Since then nothing. That was part of the deal. He didn't want Lenny to know I had been there and neither did I. It was our secret. When I rang him to ask if we could use the guesthouse, he didn't say anything, just agreed to meet us. It was as if the conversation had never taken place. That old cocaine silence — no wasted words. I think you'll like him. My guess is contact will be kept to a minimum, and with the exception of the odd delivery of carrots and kohlrabi we won't see him again until the day we leave."

The perfect neighbor. He did, as it turned out, have one fault. He was not punctual. The Greyhound hit Santa Cruz bus terminal maybe two minutes behind schedule. Half an hour later J.T. had still not arrived. Inside we sat listening to the integrated rhythms of pinball and Space Invader machines played by a small army of travelers who seemed to have nowhere to go. Muzak to our ears.

The concert was interrupted by a short scene from a spaghetti western, as the sunlight streaming in through the doorway was momentarily eclipsed by a figure arriving. The whole place looked up as a man roughly the size of a bear walked in. The bear was my first thought. The second was that for such a large animal he was remarkably light on his feet. In fact, the proportions were altogether unusual: a big square head on broad stacked shoulders and massive torso, but from the waist down the body tapered unexpectedly to reveal slim, almost boyish

136

hips and long, well-formed legs. It was like on those games of cards where you match the right top to the wrong body, making Mr. Bun a fishmonger. I moved my eyes back up to his face. He had a surprisingly gentle appearance: untidy brown hair and beard with dark eyes, like small lumps of coal, set back behind John Lennon glasses. Long before he stopped in front of us, I knew this had to be J.T.

Elly had risen to greet him, but still he towered above her. He must, I calculated, have been at least six feet four. She made a small, almost shy gesture, putting both her hands on his arms and squeezing slightly. I wondered if he even registered the pressure. He stared down at her and nodded.

"I'm late." An earth-mumble of an apology. Elly tossed it aside and put out a hand toward me. "J.T., this is Marla, a very old friend from England."

I came up to his shoulder. It was not a usual experience for me. I caught a glimpse of myself miniaturized in his glasses. What next? A handshake seemed too formal, anything else too forward. I nodded. He almost did the same.

Formalities over, he bent down and scooped up our bags, Gulliver picking up Lilliputian boulders. Outside, a battered blue pickup truck was parked halfway up the pavement. He tossed the cases in the back and opened the door for us.

We piled in. I sat at the far end, near the window, Elly in the middle, crushed between his huge bulk and my large one. The ride had the expectation of silence about it. It seemed to be a silence that he carried with him, and that infected people as and when he came across them. I settled my attention on the scenery: downtown Santa Cruz, sunshine everywhere, flattening the shadows, toasting the air. The pace of life seemed sleepy after New York. In the sixties this little town had been a mecca of easy living, with its radical new university, its endless sunshine, and its surf. Many had come here to freeload on sun, sea, and food stamps. And many, it appeared, had never left. We passed half-dressed bodies in faded denim loitering on the pavements and in the street cafés, long-haired blond angels on the way home from the beach, the commuters of pleasure. Beside me Elly was laying down cables of communication between herself and this giant.

"Lenny sends his regards. Said he might come out sometime next week."

"Uh-huh."

"He asked me to say if there was anything

you needed from the big city to let him know."

"Yeah."

At the stoplight a parade of boys in cutoffs passed in front of us, surfboards clutched clumsily under their arms. One of them had a nose covered in white zinc. They were laughing at something. In the car, Elly had turned to farming.

"How's the garden?"

"Pretty good."

What had she said, about J.T. and Lenny sitting out on each other's porches reliving the old days? It was hard to imagine such fluency. The pause grew into a silence and became a habit. We left the city and its health food shops, boutiques, and beautiful people behind. The forest began to spring up again, fringing the roads and dappling sunlight onto the truck. We were traveling due north. About ten miles outside town we turned west, up through a road which wound high and crinkly into the hills. J.T. drove it like a straight highway. The truck seemed to enjoy itself, as if it knew the way home.

At the top of one of the bends, opposite a lonely clump of mailboxes, we braked sharply and swung left down a dirt track. The pickup's wheels spun on the dry earth.

We trundled onward, heavy trees roofing the sky and cutting out the light.

In the distance an explosion of sunlight promised a more open sweep of land. The truck slowed down to greet it. Then all at once we were free from the trees, on the edge of a great rolling open plateau, wide meadowland, corn-colored with the sun, while ahead the horizon fell off into what looked like a sheer drop, and along the top of it a band of pointillist blue and silver — the Pacific Ocean, for all the world like a retouched picture postcard.

Elly flashed me a grin. "See," it said, "I told you it was spectacular." If J.T. registered the admiration, he didn't show it.

We drove across the plateau until the track began to slope toward the edge of the canyon. A small house appeared on the right of the skyline, all wood and glass surrounded by a huge vegetable plot with a line of gigantic sunflowers marking its boundaries. This surely was J.T.'s Garden of Eden. I searched for ours, but when I caught sight of it a few moments later, it seemed to make no sense. All I could see in the distance was a roof covered in grass, sloping down into the meadow. A house with no back to it? Closer, the illusion proved to be fact. The roof was indeed meadow, the building itself gouged out of the hillside like some twentieth-century cave. The entire frontage was glass, just one huge transparent wall leading out onto a wooden deck with a wild uninterrupted view of the chasm as it plunged down toward the ocean.

"Extraordinary," I muttered, as the car bounced its way toward the horizon.

"Yep, and not an architect's drawing in sight, isn't that right, J.T.?"

J.T., needless to say, said nothing. But somehow you could tell he was pleased. Houses, market gardens, kilos of cocaine. It was becoming clear that there was more to J.T. than a couple of initials. We reached the house and parked in a small gravel square just beneath it. As the noise of the engine died away, a great, magnificent silence came gusting in through the windows, broken only by the occasional cricket chafing its limbs in baked slumber. J.T. got out. The slam of the car door was like a gunshot in church. We followed quietly.

In through the glass door, wooden floors hot with the sun ran into cool shady places filled with cushions and easy chairs. At the back, tucked in against the side of the hill, a kitchen ready for visitors, two large brown bags of groceries on the worktop. Above, up an iron spiral staircase, I could make out two simple bedrooms. J.T. put down the bags and turned to Elly.

"I'll bring you some vegetables. If you need a car, the VW's got the keys in the glove compartment. See you around."

Then, with a cursory nod, he was gone. We stood where he had left us and listened while the sound of the engine rose, then faded as the truck crossed back over the meadow to the other house. The silence returned. We looked out over the canyon, shimmering in the haze of the sun. The view went on forever. It was like being in an American supermarket: the same sense of chronic exaggeration. Why have so much beauty when a little would do?

"Baby laxative," Elly muttered into the still air.

"What?"

"Baby laxative. One of the perfect cuts. White and fluffy. J.T. probably owes a portion of his canyon to it. Along with borax, baking soda, talcum powder, sulphate, and benzocaine, to mention but a few. The only use I've ever found for chemistry O level. They should teach special classes to young Americans. Professional studies. Absurd, isn't it?"

But then who ever expected the world to

make sense? All this based on a million burned-out membranes. So what? Henry Ford made his fortune out of lead pollution. America belonged to self-made men. What about the women? Left to my own devices, I would be curled in a London bed with the soft drone of the World Service as an ally against insomnia. London darkness and cocaine empires in the sun: the two images were further apart than the miles that divided them. Yet because of Elly I belonged here. Temporarily at least. She slipped her arm through mine and pulled me toward the edge of the deck.

"Come on, teacher. I'll show you where the lizards sunbathe."

PART TWO

. . . the whole truth . . .

Seven

There now followed a short intermission. Four and a half days to be exact, during which time our being together became just a way of life, careless, easy, undisturbed. J.T. was as good as his word. When I woke early that first morning, bullied awake by the light, I found a box of vegetables on the deck by the door — onions, beets, and lettuce, topped by a layer of Bugs Bunny carrots, large and sprouting. Elly rose an hour later, complaining that she couldn't sleep because of the silence. And so together we set about constructing the day as a prototype for the times to come.

First came breakfast, hot rolls and coffee on the deck amid a subtle percussion of gecko calls. Then the morning spent frying slowly, Elly stretched out coated in sweat and suntan oil, while I reclined next to her on a sunbed, half clothed, like some overweight Matisse model, a large parasol angled over me, shading my view of the canyon. By 2:00 P.M. it proved too hot even

147

for sun worshipers, and so we would retire indoors for the quiet hours, when we might sleep or read, or listen to music. Then, as the sun grew lower, we would venture out for small walks into the belly of the canyon or up across the meadow. But we never made it down to the sea or out to the road, for we were not interested in entering the world or in meeting its inhabitants. And by the time we got back, it was only a short run to the final act of the sunset, which we watched from the best seats in the house, returning to them after dinner to chatter our way into the night silence. And in this way, gradually, our togetherness ceased to be a novelty. Our conversations became less greedy and intense, we laughed and gossiped more, and thus, little by little, we caught up on each other's lives.

And so to the fourth day. Midmorning and the wood on the deck was already too hot for bare feet. We had been up a long time thanks to a phone call which had woken us on the edge of dawn, and which rang and rang until Elly stumbled downstairs, only to find the noise stopping just as she lifted the receiver. We drank coffee as the sun came up, and by nine-thirty we were cooking, Elly already two shades darker than on her arrival, staked out in the sun like a strip of salt beef curing for winter, while Marla, our fair-skinned sultana, perspired pleasurably under her parasol.

The talk had meandered through mutual friends and enemies and had progressed on to teaching and the glories of Anglo-Saxon history. Elly, as always, remained unconvinced. Like most people (like Lenny), she thinks it strange that I should find such warmth and satisfaction in the cold, dark world of pre-Norman Britain. We had sat through the same history lessons at the age of thirteen, but what had fired me had frozen her. And many others. People do not seem to understand the delights of an age when myth, religion, and reality fed into one another; when a Christian culture could absorb pagan gods and goblins, and when it produced art so beautiful that medieval monks later believed it to have been the work of angels. But then to each her secret garden. And if mine remains a private passion and one that I cannot always communicate to my yearly flock, maybe that is all to the good. I simply help to keep the academic population culled. The world has enough Anglo-Saxon historians, anyway. They are, after all, of limited use.

And so we passed on to other things. In a spot near the edge of the deck, I caught sight of a lizard petrified in the heat, his head half turned toward me, chin thrust outward, lidless eyes immobile. We attempted to stare each other out. I weakened first, blinking only to discover he had disappeared without seeming to move. I turned back to find Elly watching me.

"You know you look good, Marla," she said softly. "Getting older suits you."

"I know. I'm like wine. Give me another thirty years, and I'll be irresistible. Cheeky but pretentious."

"Seriously, I mean it. I always knew that's how it would be. Don't you remember me telling you?"

"Constantly."

"Cynic," she said fondly. "My God, it all seems so long ago. Do you ever think about those days?"

"Yes," I said, this time truthfully.

"When we were young and easy under the apple blossom."

"Boughs," I corrected. "Third-form poetry competition. You'd just had a brace fitted, and you couldn't say your s's properly."

"Pedant." She laughed. "Boy, what recall. What else do you remember?"

"The school play when you caught measles just before the first night. The day we played truant to watch a partial eclipse of the sun. And the time you stole a bottle of sherry from the staff dining room."

She whooped with pleasure. "Yeah, I remember that one. Fourth-year speech day. You'd won that book for history composition. What was it? It had a red cover —"

"W. Harrison Ainsworth. *The Tower of London*."

"That was it. And while everyone was singing the school hymn I slipped out, grabbed the bottle, and stashed it at the back of one of the kilns in the pottery studio. We drank it after school. Got out of our skulls. We must have been all of fourteen. We swore undying love to each other, never to be interrupted by such gross invaders as 'men.' " She smiled wistfully. "I suppose every generation of fourteen-year-olds discovers their own women's movement in the equivalent of some art room binge . . . until, that is, the boys come along."

I took pity on her. "So, sixteen years later we're still here, aren't we? Drinking companions always survive."

She nodded but didn't look at me. "I suppose I was afraid that you'd be shocked," she added after a while.

"Why should I?" I said evenly. "It was a cheap brand, and anyway, I've always been suspicious of traditional morality."

"I wasn't talking about the sherry."

"I know," I said softly. "Neither was I. Remember, you're talking to one of the original National Health junkies here. Mogadon Marla — big girl, big dosage."

She shook her head. "That's different."

I thought about it. "Maybe. But I'm still not shocked."

Sunshine and friendship. We sat quietly enjoying the warmth.

"It never worried me at first, you know. I used to think he was simply performing a service for people willing to pay for it. Why should smuggling cocaine be any more immoral than selling cars? Drugs were just the sweeties that the adults wouldn't let us have. One of the rules they made to keep control." She frowned. "Maybe I just ate too many."

"You had a choice."

"Oooh, you sound like Lenny."

"It's true. You didn't have to take it. Any more than the rest of America does. It's like seat belts. People don't like being told what's good for them. America is a grown-up country. I don't see why you should have to take on the guilt for her greed for pleasure."

"Even when that greed fucks up other countries?"

"What does that mean?"

"Oh, come on, Marla. You know what the cocaine trade has done for most of South America. The rich have got richer and everyone else has been fucked over."

"So?"

"So, it's immoral."

"So is all manner of exploitation. How would Lenny defend himself?"

"You want the long or the short version?" She took an exaggerated breath. "In brief, he would say that he pays a good price for his merchandise, that some of that money goes to those who need it, and that his reward is simply commensurate with the risks he takes. America has been mugging her southern namesake economically for centuries. The only real reason this cause is holier than thou is because the government dares not legalize it, and therefore can't get its hands on any of the profits." She shrugged. "He's right, of course. I told you, it's a very traditional business. A perfect example of aggressive capitalism."

"And that's why you think you should leave him? Because of his politics. Everything would be fine if he became a social worker, is that it?"

She put up a hand in mock defeat. "All right, I know, I'm only using it as an excuse.

You always were good at cutting through the bullshit, Marla. I bet you scare the hell out of your students."

"Absolutely," I said, allowing her to change the subject. "It's a reign of terror."

"Yeah, well it was always like that. Christ, you even used to intimidate your own teachers. Don't look so surprised. You must have known that. You always seemed more adult than they were; sitting there fourth row from the front, eyes fixed on them, chalking up mental scores for their performance. It was one of the best things about being your friend. It bought me protection from them."

"I think we must have gone to different schools," I said mildly. "I don't remember any of this."

"Aaah, well. That's because you were so caught up in your own anxieties. But it's true. I spent most of my adolescence basking in the received glory of your brain. I kept hoping some of it would rub off on me. That I would become more brilliant, more silent, more original. And then, of course, my father would love me instead of ignoring me. I tell you, you were my idol, my excitement, my passage to adulthood."

It was like being told a fairy story that you knew by heart with the role of the heroes and villains suddenly changed around. Could the truth really be so multilayered? I should know. After all, history is just other people's view of events. The living, presumably, see it all quite differently. As I had. Part of me didn't want to dig back that far, blow the dust off that particular trunk of memories and start unpacking all the pain and confusion.

"Don't worry," she said gently. "I know it didn't feel like that for you. But things have gotten better. Little by little. And you've changed, you know. Even since we last saw each other. I don't know if I can describe it, but you're more relaxed somehow, as if you've got a better hold on the world. It's quite a transformation, Marla. Maybe it comes from teaching."

"And maybe it comes from having to fend for myself without you," I said quietly, not looking at her but feeling a pulse of electricity pass between us.

She met me head-on. "In which case I was right to leave. We couldn't have lived the rest of our lives in each other's pockets. We both knew that. You were better off without me. I just reminded you of the past. Look at you now. You've come through, even if you don't like to admit it. In some ways you've done better than me."

If it was true it didn't hurt less. For either of us.

"I missed you, too, you know," she said with sudden ferocity. "It wasn't all one-way."

I studied a crack in the grain of the deck. "I know that."

Four, five, six heartbeats. The silence was alive between us. It could have taken us anywhere. Her choice.

"What about men, Marla? Extramural activities. Give me a progress report. Are you still chewing them up and spitting them out?"

I had been waiting for the question. A head count for the past two years revealed a visiting academic from Finland and someone I had met at a concert. I selected and embroidered. "You'd have been proud of me. There was one who lingered for almost a month."

"What happened?"

"He went back to his wife in Helsinki."

"How did you feel?"

"I had a lot of work to do."

"Coward," she said, but with great affection.

"Well, you know me. All cats are gray in the dark."

"Oh, Marla, sometimes you don't even

tell the truth to yourself, you do know that, don't you? Maybe if just once you cast off from the side of the pool, you'd discover that you could swim."

"Maybe."

"I tell you — Shit," she muttered angrily, sitting up and reaching for her T-shirt. "We've got company."

I glanced behind me to see J.T., tree-trunk body encased in checked shirt, wicker basket in hand, standing on the edge of the deck looking for all the world like a renegade extra from *Seven Brides for Seven Brothers.* Such was the perfection of his catwalk that neither of us had heard him. I was glad we had been talking quietly. Glad also for the excuse to stop. Elly scrambled to her feet. I stayed where I was.

"Fresh vegetables," he mumbled, crossing over and putting the basket on the table. He stood for a second, as if poised for a fast retreat. Except this time he didn't leave: this time, quite out of character, he accepted Elly's automatic offer of refreshment and followed her across to the chair next to mine. He lowered his bulk into it while she sped indoors to raid the fridge.

We sat for a few moments judging each other's commitment to silence. For such a big man, he imposed surprisingly little of himself on an atmosphere — not at all like Lenny arriving on the scene. On the other hand, he didn't seem ill at ease. In fact, close to, his stillness felt more like a deliberate strategy than shyness, almost as if he had made a conscious decision to be this withdrawn. On a desert island we might not have talked for years. For Elly's sake I offered up a few clichés.

"It's a beautiful view. You must enjoy living here."

He said nothing, not even the habitual grunt. I was counting to ten before graduating on to the weather when he looked straight at me, the sunlight on his glasses obscuring his eyes. "Is she OK?"

I was impressed by the way I contained my surprise. "Yes," I said. "She is."

"How about her and Lenny?"

I took time with that one, picking my way to the right words. "There are still problems. Areas of conflict."

Behind us came the sounds of glasses and bottles clinking, a fridge door closing. He looked out over the canyon, squinting into the sun. "You should see it when the mist comes in." He was addressing the ocean. "Rolls right up in the middle of the night. Thick as cotton balls. Sometimes you can't even see where the deck ends. Lasts for days." He sniffed. "Is she going to leave him?"

This time I was shocked by the question. Or maybe it was just the number of words, like hearing a monk breaking a vow of silence. Shocked, but also fascinated. "Why? Do you think she should?"

He looked at me sharply, and there was anger in the movement, as if I had said something self-evidently stupid. But now was not the time to explain. The screen door was already opening, and we could both hear her coming toward us, tray in hand. He returned to his study of the horizon.

After which he didn't stay long. The beer took him no time at all, and he gave the impression of being a man who had suddenly remembered an urgent appointment. Elly did most of the talking. Pleasantries. Half of me listened; the other half worked at lasering through those pebble wedges to the eyes behind. They gave nothing away. It was becoming a habit, these snatched conversations with cocaine men. First Lenny amid potted palms, now J.T. by a canyon. Whispers in cloisters. The equivalent of a professional tic. Did it really come with the job? Had he taught Lenny or had Lenny tutored him? Maybe I should ask. There was no reason why he should have the monopoly on curiosity.

He must have heard the thought forming, because he picked that instant to make his getaway, squashing his beer can in one hand and delivering a monosyllabic speech of farewell before padding off into the high noon sunshine. We watched him go.

"Strange," murmured Elly. "He didn't say anything. I wonder what he wanted."

"Hungry for human contact, I expect. He asked how you were."

"Did he?" She frowned. "I should have talked to him, gone round to see him. But what would I have said? 'I'm sorry I didn't take your advice. You were right.' I can't imagine the conversation. You know, it's funny, but I think he makes me shy. Me, old blabbermouth. Can you believe it?"

"Maybe he holds a torch for you."

"J.T.? Never." She laughed. "He's impenetrable. I don't think he needs people at all. All his loyalties go to his lettuces."

"So he knows nothing. How come Lenny doesn't tell him?"

"How come stones don't talk? I told you, their camaraderie is professional. It doesn't extend to emotional confessions. Real men don't eat humble pie, remember? Come on, let's get out of the frying pan."

160

In the shadows at the back of the house, we tried to recapture the rhythm of the day. Elly was doodling, reproducing bits of me in quick, sure pencil strokes. It reminded me of the old days. There had been a time when she always had a pencil in her hand: cartoons doodled on school notebooks, pupils and teachers as animals and monsters. I sat obediently still for her, a book on my lap. Illustrations from the Lindisfarne Gospels, snakes and monsters curled around the word of God. The truth according to the Bible. But on this particular afternoon not even the genius of Bishop Eadfrid's pen could hold my attention. It was hot in the shadows, and the decorated words danced on the page. We fell into a sleepy silence. After a while I looked up. The pencil had slipped from Elly's hand, and she was curled like a cat on one of the floor cushions, eyes closed.

I put down the book and went outside. Day five. Progress report. We had heard nothing from Lenny since our arrival. That much was perfect. Despite her sadness, Elly was growing stronger. Her own description had been accurate. It was like watching a body fighting back an infection, manufacturing antibodies to expel the invader. From what I could tell, the balance of power was already shifting away from that late-night despair of the Manhattan balcony. Now there were signs of anger poking through, the odd glimpse of another, younger Elly, one who did not approve of bloodsucking as courtship ritual. The longer Lenny stayed away, the further the distance between them. With luck we would not need his mystery tour to England. It might prove a voluntary repatriation. Things were going better than I could have hoped.

I walked up from the deck onto the meadow. From the row of the hill everything was quiet, the only sign of life a solitary bird wheeling overhead in search of shade. Close to, the ground was parched and cracking in the heat. Any garden would now be in need of constant attention. Lenny may have had trouble with true love, but Elly was right, his partner clearly had a serious relationship with his vegetable patch. From where I stood, I could just make out the house and its enclosure, marked by the giant sunflower ring of confidence. I decided, on what seemed like impulse, to pay a call on his estate and ask a few questions of my own.

The place felt deserted, although both the pickup and the lovingly preserved VW were parked on the gravel. J.T.'s home was altogether a more modest statement than the guesthouse, smacking more of solidity than of imagination, while its view, although magnificent, did not have quite the wild extravagance of the jungle canyon to recommend it.

The main garden was a large enclosure to one side of the house. The place was packed with crops, jostling against each other for growing space. Corn, lettuce, beans, all of them California big and pushy. To one end there was a small herb garden, the soil newly watered, and nearby a flower bed partly protected from the sun by a carefully erected canopy.

I picked a few sprigs of mint and crushed them in the palm of my hand. Their smell was sharp and sweet. I walked up onto the patio surrounding the house. My feet creaked on the boards, and somewhere in the distance I heard chickens cackling. At the far end there was a hot tub, covered with a wooden barrel lid. I was beginning to feel like an intruder. What should I say if I came across him now, face pressed up against the window, staring out at me? "Good afternoon. I've come to ask some questions about your questions"? The idea of being thus caught unnerved me. I marched up to the front of the house and knocked smartly.

Nothing. I tried the handle, and the door clicked open at my touch. Inside I glimpsed a room, almost monklike in its sparseness: bare wooden boards, two chairs in one corner, a table, and a couch that looked as if it doubled as a bed. The only color in the place came from an Indian bedspread draped over one of the chairs and a small rug with bright, intricate weaving, probably South American, on one wall. Apart from that there was order, space, and precision. And no J.T.

It was only as I pulled the door behind me that I noticed a smaller, more makeshift hut at the back of the house, partly obscured by trees. Why not? Such a substantial garden deserves a gardening shed. Even as I approached I had a sudden sense that I would find him there. Still, something made me go to the window rather than the door. I was careful not to make any noise. Like J.T., I have discovered that big people can make soft footfalls. It is one of a number of ways to do what you want without having to be noticed. Peering in through a corner of the glass, I saw what was, in fact, some kind of study: a desk, a filing cabinet, and on the wall a large diagram of what looked like the night sky. What had Elly said about him? Vegetables and stars? Maybe this was where he noted his findings, although there was no sign of a telescope. On the desk there were scatterings of paper, and the wastepaper basket was full. And then there was the bunk. The bunk on which J.T. was lying.

He was sprawled flat on his back, asleep, his head turned away from me and his arms and legs flung out at awkward angles. He was wearing loose cotton trousers and a T-shirt, which had ridden up over his chest, exposing a carpet of dark fuzzy hair. I remember thinking there was something in the way he lay which reminded me of a grossly overgrown child. The sensation of voyeurism both fascinated and repelled me. I would not like to be so observed. Then, quite suddenly, he moved his head, pointing his face up toward the ceiling. It was a deliberate gesture, not the careless kind that people make in their sleep. It was then I realized that his eyes were open. I pulled my head back abruptly, but not so fast that he might not have registered a shadow of movement. I decided not to announce myself formally. Clearly this was not visiting hour.

I was halfway to the vegetable plot when I heard the door being flung open, and a shout pulled me to a halt. "What do you want?"

There was real aggression in his voice. I swung round, defending with an attack. "I knocked at the house. There was no answer."

He did not respond, just stood staring at me, squinting into the sun, head cocked to one side like a blind man sensing direction. "You alone?" he said at last. "Where's Elly?"

"Asleep."

We stood growling, each waiting for the other to make the next move. Technically, I was the trespasser. So why was I here? "Elly told me you were something of a stargazer. I was wondering if you had a chart or map I might borrow." Not bad, conjured as it was out of thin air.

"Why?"

I had to hand it to him. He was even harder to have a conversation with than I was. "Because I'm interested," I barked back. It was not a total lie. Who isn't curious about infinity?

His face creased into an unexpected, almost sly smile. It was obvious to both of us he didn't believe me. But I didn't care. The pause began to lengthen, but this time I stood my ground. I didn't mind silence either. After a while he turned on his heel and walked back toward the hut. I understood I was not being invited to follow. I waited, paying unnecessary attention to a small, fresh mound of earth near my foot. He took his time. I wondered vaguely what I should say when he returned. I had gone back to playing footsie with the earth mound when he arrived. Now, it seemed, he wanted to join in.

"Gophers," he said, looking down at my feet.

"What?"

"Gophers. Little bastards. They chew their way through everything. First couple of months after we laid the electric cables I kept getting power failures. Spent days digging up the cable only to find teeth marks right through it. In the end I had to take up the whole damn thing — miles of it — case it in steel and stick it back again. Now they just break their teeth on it and go for the plants instead. Here . . ."

He held out the map but stood his ground. There was four or five feet still between us. I was meant to go to him. As I walked, I was aware of his eyes on me. The scrutiny had nothing to do with sexuality. It was more abstract than that. I wondered what he thought he saw. I put out my hand to receive the chart. "Thank you." This time we looked at each other. "I wanted to talk about Elly."

It was a calculated risk. I am not the kind of person to put everything on one throw of the dice. The length of his speech and the fact that he had held on to the map just a fraction too long told me he wanted to talk too. Or so I thought. He made a small impatient movement and scowled in the direction of the truck. "I have to go pick up some feed for the animals."

"I see," I said evenly. "Well, don't let me stand in your way."

He was still frowning as he strode past me to the truck. It was hard to know at what point he changed his mind.

"You might as well come along for the ride," he grumbled, flinging open the driver's door. I must have shot a look across the hill, because he added curtly, "We'll be back before she wakes."

The journey did not prove conducive to chatter: both of us straight-backed, eyes stapled to a road which whipped and snarled its way through the mountains. It was his fault. He drove deliberately too fast, taking corners in third gear and straight stretches with his foot down. After the fourth bend I had to catch hold of the door strap to avoid being flung against him. He was in an awful hurry. Was this plain bad temper or his way of trying to impress? After a few miles he seemed to ease up a little. The wind, which had been whipping in through the open window, calmed down and blew hot again.

"How long have you known each other?" His voice, even though I was expecting it, made me jump. I shot him a look, but his eyes were firmly on the driving. One of the screws which joined the metal arm of his glasses to the lens frame was loose, I noticed. For a man who owned a chunk of the Pacific coastline, he wore pretty cheap spectacles.

"Eighteen years and five months," I said, talking to the windscreen.

"And when did you last see her?"

"Two years ago."

"You think she's changed?"

"No, not really. Not underneath."

In front of us, from round a bend, a red estate car appeared, moving fast. The road didn't seem wide enough for both of us. He put his foot down on the accelerator. I felt my body snap into attention. The cars rushed toward each other. And sliced past. Just. I let out a breath I was not aware I had been holding.

"She's stayed off the coke?" he said, perversely slowing down now.

"Yes."

"But she's still strung out on Lenny, right?" This time he did look at me, a fast poking glance that seemed to have a fist of anger in it. Interesting how I found his bad temper easier to handle than Lenny's slimy charm. "Yes," I said, finding his phrase surprisingly satisfying. "She's still strung out on Lenny."

He grunted. We were approaching a small settlement, a sprinkling of houses and the odd store, breaking open the forest and widening the road. In the sunshine it seemed picturesque and romantic, the kind of place where Sissy Spacek might have come from. J.T. screeched into the forecourt of what looked like the outhouse to a farm.

"Wait here," he mumbled, snapping open the door and sliding out. I watched him stride across the space. It suited him, this landscape. He was built for it.

He disappeared inside the barn door. I sat and wondered what they did here when it rained. From a large wooden cabin across the road a woman came out and stood on the porch, watching me watching her. She had long, silvery gray hair and was wearing dungarees with a skimpy T-shirt, which showed off her brown arms and shoulders. There was something in the way she held herself that was both lazy and alert at the same time. She was very attractive, not so much from her looks as from a kind of careless sexuality which clung to her almost without her noticing it. She was the sort of woman writers create as one-night stands for heroes-of-the-road novels. Someone who gave of herself without having to check if anything had been lost. Reality or male fantasy? If I got out of the truck and went up and asked her, would she tell me? How is it that other people are always such mysteries? Maybe she was thinking the same about me. The interest was certainly mutual.

Then, suddenly, she straightened herself and walked off the porch toward the road, her attention caught by something else. Or someone else. From the barn J.T. emerged, carrying a sack of what might have been grain. They saw each other, and communication flashed between them. I couldn't read it, but there was something in the way her head rose up that spoke of belligerence or defiance. Then it was over, and she turned on her heel, shooting me one last glance before walking lazily back to the house. The screen door slammed behind her. Old flames after the heat had died down? None of my business.

Back on the road, J.T. seemed preoccupied. Bad tempered again. "I don't know how much you know," he said at last, almost impatiently.

"Enough."

"And how much is that?"

"I know that you and Lenny used to work together, and I know what it is you did. And that you don't do it anymore." Pause. "I also know that you gave Elly help when she needed it."

We drove for a few moments in silence. "And where do you fit in?"

"I'm here because she asked me to come."

He stretched slightly at the wheel, rubbing his back against the seat and wiping one hand on his thigh. I studied the legs reaching down to the pedals, slim, almost elegant, so mismatched with the rest of his body. His legs, my hair. Maybe he too would have been grateful for a way of homogenizing his image. Or would he?

"You should get her out of it." It was so quiet and mumbled that I almost missed it. But there it was, the one I had been waiting for.

"Why?"

He made a harsh clicking sound, another statement of frustration at my chronic obtuseness. "She doesn't fit, that's why. She never has. He told her lies and she believed them. But even she can't be fooled forever.

Things have changed. It's not a game any-more."

Talking in tongues. "What does that mean?"

He scowled. "You asked me what I thought, and I told you. What Lenny does is dangerous. Especially the way he does it. You should get her out while you can. His luck won't last forever."

Ahead of us the red mailboxes appeared, standing sentry by the turnoff. The journey back had taken no time at all. He took the corner fast and had to brake as we hit the dust path. As the truck whined in protest, he muttered something. I thought I caught the words ". . . before it's too late."

"What?"

But he shook his head. Stubborn silence. I felt rushed. And bullied. What gave him the right? "If you think all this, why don't you tell her yourself?"

"Because she's your friend, not mine," he said curtly.

"And what about Lenny? Whose friend is he?"

This time he looked at me. A kind of fury. "Listen, Lenny and I worked together, right? That means we got certain obliga-tions to each other. She isn't one of them. Got it?"

173

He made it clear this was the end of the conversation. I sat with my anger clasped tight between my hands. On the brow of the hill he stopped. It was my cue for an exit. I stayed put.

"So, can I tell her what you've said? Or was it all 'confidential'?"

There was only a hint of mockery in my voice, but I have no doubt he heard it. "There's nothing to tell," he said, as if the whole subject suddenly bored him. "We just went for a ride, that's all."

I got out of the car and slammed the door.

"Here." He called me back, holding out the star map through the open window. "Take it. You could learn a lot from looking at what's already around you." And letting it fall to the ground, he drove away.

I stood watching the truck grow smaller in the distance. Then I picked up the map and began to walk. The exercise made me feel better, less churned up. And so I crossed the ridge back to the little wooden house on the edge of the world where Elly was sleeping peacefully.

Eight

Except Elly wasn't there. In the hollow of the cushion where she had been lying was a note, written in faint drawing pencil:

A short walk in the canyon. Back by teatime or call out the huskies.

It had no time on it. The kitchen clock read 3:40 P.M. I thought about trying to catch her up, but there was no way of knowing how long she'd been gone, and from our experience of canyon walks I knew the path was not easy to follow. If she strayed and I missed her, we would never find each other. Better to wait. I settled myself in a chair near the fireplace and started in on the meaning of life.

The question was, Should I tell Elly? Or, to be more precise, what was there to tell? Even now the conversation shimmered and slid in and out of my grasp like a fish in fast water, full of atmosphere but with little meaning. What exactly had been said? That

J.T. thought she should leave Lenny. That came as no surprise. He had said as much before. What else? That she should do it soon, before it was too late. Because Lenny's luck would not last forever. Those were the words that carried the chill. Were they just some strange prognostication gained from stargazing, or did J.T. know something? In which case, how did he know, and more important, why didn't he tell Lenny?

Consider J.T. What made him so incorruptible? He was as much an unknown as Lenny. More so. Elly had at least loved and lived with Lenny. She knew him. By her own admission, she knew nothing about the man who claimed to be his friend. A man who until a few years ago had earned his living by dissembling, fooling most of the people most of the time. The fact that I instinctively trusted him more than I did Lenny was based on a number of things. As Elly herself had put it, he shone less, and therefore seemed more real. His anger felt safer than Lenny's charm. He was not the one who had hurt Elly, so he could not be blamed. Most of all, it appeared, he was on my side. But with what motive? For one of nature's loners, he was getting very involved. Might it not be that he was jealous of Lenny? There were reasons enough. Lenny was fabulous. Lenny was charmed. Where J.T. had almost got busted, Lenny walked the tightrope with wit and with style. And he walked it with Elly. Where was J.T.'s comfort — a large garden and a single bed? Maybe he got his kicks from undermining others. Nothing he said could be backed up. He had even warned me against repeating it to Elly — a protection, no doubt, against it getting back to Lenny, who would surely see it as a betrayal. The more I thought about it, the more worms I could see squirming under the surface.

If I told Elly the facts, they amounted to nothing. And if I interpreted the innuendo, wouldn't she be obliged to warn Lenny? And mightn't that, in some way, bring them closer together? No, malice or make-believe, there was nothing to tell. I felt better.

I'm not sure when I realized that she had been away too long. There is a point during California afternoons when the heat is so close and so powerful that it brings everything to a temporary standstill. Time bears no relationship to the hands on the clock. Maybe it was this, or maybe I had simply dozed for a while without knowing it, tumbled into a kind of waking daydream. Whatever the reason, I didn't at first realize how late it had become.

In the kitchen I flicked on the radio while the kettle boiled. The FM station told me it was 6:08 P.M. Even assuming Elly had left the house the minute before I arrived, she had been away for two and a half hours. I went out on the deck to watch for her.

The sun had started moving again, mixing the color palette with a little glitter, playing to the gallery now. In the canyon, a ghost of a wind was ruffling the heads of the trees. I kept thinking I had caught sight of her, or made out the sound of her feet on bracken near the house, but it was simply the breeze playing tricks, and she never appeared. If it hadn't been for J.T.'s conversation, I doubt whether I would have thought twice about the delay. City girls always misjudge landscapes, and in my time I had been on more than one walk with Elly where a half-hour stroll turned into a minor marathon. As a child I had picked up my mother's fear when my father was late home from work. He used to travel a lot in those early days, and one evening the radio had given news of a multiple pileup on a motorway he should have been driving along. He was two hours late that night due to the traffic jam caused. He called my mother from the nearest service station, but the damage was done, and ever after she suffered nightmares of oxyacetylene torches cutting through buckled car frames on even the simplest of journeys. Her anxieties were so great they even blocked my own, but as I grow older I find that I too have to quieten my imagination when people are late from car trips. Traditionally, though, the fear is limited to vehicles. When walking, people always come back to me.

J.T.'s whispers left shadows in the sunshine. It was late. She should have been back. At 7:00 P.M. I decided to go and look for her. I was upstairs changing into walking shoes when the phone rang. Elly, stranded somewhere, needing a lift. I got down the stairs fast, but it stopped ringing just as I reached it. Still, if it was her, she would call again, I waited. Five minutes later it rang. This time my hand was over the receiver.

"Elly?"

Nothing. Silence. Then a man's voice. "Hi. How are you today?" in a flat, dead tone. A long pause. Then, "Have a nice evening. And see you soon, huh?" with the same dull death in the voice. Then the line disconnected.

I looked down at the receiver and felt a chill inside me. I remembered again the other phone call, at dawn; I heard J.T.'s mumblings over the car engine — "Things have changed. It's not a game anymore." And suddenly I was frightened for Elly.

From the deck I shouted her name over the canyon. My voice burst into the silence and seemed to carry halfway to the ocean, but I couldn't be sure how far it would penetrate the undergrowth. I clambered down onto the path and started walking. For the first quarter mile it was familiar. We had been here twice before and had trampled down the top layer of summer growth. But we had never got that far. At night sometimes you could hear coyotes howling in the belly of the canyon, and we had been careful not to stray from the path. I reached what I thought was our limit. The track plunged downward. I followed. Fifty yards on I came to a small clearing, with two separate paths branching off from it. I shouted again. The sound returned empty. Which way? Above me the canyon had become a cliff. I could see nothing but trees, no sign of the house. What if she had arrived home and was standing out on the deck looking for me? Or had made it down as far as the road and was stranded with no way of getting back? Or maybe she really was lost in the canyon. In which case I was going to need help. J.T.? Who else was there to ask? I hesitated for a moment, then turned and forged my way back up toward the house.

The light was already beginning to fade as I pulled myself onto the deck, soaked with sweat and a little the worse for wear. It was then I heard it, the sound of a car engine, the crunch of wheels on gravel. I ran to the top of the stairs in time to see a youngish man in Yuppie casuals getting out of the driver's seat and walking round to the passenger door. Elly emerged, a hand on his arm. She saw me immediately and waved, but as she walked toward me I saw she was limping.

She must have read some of the last few hours in my face, because when she reached me she grabbed hold of my hand and squeezed tightly.

"Oh, God, Marla. I'm sorry. You were worried. I knew you would be. I got totally lost, completely fucked up my sense of direction. It took me hours to get out of the canyon. And when I got to the road I didn't have any money. I had to hitch a lift back."

"What happened to your foot?"

She made a face. "I slipped down a gopher hole. My fault — it's these plastic shoes, not made for mountaineering. Can you believe it? Typical. I'm OK. But what about you? How did you get all those scratches?"

I looked down at my arms. "I went looking for you."

"Oh, you didn't." She groaned and laughed. "Jesus, what a pair we are. I'm sorry."

Behind her, Sir Galahad hovered nervously. "What about him?" I said, gesturing with my eyes.

"Oh shit, Frank. He gave me a lift from the road. Went miles out of his way. He's really sweet. Can we give him a drink or something, just to say thank you?"

I studied the rather awkward figure, smooth plump face, and clumsy half smile. Another lame dog. In the old days Ely had been in the habit of collecting them. It had been my habit to be rude to them. I avoided temptation by becoming the waitress.

By the time I returned with bottle and glasses, Frank was halfway in love. It wasn't her fault. I had seen it happen often enough before. For her, charm was just a way of getting on with the world, her social vocabulary for tricky situations. It was just that some people took it more seriously, saw in it what they were looking for rather than what was actually there. Poor Elly. The irony of her relationship with Lenny was that in some way she had been snared by her own trap. But not forever.

I sat and watched her scattering stardust. And I even began to feel a little sorry for this hapless computer salesman from Portland, Oregon, on his way home after visiting his children and so obviously looking for a little romance after the breakup of his marriage. His life story came out without the asking, and when he finally took the hint from our empty glasses and allowed Elly to accompany him out to the car, I've no doubt that he asked whether he could see her again, and that she gently deflected the request and kissed him on the cheek to see him on his way. Funny. There are times now when I wonder what happened to him. Although I can't say I really care.

Later, after food, showers, and liberal doses of witch hazel, we settled ourselves back out in the night to stargaze our way to sleep. Life was normal again, and my anxieties had evaporated, explained away by a series of coincidences. So J.T. nursed a nugget of envy against Lenny, and some nutter had plucked our phone number out of the air. There had been no return calls. Silly to have been so disturbed. In the life I came from, there was never this much drama. Hardly surprising then that I overreacted.

It was half an hour later that Elly recounted her journey through the chasm, and the fear returned.

"Actually, I have something to tell you. Something that happened this afternoon. A rather strange story. You'll probably think it's nothing."

"Try me."

"Well . . . I came across these two guys, halfway down the canyon. They were camping out."

"What's so strange about that?"

"Nothing. Only it was just a pretty crazy place to camp, that's all. If you wanted to go trekking, there are a zillion more beautiful spots — all higher up than that — where the views are magnificent. You can't see a thing from down there."

"Maybe they weren't interested in views. Maybe they wanted to be near the ocean."

She shrugged. "Yeah, except this place was miles from the sea. And if they were beaching it, then it's the wrong piece of coast altogether. It's all rock down there."

"So, they were looking for privacy. Two consenting adults on holiday. I don't understand what was so strange about them, Elly."

She chewed at the side of her cheek.

"Well . . . ," I prompted.

"OK. There was something else, but it's

probably nothing. They had a telescope with them."

I don't know what I was expecting. But not this. "A telescope? What kind of telescope?"

"I dunno. A regular long-distance telescope, I suppose. It was on a stand."

"Well, that answers your question, doesn't it? If it was that big, they could hardly hump it up into the hills. They were obviously stargazers. That's no doubt why J.T. picked this place. The greatest aurora borealis on the West Coast. It's probably a regular Santa Cruz habit, the biggest thing since skateboarding."

"Yeah. Probably."

"Elly . . . ?"

She shook her head impatiently. "Marla, I know you're going to find this stupid, but if they were stargazing, then all I can say is they had the telescope in totally the wrong direction. It wasn't looking up at the sky. It was pointing directly at this house."

There it was, the tweezer nip in the soft flesh of my stomach. "Are you sure?"

"No, of course I'm not sure. But there's a point toward the bottom of the canyon where there's a clear break upward. It's why at night sometimes we can spot car beams moving along the line of the coast road.

Looking upward from there, you'd have a direct line to the house. With the naked eye it's tiny, just a smudge against the hillside. But with a powerful telescope . . ."

"Listen, I'm sure there's a simple explanation to all this," I heard myself say. "Of course they didn't have the thing pointed at the sky. It's daylight. What stars could they see? They were probably testing out its strength on the landscape." Elly said nothing, and I went on. "At worst you just came across a couple of weirdos who like watching women sunbathe five miles away."

She smiled, but you could see she wasn't convinced.

"If you were so intrigued, why didn't you just ask them what they were doing there? Were they so mysterious?"

"That's the bit I can't explain. Maybe they just gave me a fright. I came upon them so suddenly. It was so silent and empty down there. When I heard their voices, I nearly jumped out of my skin. I spotted them, so I was the one who got the shock."

"Did they see you?"

"No, though they heard me, made a big deal about scouting around in the undergrowth to check out the noise. But they misjudged the direction. By the time they got

186

back to the camp, I had slipped down below them and could see without being seen."

"See what?"

"Not a lot. One of them had his back to me — he was playing about with some piece of machinery. The other was smoking a cigarette and talking into some kind of walkie-talkie."

"There," I said firmly. "What more do you want? They were a couple of tame scientists."

"They didn't look like scientists," she said almost sullenly.

"And since when could you tell a doctor without a white coat?" I teased her. "Seriously, think about it. If they were Peeping Toms, then why weren't they in a more convenient spot? This is California after all. Half the people in this state regularly take off their clothes in public. They don't need a telescope to see that. And if they didn't look like scientists, then that's America for you — no proper dress code. It's been impossible to tell a professional since the sixties, you know that. You should see the visiting academics we get at UC — they look like video stars."

This time she laughed. I took it as a sign of surrender. We fell silent. From inside the house the hall light was leaking out onto the deck, reaching almost to where we were sitting. Just twenty-four hours ago we had sat here, cocooned in the knowledge of our isolation. Now, there was just the thinnest thread of possibility that with the house lit up . . . I had the feeling she was thinking the same thing.

"I suppose I'm just getting paranoid in my old age," she said, focusing in the distance on the occasional flickering car beam crossing the base of the canyon. "An occupational hazard from sleeping too many nights next to a man who breaks the law."

"What kind of paranoia?"

"Oh, I dunno. Cops and robbers, I suppose. Stupid really. It's so safe. Or at least that's how Lenny makes it feel. But you hear stories."

"Such as?"

"Big fish eating little fish . . . little fish fighting back, that kind of thing. I don't usually take any notice. There was a time when every newspaper and periodical carried its own shock-horror tale about the corruption and violence of the cocaine trade. Mutilated bodies in canyons, shoot-outs in mountain strongholds, all good sensational stuff. Gave me the creeps. I stopped wanting to know. What the eye doesn't see . . . But then it all seemed so far removed from Lenny. Even when I asked he wouldn't tell me. I'm just the gangster's moll, remember."

J.T. was only half right. She may have been naïve, but she was still wise enough to be frightened. There they were again, his words caught like small chicken bones in my throat. Except this time, however much I swallowed, I couldn't dislodge them. But tonight was not the time for such thoughts.

"Listen, if it still worries you tomorrow, we'll go and talk to J.T. Who knows? They might even be trespassing on his land. He could go down with a shotgun and run them off."

"Naaw . . . in the morning it'll all be dissolved by the sunshine," she said, gathering up the glasses and drifting back toward the house. Inside, as I locked up, she moved to put out the light.

"Hey, Marla." I turned. In her hand was the telephone receiver. "Did you know the phone was off the hook?"

I stared at it, rerunning the haste with which I had replaced it, and hearing again the flat, menacing voice on the other end of the line. Then I remembered something else. Elly's words out on the deck. ". . . the other was smoking a cigarette and talking into some kind of walkie-talkie." Immediately my good sense marched in and stamped on the suspicion. I kept my foot hard down until all traces of it had been crushed. Elly was talking.

". . . Marla?"

"What?"

"I asked if someone called."

"Yes . . . Wrong number." It was a quick lie, based on instinct rather than judgment.

"I bet it was the same mental defective who called this morning. God, what's the point of being ex-directory when you're pestered by idiots. Might as well be in the book." She slid the receiver back into its cradle. "Bags I the bathroom first."

As the water ran, I kept vigil over the telephone. Then, as I heard her snap out the bathroom light and cross the floor to the bedroom, I lifted the receiver gently and wedged it just out of its cradle.

Later, as we lay out on our mattresses on the upstairs verandah, staring out into the great dome of the night sky with the haze of the Milky Way a faint cloud against the darkness, I thought of stargazing. And more.

"I have an idea," I said, and my voice sounded huge in the night. "I was thinking of going back via Paris. To visit Gem. I haven't seen her for a while now, and she's

190

been ill recently. She still asks after you. I wondered if you'd like to come along. Just for a visit."

The pause that followed was so long I wondered if she might really have fallen asleep. Then her voice, small and clear said, "Yes, I'll think about it."

After that we both lay awake for some time.

Nine

In the morning, over breakfast, we decided to take the car and spend the day away from the house, as if it was an on the spur of the moment decision, unconnected with the night before. We walked over to J.T.'s to pick up the VW, and perhaps, had he been there, one of us might have said something, but as it was the house and hut were empty. Like a modern-day *Marie Celeste*, the imprint of a human hand was still warm around the place. The garden soil was dark with fresh watering, and in their pens the chickens had just been fed, heads bobbing up and down to catch the last of the grain. But in the drive the blue pickup was gone, leaving the fashionably old VW snoozing like some snub-nosed animal in the morning haze. Elly disappeared into the house to leave a note, and then, finding the keys in the glove compartment, we set off, leaving it all behind us.

From Santa Cruz we headed out along Highway One toward Carmel and Big Sur.

A few miles out of the city the horizon leveled off and the trees and shrubbery dropped away. The highway glistened mirage-wet in the heat, while to either side stretched long level fields encrusted with artichokes and alfalfa. Nearer to Sand City nothing grew, just wild white expanses of sand dunes, sloping gently to the sea and throwing up sand mists to filter the light. It was like driving into instant science fiction: the horizon designed for the classic long shot of giant tentacles waving into view, followed by a hideous, gaping mouth, eager to crunch up the inevitable unwary Cadillac with its young courting couple canoodling in the back. I have never understood what audiences get so upset about. The mutants are invariably more interesting than the families they consume.

In homage we ran through a list of monsters we were most sorry to have seen destroyed, and our movie reminiscences got us as far as Monterey.

There we decided to stop for coffee, to investigate old memories of this little coastal community; Steinbeck country, which had given up its literary associations in favor of style, booming during the late sixties with artists' studios, restaurants, shops, and bars. A generation later it was already tumbling down the other side of the parabola of fashion, a town after the gold rush had passed through. It proved that you should never go back. But the road ahead was yellow-bricked with memory, and we decided to carry on regardless.

Nature disappointed less. We picnicked on the Monterey peninsula, seventeen miles of rolling coastline where the wind still sculptured the trees horizontal and the cliffs plunged down to an inhospitable Pacific, glistening blue-green under the sun. And it was there that Elly suggested we spend the afternoon in Big Sur and book a table for dinner at Nepenthe, to test out her one last solid-gold memory.

Nepenthe is the kind of place, perched as it is on the edge of the cliffs, which stays clear in memory when other things around it fade and are washed away. Elly had come here first as a chubby eighteen-year-old. An Americanophile to the core, she had come to California in the three months between school and university, eking out a living by looking after rich children in a modest mansion not far from the coast. It was the end of the sixties, and professional America was indulging itself in the new morality. The lawyer's family she dropped into was having marital problems John Updike *Couples*

194

style, and that didn't leave them a lot of space for their children. Nepenthe had been Elly's leaving present from the parents, a statement of their gratitude for all the free time she had given them to experiment with the destruction of their marriage. I knew all these things because those three months had been the first time that Elly and I had ever been separated, and she had written to me regularly, weekly installments of soap. Her letter composed the day after was a classic, detailing the disintegration of the evening as the husband got drunk and made a pass at the waitress, while the wife ordered a taxi home at enormous expense and left without him. Elly, as usual, had been caught in the middle. Two months after she got home to England, she heard that divorce proceedings had begun. Twelve years on, she had lost track of the characters, but the memory of the setting remained clear.

This time she played the role of the host. We sat out on the verandah with the sunset in front of us, easy little rich girls, less glamorous perhaps than the rest of the clientele, but with enough money to buy our way into their charmed circle for the night.

So we indulged ourselves, and at the end of the meal, when the waiter brought the bill, Elly hissed at me to keep my wallet in

my bag and, with a certain sense of ceremony, laid out two crisp hundred-dollar
notes in between the white folds of the
napkin and waved away the change. But it
was so much money that neither of us could
be quite casual about it.

"We're both wondering if I'll miss the
money, right?" she said after a while. "The
answer is I don't know. I've tried hard not to
become dependent on it, but it does rather
seep in through the cracks. Wealth. It's like
all the best drugs. You don't notice it until
you're hooked."

"So? You've already shown you can break
one addiction. If it worries you, you could
always use my building society as a diner for
a while. Small doses until you feel strong
enough to go it alone."

"Marla . . ."

"No, I mean it. People keep whole families on my salary. You could become an in-
terior designer. Do for me what you did for
Hermosa."

"Oh sure — you really want to live in an
overpriced goldfish bowl. Thanks, but no
thanks."

"So, why don't you ask Lenny for ali-
mony? In lieu of services rendered?"

"Because he'd give it, that's why. And I
want his charity even less than I want yours.

Don't worry. It's no big deal. I've been poor before. It's just a question of acclimatization. The money will be the least of my worries." She finished her coffee. "Come on. Franklin's head is burning a hole in my pocket. Let's have a brandy to celebrate our friendship. We're probably the oldest surviving relationship in this restaurant, let alone in the state of California."

By the time we got back on the freeway, the roads were empty of traffic. I was beginning to wonder if we shouldn't have decided to stay the night somewhere when the engine started to make its feelings on the matter known. For a while we both tried to ignore the grumblings coming from under the bonnet, but we were still some way outside Santa Cruz when the car spluttered, then juddered, and finally choked itself to a congested, graceless halt on the hard shoulder. Elly turned the key in the ignition. The engine gurgled into life again, but with a rasping, desperate sound that made us suspect the worst. We crept along for a few miles in the slow lane, trying to believe in miracles, but all three of us knew there would be no getting home that night. It was after midnight. A tow or a mechanic would take hours, even if we could find a phone. And, as Elly put it, the prospect of sitting out on a dark, deserted highway waiting for the tap of a disembodied fist on the windscreen was a little too close to urban legend for comfort. The only thing to be done was to try to get off the freeway and find a place to stay until morning. Sand City was creeping up around us, the sand dunes dark and eerie in the light of a half-moon. To one side, off the road, there was the gaping carcass of a hotel which looked as if it had been built for a totally different landscape, before the sand had flowed in, bringing commercial disaster in its wake.

We panted on, and at the next side road, chugged our way toward what must once have been the outskirts of the town. In the distance we reentered B-movie territory, with a flickering neon sign above an arrow pointing left, announcing, SAND CITY MOTEL, with both the C and E missing. We grinned at each other, half anticipating swirling mists and a Rod Serling voice introducing *The Twilight Zone.* Fifty yards down the side road, there it was, a set of ten rather sad bungalows, two with their lights on, the rest dark. Who could possibly choose to spend the night here? We tossed a coin to decide which one of us would make the introduction. Elly won.

The owner, whom I roused from a back-room television den, didn't look anything like Norman Bates and treated the whole transaction as if it was just his job. It made me wonder if we Europeans are the only ones to conjure up an instant vision of *Psycho* on journeys into the unknown. Americans at least had experience of motels long before that particular highway was removed and Norman's mother slept once too often with her new lover. In England we expect landladies to be thin-lipped and sullen. Who knows, perhaps a streak of the psychotic is occupational in motel owners? I did not stay to find out.

Inside the room, safely locked, we tried phoning J.T. to explain our absence. But there was no answer. It was after 1:00 A.M. He must still have been out, cruising the Santa Cruz bars on his night on the town. Elly let it ring, just in case, propping the receiver under one ear, while we lay in bed watching reruns of *Lou Grant* on a television which had seen better days. After ten minutes she gave up. Lou Grant put the *L.A. Trib* to bed and we went to sleep.

Her cry woke me from what must have been the deepest part of sleep, because I remember a sensation of dizziness as I rushed back to consciousness. She was sitting upright, one hand over her eyes, as if she had been struck by a sudden blinding migraine. I got up and went to her, putting my arm around her shoulders. "Elly, what is it? What's wrong?"

"Oooh, it's nothing." She shivered violently. "Just a bad dream, that's all. A touch of Brian De Palma in the canyon. I must have scared myself awake."

I leaned over and switched on the bedside light. She winced in the glare. "I'll get you a glass of water," I said, taking a sheet with me for protection. In the bathroom a small spider was resting halfway up the sink. I gave him the thumbs-up and ran the water from the bath. Elly gulped at it greedily.

"Do you want to talk about it?"

She shrugged. "There's nothing to tell really. I dreamt I was in the guesthouse on my own at night, asleep on the verandah outside. I woke suddenly to see this figure standing in the doorway, watching me. I cried out, but he began to come toward me. I scrambled up, but there was nowhere to go. He was blocking my path into the house. I desperately started to climb over the side of the verandah to drop down onto the deck below, but just as I was hanging there, about to let go, I spotted something in the corner, the shadow of someone crouching, waiting to pounce. That's when I woke up. It scared the shit out of me. Stupid, eh?" She grinned wearily. "It must have been the lobster. Seafood revenge. It's OK. I'm all right now. Just give me a minute."

I walked over to the window, where a dull, dirty light was filtering in through the curtains. I peered outside. For the first few yards the lamp above the door threw down a semicircle of yellowish haze. Beyond there was nothing. Somehow the light made the darkness seem blacker. Sand City USA. Once again we were alone in a lost landscape. What was it about this country that seemed so alien when the night fell? Maybe it was just the size.

I said nothing but kept my eyes focused on the darkness. Finally, when it came down to it, it was her battle and not mine.

"You know, I really did believe it was the golden land," she said, more to herself than to me. "The place where anything was possible so long as you had the energy; and that energy was something everyone had, like a natural resource. Funny. I must have squandered mine along the way. It's certainly taken me long enough to realize there are some things you can't change . . . some people —" She broke off.

Peering into the night, I imagined waves of Indian warriors crouching in the blackness, light-footed, intent on mischief. I tensed myself for the war cries. Elly and Marla's last stand. One for the history books. Not bad as endings go. Time passed. Outside everything stayed the same.

"You know, I think I would like to go to Paris. For a visit. If that's all right with you."

I let the curtain fall softly back into place. The world contracted and became more domestic. Manageable. I turned to face her. She was sitting huddled, staring at the wall, frowning, as if the problem were not yet completely solved. I felt, as if we had been in the room for days, working it over, sorting it out. For a moment of triumph, it was all very subdued. She looked up at me and smiled. I smiled back. It seemed enough. She settled herself back down under the covers. "I think I'll be able to sleep now. How about you?"

"I think so too." I got into bed and lay there for a while, feeling a kind of satisfaction. I also felt her sadness. Beginnings are endings too. Eventually her breathing evened out into a regular pattern of sleep. I called her name softly; she did not respond. I turned over and closed my eyes. The next thing I recall was the sound of a car door slamming and a motel morning dragging me out of sleep.

★ ★ ★

The first day of the rest of our lives. It did not stand on ceremony. Sand City welcomed us begrudgingly. The girl at the breakfast diner was impatient, though we were the only customers in the place, and even the eggs did not seem sunny-side up. We said very little. Elly was light and shade, the exhilaration of a decision made and the knowledge of the battle to come. I did not intrude. The car limped faithfully into town, only to die quietly a hundred yards from the garage. We pushed it the rest of the way and stood like worried parents as the doctor prodded and poked under the bonnet.

"Fuel-flow problems," he announced in a voice that had traveled a long way to get to California. "I ain't got the right parts here, but I can fix her up temporary like, so you can git home. Take me a couple of hours, though."

We left him to it and headed for the beach. Sand City — it meant what it said. Miles of it, dazzling white under the sun, tons of it, pounding in on every roll of surf. Even the air was blurred with sand mist, sticking to your skin and stinging your eyes. We lasted just over an hour, watching a few mad surfers become waterlogged with

203

failure. Then we took refuge in a darkened bar, where we drank tequila sunrises without the tequila and felt the windburn on our faces.

By 2:00 P.M. the car was better, if not well. We took it easy, pootling the back roads and chugging our way up the hills toward home. An hour and a half later we reached the mailboxes, and although I would not have admitted it, I was glad to arrive back in daylight. From the summit of the ridge we looked down onto the J.T. homestead, still uninhabited, the truck nowhere to be seen. We left the VW in the drive and walked back across the meadow.

We were perhaps fifteen yards from the house when the telephone began to ring. Before I could quicken my pace, Elly had made a run for it. By the time I stepped in through the glass door, she was talking animatedly, her back turned away from me. I didn't need to hear the words to know that this was no death's voice intoning platitudes. Her body language gave away the identity of the caller. Inside the house, the air was stale from a day's baking, but otherwise everything felt just as we had left it. Outside, the canyon seemed empty in the heat. Just bad dreams?

She came out and joined me, squatting on

the floor next to me and wrapping her arms around her knees. She looked uneasy.

"Lenny," I said, to save her the trouble.

She nodded. "He's been ringing since yesterday. Both here and J.T.'s. Trying to get in touch urgently." She hesitated.

"When's he coming?" I said evenly.

"Tonight." She pulled a face. "I'm sorry. Nothing I could do. He'd made all the arrangements, was just walking out the door. He gets into San Francisco at nine P.M. Wants us to meet him at the airport and go into town for the night. There's someone he has to see tomorrow. It means we have to book a cab to pick us up, then hire a car in Santa Cruz —"

"*You* have to book a cab, you mean," I said deliberately. "I'm not going."

"Don't be stupid, Marla, you —"

"I'm not going." This time more firmly. "You need to see him on your own. If you have things to say to each other, you can't say them when I'm there."

She frowned. "What we have to say can wait. I'll talk to him later. I don't want to leave you here on your own."

"Elly," I said quietly. "You should talk to him now. It won't get any easier tomorrow or the day after."

"I know that, but —"

"But nothing. What are you waiting for?"

"I don't want to leave you alone," she said again, this time with what I recognized to be a note of Elly stubbornness in her voice.

"And I don't want to come with you. I want to stay here."

"And what will you do?"

"Oh, read a book, eat a steak, drink a bottle of wine, watch the sunset. It'll be hell, but I'll manage somehow."

"Seriously."

"Seriously, I'll be fine, Elly, don't use me as an excuse. You have to tell him, and you have to do it alone. Now is the perfect opportunity. We've spent the last two years at opposite ends of the earth. Eighty miles for a night won't destroy us. If I feel like company I can always go and spend the evening with the chickens."

"And what if J.T. doesn't come back?"

"Of course he'll come back. Even if he's drunk and incapable in some Santa Cruz brothel, he's not the kind of man to neglect his animals. I'll be all right. I promise."

She gave me one last look, to which I steadfastly lied. Then she nodded. "OK. You win. I'll go alone."

It was just after 7:00 P.M. when the taxi arrived. The time of day when the light is drunk on its own beauty and generous to

206

everything and everyone. Elly looked magical, her skin warm with the sun and her eyes bright with the prospect of conflict. Were I Lenny, I would treasure her more than cocaine, I thought, and told her as much as we walked together to the car. She laughed and climbed in, holding my hand through the open window. "Don't worry, I'm stronger than I look."

"I know. It's him I'm worried about."

"I'll call you tomorrow evening. Take care. And remember, if you feel at all —"

"I know. Give a little whistle. If you don't leave now, you're not going to make it in time."

I stood and waved until I could no longer make out her hand held in salute out the window, and all I could see was the cloud of dust as the wheels churned up dry earth crossing the ridge. Then I went back to the house, poured myself a stiff drink, and thought about how anxious I really was.

Logically, I knew I had nothing to fear. Two stargazers and a disembodied voice on the other end of a telephone. Both separate, innocent facts. Only paranoia made them threatening. I understood that in many ways I was infinitely safer here, in the middle of nowhere, then I would ever have been in the center of a town. Anyway, I am lucky.

Unlike Elly's, my fantasies of evil are not of the Brian De Palma kind. I live alone in one of the biggest cities in the world; I walk its dark streets late at night, take shortcuts down its alleys. People do not challenge me — if anything they steer clear of me. I do not smell vulnerable. And if sometimes I lie awake at night, it is not because I hear noises on the stairs. No. I would treat this night as any other, wrap myself in a little history and enjoy the quiet. And if I did look over my shoulder once or twice, it would be in the almost certain knowledge that there was nothing to be seen.

It was less than an hour later, when the sun was halfway through its flashy nosedive into the ocean, that I found the Santa Monica parking ticket in the undergrowth and my anxiety became more concrete.

Ten

I certainly wasn't looking for it. In fact, if it hadn't been for the animal, whatever it was, I would never have spotted it. But when I heard the bright, crackling sound of dead grasses rustling near the edge of the deck, and saw the undergrowth shiver, it was simple curiosity — a town girl's fascination with nature — that made me want to discover what it was. It had sounded too loud and too careless to be any kind of lizard, and my immediate thought had been one of J.T.'s gophers coming up for air. I had a vision of a wide-eyed cartoon-type rodent with Bugs Bunny teeth and a "What's up, Doc?" kind of mischief. Maybe they were taking time off from the lengthy process of gnawing through steel coating. I was interested to make the acquaintance of one of the "little bastards."

I got up from my chair and lowered myself from the deck to the spot where the noise had come from. Nothing. Of course. I pushed aside the grass in the hope of coming across some telltale mound of fresh earth. It was then that the flash of orange caught my eye: a piece of soft cardboard no bigger than a calling card but fierce in color. I picked it up, curious to know what remnant of California history I had excavated. I didn't notice the date at first, although I remember thinking that it looked newish. For those few moments it seemed I had chanced upon a common or garden-variety parking ticket from a Santa Monica car park. It was not until I had carried my spoils back up to the deck and there indulged my historian's mania for tidiness and accuracy that I deciphered the date. The ticket had been punched out at 1:45 P.M. on August 2. It took the teleprinter in my brain about thirty seconds to assess the significance and start spewing out conclusions.

Today was the eighth. That made the second a Saturday, the day we had arrived from New York. We had reached the house in the late afternoon. The ticket could not possibly have been dropped before then. Santa Monica was in Los Angeles, which in a fast car was five or six hours from here. Even substituting planes for cars, by the time airports had been reached and schedules allowed for, the owner of the ticket could hardly have arrived here before we did. Which meant they must have arrived after. But apart from J.T. (could he have been in Los Angeles that morning?), the only visitor we had had was Sir Frank Galahad, and his story had not included Santa Monica. He had not seemed the kind of man to lie. That left the thirty hours while we had been away on the coast. At some point during that time someone had been here, someone who had, perhaps, walked up from a campsite down below?

In the canyon, twilight was chipping away at the definition of the landscape. There must be a rational explanation. It was 8:00 P.M. The day was living on borrowed time. Elly was eighty miles away. J.T., for all I knew, was unconscious in some Santa Cruz bar. I was alone in a house that was totally isolated, with no transport and no one to call. There had to be a rational explanation. I set about constructing one. While we were away, someone — a hiker, maybe even a visitor for J.T., who not finding him at home had tried the guesthouse instead — someone had stood on or near the deck. Maybe they had reached in their pocket for a cigarette and the ticket had tumbled out, obscured immediately by the undergrowth. What could be more innocent than that? They had stood smoking, admiring the view

— I would have done the same — then gone their way. Why not?

I looked back at the house, with its elegant frontage, crimson in the last flush of sunset. It would have looked inviting to the curious visitor. Such an unusual building, after all. Wouldn't they, perhaps, have been tempted to go inside? As it happened, the door wasn't locked. We had expected to be away for only a few hours. If I had been them I might have sneaked a look.

I justified the second search by the fact that the lights needed to be put on anyway, and I could tidy up a little of the debris left by Elly's sudden departure. I found an empty wine bottle by the cushion and a book on the telephone table. Surely Elly had left them there? Upstairs in the bedroom, clothes were strewn all around — Elly had had some trouble deciding what to wear. I folded them up and put them back into her suitcase. The place became normal again. No one had been there. Out on the verandah, the mattresses lay side by side, the bedclothes disheveled and unmade. I would not sleep outside tonight. I bent down to pull one of the mattresses indoors — the action saved my life.

I saw the footprint first. There it was, right in front of me on a piece of sheet trailing across the floor, the faint but distinct imprint of a large boot with a ridge of patterned grooves across the sole. It did not belong to either Elly or me. She had Cinderella feet, while mine, big boned and solid as I am, don't reach such circus proportions.

It was then that I saw it move: out of the corner of my eye, a stream of mercury slithering under the sheet. This time my reflexes worked faster than my brain. I was already up and moving when the rattle-hiss hit the air and a black shimmerhead broke cover, reared up, and lunged in the direction of flesh. It missed the bare skin of my legs by a breath — I could feel the rush of air it disturbed. It reared back to strike again, but I was out of range, across the no-man's-land of the verandah into the bedroom, slamming the door behind me and registering as I did so the thud of snake head against wood. I felt its rage as it recoiled from the blow and imagined it slithering back on itself, gliding along the edge of the verandah and curling itself around the pole that connected the balcony with the deck below. Elly's dream flashed through my mind, and I flung myself downstairs. The glass door was open an inch or two. I rammed it shut and locked it. In the back of my head, a pulse was pounding. I sat on the bottom step of the spiral staircase and took deep breaths. The thumping receded, and my brain started functioning again. A simple cause and effect equation. Town girl I may be, but it didn't take Desmond Morris to recognize the death rattle from the room above. Someone had just tried to kill me. I congratulated myself on my continuing survival. Then I began to think about all the other snakes in the house.

That decided it. I suppose I could just have barricaded myself in and slugged it out with the fear and the darkness, but who was I to say they wouldn't come back? For the first time I began to appreciate the power of Brian De Palma. Outside there was twilight enough to make the journey to J.T.'s. If I left it any later, I would have to face the path at night. At J.T.'s there were animals. And a car — ill certainly, but technically still alive. There might even be J.T. by now, broad shouldered and calm, sitting at his table cutting up kohlrabi and studying his star map. The picture was absurd and comforting at the same time. J.T., up until now as much a contender for mistrust as anyone else, reborn as a symbol of sanctuary. I had no other choice.

Stuffing a few books into my bag and liberating the rest of a bottle of Scotch, I switched off every light in the place and, hawkeyed for snake movement, slid out of the door and crossed the deck. A gleam of light winked up at me from the bottom of the canyon. It could well have been just the headlight of a passing car; I didn't stop to check. Striding out toward the brow of the hill, I did not look back.

I reached J.T.'s breathless, to be greeted by a cacophony of animal voices raised more in hunger than in welcome. The walk had restored a measure of sanity, and I even contemplated stopping to feed the chickens before continuing my flight. But the chicken pen was at the edge of the trees, where the air was already thickening into night. If the roles had been reversed, would they have fed me? Survival first, charity later. I headed for the car.

Inside I muttered a few incantations, slid the key into the ignition, and turned. The engine coughed politely and died. I tried again. So did the engine. Again it failed. I sat back and closed my eyes. This time it caught. I put my foot on the gas, and the engine roared into life. Now the real problem began. It was almost three years since a Ford transit van had written off my Deux Chevaux and given me the perfect excuse to stop driving. Three years for someone to whom mechanical skills do not come easily. They say that in emergencies people remember things they thought they had forgotten. But who are "they," and how can they be so sure?

I put down the clutch and fumbled for reverse. We backed out of the drive a good deal faster than anticipated, but at least we were moving. First gear took us onto the path, slower and with a judder that was not entirely my incompetence. The headlights, when I located them, were not strong. But they picked up the contours of the path sufficiently for me to follow it over the ridge toward the line of trees which marked the beginning of the path to the world outside.

We were halfway down the avenue, with the trees arching overhead cutting out the remainder of the light, when the engine began its death throes. Whoever had been up there watching over me when the snake's head missed its target had evidently been called away on more urgent business. I was on my own now. I pumped the gas frantically. The car whimpered softly, then expired. I turned the key. Nothing. This time there would be no raising from the dead. Outside, the darkness rubbed itself up against the windows and the silence howled.

What next? Leave the car and walk the rest of the road until I found a lift? On the entire drive in daylight we had passed only two cars. What chance was there at night? Or stay where I was until morning? Or till J.T. came home, taking the corner in memory of racing drivers, speeding straight into the tender frame of the VW? My stomach starting producing ice chips. I sent a message ordering it to stop, but it didn't seem to get through.

It got me out of the car, though, pushing and shoving the tin lump off the path. It was useless. The lane was wide enough for only one vehicle; however hard I tried, I wouldn't clear the path. In reverse we got ten, maybe fifteen yards back. Then the rear wheel hit a rut and wouldn't budge. Back inside the car, sweating, I strapped myself into the passenger seat near to the horn and turned on every light I could find. The path in front leapt into muddy yellow focus, catching a moth flitting in search of food. It wasn't great, but it would have to do. I took more than a few mouthfuls of Scotch and, getting out a book, prepared to sit it out.

I have no idea when the lights finally died. Or when I fell asleep. I know only that the last time I looked at my watch it was 12:54 A.M., and both myself and the lights seemed to be fading. I remember turning off the inside lamp to conserve energy and snapping myself back into life. I was feeling almost alert as I began my introductory lecture on monastic life in early Christian Britain. I couldn't tell you how far I got, though I have a dim recollection of starting to slide around the time of the Vikings' destruction of Lindisfarne.

The Ford truck's destruction of the VW came twelve centuries later, at exactly 3:06 A.M. A fact I know for certain because it was the moment my watch stopped on propelled contact with the dashboard. I was lucky. As J.T. put it later, if it hadn't been for the skunk which nipped between his wheels just as he turned the corner by the mailboxes, he might have been traveling a good deal faster than the thirty miles an hour he was doing when his headlights picked up the sudden gleam of tin and glass in the middle of the path and he slammed on his brakes, bracing himself against impact.

The blow lifted me out of sleep and my seat at the same instant, picking me up to fling me backward and then forward. The seat belt and my rag-doll limbs saved me from real injury, but I registered a sharp pain as my chest and the belt welded themselves together temporarily. Out through the windscreen I saw the nose of the truck rutting itself into the bonnet of the VW and, beyond, a door flung open, with a large figure staggering out. I remember thinking that it wasn't quite J.T., but I couldn't work out what was different. The whole scene seemed to be taking place somewhere else, somewhere where I was not. The illusion was destroyed when the driver's door was wrenched open and the great bear's head pushed in.

"Elly, are you all right?" it roared. It was then that I realized the deliberate mistake. The Bear did not have its glasses on.

"It's not Elly. It's me," I shouted but couldn't be sure if I had opened my mouth to let the sound out. "Marla," I tried again. I pulled myself free from the seat belt and made an attempt to get out of the open door. But it wasn't just my mouth that didn't work. My legs seemed to be giving trouble too. I found myself sprawled on the ground with J.T. towering above me like some monstrous high-rise building. I could feel a violence in him, and the sense that once released it would not be controlled. He took my hand and began hauling me up from the ground. I thought for a moment he was going to hit me, and I flinched away from him.

"What the hell . . ." his voice growled in the night. It was then, with a grace and style entirely my own, that I vomited over his shoes.

"Drink it."

I could smell the vomit on my breath. I didn't want the Scotch, but I needed its antiseptic qualities. I took a gulp and liked the way it flowed like hot lava down my throat, scalding and melting the ice chips still lodged somewhere in the bottom of my stomach. Maybe if I drank some more I might even feel normal.

"That's enough." He took the flask from my hands and, holding it up, poured a small river down his own throat. I wondered if he could taste my breath on the rim. I was sitting on a log by the side of the path, his jacket round my shoulders. He was crouched in front of me, squinting through the crazy paving of one smashed lens, the other mercifully untouched. I was glad he was there.

"You all right now?"

I nodded.

"So, tell me."

I did, making it as simple and as accurate as I could. And the sound of my own voice reassured me somewhat, which was all to the good, because when I reached the part about the telescope and the phone calls, thunder began to grow in him, a great rolling wave of it, which exploded over me as the snake sent me scuttling across the ridge for cover.

"Motherfuckers . . . stupid motherfuckers. Jesus, what kind of stunt —" He broke off, and the night shivered with his fury. He wrenched his attention back to me. "You sure about the snake? You sure it was a rattler?"

"I didn't stop to check its fangs, if that's what you mean. Yes, of course I'm sure."

"God damn . . . I told them. Assholes."

I suppose I might have got there faster, but I arrived in the end. "What do you mean? I don't understand. Do you know these people?"

He stared at me as if he hadn't heard a word I'd said.

"Tell me." My voice, it now became obvious, was not entirely back within my control. We both noticed it rise too sharply.

"Yeah," he growled. "I know them."

"Who are they?"

"No one. Hired hands. Doing someone else's dirty work."

"Whose?"

"But she didn't see any of it, right? The

221

footprint, the snake, the phone calls . . . she doesn't know about them?"

"I said, whose? Answer me, for Christ's sake."

"No, God damn it, you answer me first. She doesn't know about that stuff?"

"No." I took an angry gulp of air. "No, she doesn't."

"And she and Lenny won't be back until tomorrow. They're staying in the city. You certain of that?"

"Yes, I'm certain. She said she'd call, listen —"

"No, you listen. I'm going to have to leave you . . ."

"Like hell you are." The words erupted so powerfully that even he had to pay attention. "What is this? What the fuck's going on? Tell me. I have a right to know."

"You will." He was gentler now, concentrating on me hard. "But not now. Now I gotta do something, and you can't come with me."

"I'm not staying here."

"No, I'll take you back to the house. You'll be safe there. They won't come back."

"How the hell do you know?"

"Because they've got eyes. They saw Elly leave. And it's not you they're interested in."

I shook my head. "I'm still not going back."

He brought his face close to mine and stared at me. I could smell the sweat on him. It was heavy and sweet and not unpleasant. I liked the bulk of him. It filled up the night and left me comforted. He nodded. "All right. You can come with me. But you'll have to stay in town. There's a place you can hang out. I'll pick you up when I'm finished. But no questions now, right? You're gonna have to wait for the story."

"Where are you going?"

"I told you, you're going to have to wait. Come on."

He pulled me up from the log and, holding tight on to my arm, guided me toward the truck. His hand was hot and damp through the sleeve of my shirt, and his grip less than gentle. There had been more physical contact between us in the last few moments than in the whole of our strange, oblique relationship. What kinds of women did he love? Ones built in his own image? Or was it always the pursuit of fantasy? I already knew the answer. "Elly, are you all right?" Every giant has its Achilles' heel. On the other hand, right now I was more worried about his eyesight.

"What about your glasses?" I said as I

clambered into the passenger seat. I wouldn't swear to it, but I think he smiled. Behind the cracked lens he closed one eye, a kind of wink.

"We were both lucky tonight. I cracked the right one. The left works fine. I just wear the glass to keep the balance. Let's go."

Half an hour later I was sitting propped up at a dimly lit bar with padded leather stools and a large fish tank above the optics, where a sluggish octopus was clinging to the glass walls. J.T. had gone, and I had nothing to do but swallow black coffee and wait for his return. Outside it was getting on for dawn, but here it was perpetual night. In the half-light the place looked sleazy, but it was also sleepy and safe. J.T. was obviously a regular. Even the bartender was discreet, or maybe drunk enough to be lacking in curiosity. No doubt this kind of thing was routine for him, all in a night's work. Whatever the conventions, no one bothered me. The pickups had all been had, and those left were too self-absorbed to care. At the far end of the bar, a man somewhere between forty and sixty sat hunched over a half-empty glass. He had looked up briefly when J.T. left but evidently found me less interesting than his liquor.

Across the room a man in a denim shirt

was shooting pool with himself, taking every shot with a kind of glazed, slow-motion concentration. He had the air of someone who had not seen daylight for months, and had no intention of breaking the habit. I watched him as he stood, leaning on his cue, staring intently at the table, deciding on the next target. There was something about him that appealed to me. I liked the way he had chosen this as real life, above and beyond anything that went on outside. It was an exotic isolation, and I was impressed by it. I thought about my own life. I too lived temperature controlled, working and watching others, always on the other side of the white line, using distance and efficiency as my version of potting every shot. Except now I had broken my own rules. By stepping into Elly's life, with all its pain and chaos, I had left the control chamber, I had become involved. And because of what had happened in the last six hours, and because I was about to learn more than even she knew, it was becoming my story as well as hers.

At the table the man had made his decision. His body stretched for maximum reach, he was trying a rebound shot to pocket the blue. A Tammy Wynette tape was soaking up the silence, but its level was low enough for me still to catch the crack as the white ball hit the blue and, at a perfect angle, sent it gliding gently toward the pocket. It was just a sigh away when momentum ran out and it came to rest, hovering on the edge of the hole. The man straightened up and regarded it with a neutral stare. I turned my attention to my cup. There was no going back now.

Eleven

It was well into dawn by the time J.T. and I emerged from the bar. My eyes were beginning to smart with tiredness. I had reached that point where sleep seems an almost unbearable temptation. On the journey back, we spoke very little. I didn't ask and he didn't volunteer. Maybe I didn't want to hear the explanation after all. As we drove over the ridge, the sky was a translucent gray-pink with shots of blue running through it, like veins under the finest of pale skins. The world was fresh and clean, and last night seemed a long time ago.

When we reached the cabin, he turned to me. "You look strung out. You wanna sleep? We can talk later. Before they get back."

I thought about how it would be after two, maybe three hours' sleep, how if anything I would be feeling even more dislocated. I shook my head. "No, I'll hear it now."

He got out of the truck. "OK. But you need to wake up. You should take a shower." I hesitated. I wasn't sure if I wanted to shower in J.T.'s house. It smacked of a complicity, an intimacy, which we didn't have, and which I was pretty sure I didn't want.

He noticed my prevarication and bent his head back in through the window of the truck. "Listen. Maybe we should get a few things straight. You and I have got some things in common. We don't like people too much, and we don't spend a lot of time with them. But you got your nose caught in this honeypot. You were the one who came back and started asking questions, and now you're gonna have to be the one to hear the answers. I know nothing about you except that you're Elly's friend and you're looking out for her. That's enough for me. I don't want to know you any better than you want to know me, and I sure as hell got better things to do than make a grab for your tush. Now, you can take your goddamned shower anywhere you like. But I'm stopping here, and since we gotta talk, I suggest you save yourself a journey. OK?"

It was the kind of speech which, had it been delivered by someone else, would have been designed to wound. But not coming from him. He was right. Left to our own devices, we would not have passed the time of day together. But some have communion thrust upon them, and one of the things we had in common was a talent for bluntness over charm. It was acceptable to lay down some ground rules. People are easily offended where sex is concerned. Not me. I took myself out of the game a long time ago. I may have crossed some boundaries that night, but not all of them. I got out of the car and slammed the door behind me.

"OK," I said. "Since you put it so eloquently, where do you keep the towels?"

The shower helped, but the cocaine worked even better. Innocent I may be, but stupid I am not. He had been awake for at least as long as I had, maybe longer, and there was something in the quality of his attention — an energy, clipped, almost impatient, that I thought I recognized. Professions can still be hobbies, and old habits die hard.

When I came out of the bathroom, he was sitting cross-legged on the floor by a small table with a slab of glass in front of him, and on it a mound of crystalline white powder. He divided off a small heap and began running it into lines along the edge of a razor blade. He handed me a glass straw and pushed the slab toward me.

"Just a little," he said, carefully watching

me. "It'll help you listen."

I did as I was told and took only what I thought I needed. It burned slightly as I drew it up into each nostril. I sat back and sniffed. Just like in the movies. Somewhere in the back of my head, I felt my brain kick-start, like a television picture jumping into sharp focus. At the same time I tasted a bitter liquid at the back of my throat. I swallowed and pushed the glass back in his direction. He hoovered up the remaining lines and picked the dust off with his fingers, running them along his gums. The ceremony completed, he sat back and snorted loudly.

"I didn't figure you for someone who did coke."

"I don't. Usually. What gave me away?"

He shrugged. "Oh, I dunno. I just got the impression you were pretty straight."

"Well, appearances can be deceptive. I thought you were supposed to have retired."

"Yeah, well, it still has its uses." He snorted again. "You want some more?"

I shook my head. He pushed the glass to the middle of the table. I waited. I got the feeling he was preparing a speech.

"One thing first, OK? Some of what you have to know goes back a way. When you've heard it, you can do one of two things with it. You can tell Elly all or some of it. Or you can keep it to yourself. But you open your mouth to anyone else, and someone will shut it for you. Do you understand?"

What is it they say about coke making you aggressive? More myths than there are ways to cut it. "Don't threaten me, J.T.," I said softly. "I'm not a member of your fraternity, and I'm not interested in becoming one. I may be straight, but I'm not stupid. Maybe we should both agree not to underestimate each other."

Even university teachers learn how to deal with smart-aleck students. I was feeling just fine. He frowned at me but said nothing. I hadn't expected him to. There was a pause. The silence before the story begins. We both recognized it. He moved his gaze from me to the little white hillock on the table between us. And when he did start talking, he kept his eyes there, as if she was the one he was really addressing.

"Me and Lenny go back a long way. But I go back further. I've been in the profession since 1970, got my training in Asia, a short tour of duty napalming villages in Vietnam. The perfect place for pleasure drugs: a lot of people looking to get wasted, and a lot of openings for anyone willing to keep the

231

supply lines fueled. I was never very good at killing, but I had a certain talent for organization. And I was lucky. Six months in I took a piece of shrapnel in the head. It put my right eye on the wounded list and left my brain fit for active service. I spent my convalescence working on a few ideas, then a couple of months later I was on my way home, with an honorable discharge, a list of contacts, and a couple of kilos of sample raw material. The best grass in the world. Bringing it all back home, they called it. Why not? No one was employing veterans anyway, and as a soldier I'd been trained to break the law. First couple of years it went just great. Then they started shipping the boys home, and folks began growing their own. It was time for a change. So I switched products.

"Down south everything was humming. I went to Colombia. There were fortunes to be made in Peru and Bolivia, but it was more primitive there, and the paranoia stakes were higher. In Colombia, so long as you got in quick and knew what you were doing, the market was still open. If you paid the right people, you could even work with the law on your side. I had money to invest. And I had experience. I took a crash course in Spanish, and by the time Lenny arrived on the scene I had a police chief in each pocket and access to an airstrip up near the coast that didn't even show on any of the official maps. I had people lining up to sell me top-quality stuff. I was set up real good. Lenny knew that. But then he knew a lot of things. He'd done his homework, and he wasn't exactly short on bucks either.

"For him it was always a career. Like others train to be lawyers, he had set his sights on Moma Coca. For a while he just watched. Hung around. I knew he was there. He was either a narc or a novice. And I was very good at spotting narcs. He moved into my hotel, and he tried hard to get to know me." He smiled. "He tried real hard. And in the end it worked."

"I thought you were the one who didn't like people. What made Lenny such an exception?"

He caught my eye briefly. "It was a long time ago. Could be I liked people more. Or could be that Lenny had a lot going for him. He was different then, less smooth, less sure. And he was hungry. When it came to detail, he didn't know shit from shinola, but he had a lot of fancy ideas. Some of them pretty neat. And he thought about things. It wasn't the most refined of professions at that time, and Bogotá had more than its fair share of assholes, people with big appetites and not enough between the ears to sustain them. Lenny was sharp, and he was good company. Maybe I saw myself in him — the eager apprentice. Whatever. I was looking to expand. Off-load some of the work. I wanted a partner, and you had to be careful who you picked. I was careful. I picked Lenny.

"And for a while there it worked just fine. I cut him in, introduced him to the right people, got him the right prices, showed him where to take his profits so they came back clean. He learned fast. People responded to him. He brought a touch of New England charm to the business. He was clever. He was also hard as nails. And he wasn't content with present success. Sure he capitalized on old routes, certain blind-spot islands in the Caribbean where you could refuel and unload your planes without ever touching customs, and where you could register yourself as a company with a suitcase full of cash, no questions asked. But for every safe scam he researched another. He opened up new routes, trial runs, sending stuff halfway across the world — places no one would look for it — then rerouting it back into the U.S. through a couple of hands he owned. It was easier

234

then, sure. But he still did it. And got off on the risks. I tell you, he had a natural aptitude for the job. You had to admire him for it."

And J.T. had. Whatever had happened since, the boys had had fun together. You could tell that from the look in his eyes. It wasn't that hard to imagine. Elly had fallen for it. Why not J.T.? Yes, they must have made an impressive duo, the gruff bear king and his slender, suave accomplice. Comrades in battle. Nothing succeeds like success. America's number-one export.

He moved his head sharply, changing the slide: "But he had his problems. His self-esteem started to expand at the same rate as his profits. A common complaint. He had some ideas about honing down the workforce. Thought if he paid the right people at the top, he could cut out a few of the middlemen. There were other guys trying the same trick, but they had a different kind of muscle behind them. I warned him what would happen, but he didn't want to hear. He was looking to graduate from my advice. We had a connection out of Rioarcha, lifting stuff through the Capos islands and in through a back door. The deal was a dream, safer than government bonds. But Lenny decided he could run it himself, cut a few

235

corners at source. He didn't pay the right person, and they walked through his locked door in Santa Marta one morning and busted him with a couple of suitcases. Lesson Number One: everyone has their own police chief when they need him. I had to come in with a lot of money and one of the big boys to get him out. He learned, never made the same mistake again. But it was too late. It put him in my debt, and it finished us. He wasn't too pleased, but he knew the score. He didn't need me anyway. He was into his own trip. Bigger risks, bigger profits. I wasn't interested. The business was already getting out of hand. The days of the small investor and the romance of the identical suitcase scam — all that was gone. With millions sticking dollar bills up their noses, the corporations were moving in, and they didn't leave a whole lot of room for independent operators.

"The Network was muscling around, making people offers they couldn't refuse. If you were real well established, you might get away with it. But the atmosphere had changed. Everything was getting rougher. Here and there. As more stuff moved, it was only a matter of time till prices dropped. And when they dropped far enough, they'd hit the streets. And that would make the old profit margins look like chickenshit. The noses of senators and record producers was one thing, the veins of street punks in L.A. ghettos was another. The authorities started to squeeze. Home and abroad. I could see it coming, and I wanted to get out. I told Lenny that if he knew what was good for him he'd do the same. But he was riding the wave and he didn't want to get off. Me — I'd already made my pile and there were other things I wanted to do. I'd bought the land, and I wanted to get down to living on it. But, like everyone else, I couldn't resist just one last trick.

"It went beautiful. No problem. Until I got back here, that is. Then, maybe ten days after I'd sent it out, the shit hit the fan. Somewhere not so far down the line some geek left his car unlocked while he went in to pick up a packet of smokes. Someone else stepped in and took it for a joyride. It had two pound's of high-grade toot in the back. When the cops found it, they got real excited. Figured they were onto something big. It ought to have been far enough away to keep me safe. But the heat was on. The government was looking for prosecutions, and promotion was based on commission. The narcs leaned real hard, and the guy talked. They sniffed their way upward. It was bad luck, that was all.

"Business had been slow. Already the glut was beginning to show, and not everyone had moved their stash. They busted one of the guys I sold to direct. In theory I was still safe. There are rules if you play the game properly. The few people you sell to are the only ones who know you. They need you as much as you need them. If you go down, you keep your mouth shut, and they do the same thing. They know there'll be someone there with the money to see them through. Good lawyers, light sentences, and their families looked after. Insurance, like any profession. It's not in their interest to go state's evidence.

"But this time my karma was bad all the way down the line. The guy himself knew the score — he would have stuck to the rules. But his old lady was something else. She was seven months pregnant and a real electric lady. She went crazy. This had been their last trick too. Enough money to make it a happy childhood, and she wasn't going to have him go down for it. The cops were very helpful. They wanted the source and they even hinted they'd lift the rap altogether if he saw things their way. He held firm, and for a while everything looked OK. Then she got real antsy. Told him he wouldn't have a wife and kid when he got out, and that if he wouldn't save himself she'd do it for him; she had her own story to tell. Even I didn't know how much she knew, but you could be pretty sure if she flung enough shit some of it would stick. To me and other people as well. I cleared the decks, cleaned out everything that could touch me, and sat back and waited.

"Then, two days after the warning, she was on her way to visit her parents up in the mountains when her car went off the side of a bridge. It was the beginning of winter. The roads were wet, she had a BMW that she drove too fast, and the river was flooding underneath. She didn't stand a chance. A lot of people were real sad, but a lot of others slept better in their beds that night.

"Tyler, her old man, went into a kind of shock. He just zoned out. Gave up talking altogether. To anyone. That included the narcs. The welfare worked well. A lot of money went into the bank account of a high-flying lawyer who played footsie with the prosecution and got some mileage out of a false signature on a search warrant. Tyler got off with a two-and-a-half-year sentence for possessing a whole lot less cocaine than they actually found. Everyone started breathing again. I laid the electricity cables on the land, threw away my Colombian visa, and went into early retirement.

"The day after the sentencing I got a wire from Lenny, congratulating me on my recovery. That summer he turned up here with Elly. Things were going fine. I was out of it. There was no competition between us, and he was riding high. He even felt like he'd mellowed out a little. Or maybe that was her. She had a kind of easiness about her then, as if she expected people to treat her right, and so they did. I'd never seen Lenny so hooked before. Anyway, whatever the reasons, we had some good times.

"Then, just after they left, something started to crawl out of the swamp. Tyler's old lady had had a sister who she was real tight with. A woman called Nellie, a good-looking broad with the same kind of electricity. I knew her from a couple of years back. She and I had played around a little, but I was into the business and it didn't work out. She took off with some guy from Vancouver Island. She came back for the funeral. Then she stayed around and started digging up the past. Tyler had been one of the boys for a while. I had never told her what I did, but she wasn't stupid. Now she began adding things up. She also began asking questions about her sister's death.

The verdict had been misadventure. The pathologist had found traces of tranqs in her blood, but Nellie wouldn't believe it. Said her sister would never have taken that kind of shit during pregnancy. She started suggesting that the death maybe wasn't such an accident after all. And she wasn't too choosy who she said it to. She even came to see me about it. I told her to drop it, that she was whipping up a storm, but she didn't listen. Maybe she needed to get back at me too."

He paused. Obviously not all the truth was for retelling. In recent memory something stirred. A good-looking woman standing outside a log cabin, watching him, long graying hair and a spark of sexual defiance in her eyes. An electric lady? Maybe.

"I think I saw her." I said quietly. "That day at the feed store. She was staring at you from across the road. I wondered why."

"Well, now you know," he said grimly. "So, do you want to tell me about your love life, or can I get on with the story?"

The sarcasm was meant for her, not me. I felt almost sorry for him. Almost. He took my silence for obedience and continued.

"About a month later I had another visit. This time from a couple of professionals. Rumor travels fast, especially through prison gratings. Tyler had heard from someone who claimed they knew that his wife's car had been 'arranged' just before that last drive. It couldn't be proved — the engine had gone right through the front seat into the bodywork — but the facts added up to a nice round total. Tyler hadn't been doing too well inside — some coke men don't — and this flipped him out. So he commissioned a couple of old friends to find out the truth. I arrived back here one night to find them waiting for me. They put a few ideas to me, batted me around for a while, then asked me what I thought. It took a while, but I finally managed to convince them I had nothing to do with it. But by then I'd given the matter some serious thought, and I had a pretty good idea who did. I put a call through to my ex-partner, told him about my visitors, and said I wanted to talk to him.

"By the time he arrived I was turning from blue to yellow and he didn't have a mark on him. He knew why I wanted to see him. He even seemed quite pleased with himself. I don't know — maybe he was expecting me to thank him. Sure the rumor was correct. It was just the paymaster they'd got wrong. I should have guessed. Lenny owed me. And he didn't like being in debt. It was his style, not mine, to secure silence with a chiseled brake cable. He had it down pat. What else could he have done? I was in trouble. It was her or me. And if I wasn't going to protect myself, then someone had to do it for me. And, after all, we were old *amigos*. He made it sound real logical, even necessary. As if there had been no way out and he'd taken the burden on his own shoulders just to help an old pal.

"Except I didn't see it quite like that. Maybe I just don't like people doing me favors. Or maybe I didn't agree with his logic. It had had nothing to do with him. It was my business, and I was the one calling the shots. I was ready for her to talk. Sure there would have been trouble, but it could have been contained. I was smelling real clean. I had a good lawyer and an even better accountant. It didn't matter to me if my cover was blown — I didn't need it any-more. I'd closed down shop anyway. It wasn't worth two deaths. Simple as that. Even if I had decided to stop the leak, there were other ways. It didn't have to be done by pushing her and a seven-month-old fetus into the Santa Cruz River. That was some-thing Lenny had not learned from me."

Playing the game fair. I seemed to have heard those sentiments before. Elly's words.

And where had she got them from? Lenny, of course. In public and in private with her, he was still the moral philosopher, the good guy, still the disciple of his teacher. And in reality? In reality I believed what I had just been told.

"Of course, there was another side to the story. You had to look at it from Lenny's point of view. After all, he was still in business, and he was right about one thing. If they'd busted me, a lot of other people would have gone down too. The ripples would have spread. And Lenny was one of the places they would have spread to. We had a whole past between us. My past, his present. Sure her death saved my ass, but it saved his as well. Mr. Nice Guy had an ulterior motive. And he knew I knew it."

He broke off and pulled the glass slab toward him, peeling off another couple of lines and running them smoothly up his nostrils. A little more energy for a little more eloquence. There had been more words than I could have believed he had in him. Maybe some of them belonged to the cocaine. He squeezed his nose between his thumb and forefinger, then snorted and cleared his throat. I imagined the jet stream of energy coursing up through his brain, winding him up, speeding him on. He pushed the slab my way. I shook my head. I had all the excitement I could handle right now, and I was so awake my head hurt.

"What happened?" I said, suddenly impatient with the silence.

"Nothing happened. I told him that somebody at his end was whispering half-truths and that if he knew what was good for him, he'd find the leak and plug it fast. I sounded tough, but we both knew the score. We were quits. He knew I had to stand by him. Mind you, he also knew what I thought of his 'favor.' But business is business. Even when you're retired you don't go out of your way to make enemies. Particularly enemies like Lenny. He's a big man now. I don't have the muscle to fight him anymore."

I wondered if that were true but decided not to ask. "So, you pretended to be friends instead?"

"We're polite to each other, if that's what you mean. A pattern of behavior has been established. He keeps in touch; I respond. Maybe he just needs to know what I'm doing. Who knows? Or maybe it's more than that. You don't make friends that often in this business. Associates yes, but not friends. For a while Lenny and I had something going. We trusted each other. We even liked each other. From what I hear those are two qualities he's not familiar with now. Could be I remind him of the old times. He always wanted to be top of the heap. Maybe now he's got there he doesn't like the drop. Something's changed in him. Sure as hell he can't relax anymore. Even the charm has barbed wire in it — I reckon you noticed that too. And this time not even she can change him. Shit, he really blew it, threw it away. He had it all. She was there for him, I saw it. But he couldn't hack it. Couldn't share. He always did have too much vanity. Spent so much time looking at himself he forgot to check on other people. She was asking for help. Any fool could see that. But he couldn't be bothered to notice. Stupid motherfucker . . ."

Things were beginning to fall into place. Why he had given Elly the advice he had. And why he had told her to keep the visit secret. She was right. In some ways J.T. was closer to Lenny than she was. He knew him better. But how much better?

"So, you think he never really gave up the job? Even when he told her he would."

He smiled lazily. "What do you think? Lenny's not a guy to do something he doesn't want to. Whatever the pressure. I think it suited him to have her believe he was giving up. Her and some other people.

Telling the truth isn't one of the strong points of this profession. And rumor has it Lenny has been getting more than a little paranoid."

"You're saying he doesn't trust her?"

"I'm saying he doesn't trust anyone. Why should she be the exception? You got any more to add, or shall I finish the story?"

I treated it as a rhetorical question. There was only a short pause.

"For a while everything went quiet. The garden was growing real good when Tyler got out of jail. Came riding into town about six months ago with a couple of 'undercover' narcs on his tail, curious to find out who his friends were. He was careful. He got a job, left his money alone, and went about his business. After a while they got bored and went back to busting punks. Everything looked good. Then, about a month out, he moved in with Nellie. He had nowhere else to go and she offered. She and her sister looked a lot alike. Maybe that gave him back the ache. Or maybe he'd never lost it. Anyway, Nellie was still cat-curious, and she started to needle him, to get him back on the scent again. So he talked to a few people, even took a trip east to check out some names.

"It was only a matter of time till Lenny

got wind of it and decided to reunite husband and wife. I went to see Tyler, to warn him off. He had kept his mouth shut when he could have talked, and I owed him. In the old days he would have listened. But, I tell you, he had changed. He used to be a real smart guy, kept things to himself, knew exactly what he was doing. But somewhere along the line he'd got turned inside out. You could taste the hatred in him. He was so eaten up with it he was vibrating. A real born-again revenge man. With nothing to lose. Except it wasn't me he was after. He even apologized for having my ribs cracked. A simple case of mistaken identity. He knew that now. I didn't bother to deny it. There was no point in lying. I just told him that paying back wouldn't achieve anything, that it was finished and he should get on with his life. Only he wasn't interested in living in the present. The house was full of pictures of her. It was like some goddamned shrine with Nellie as high priestess, and him full of Bible fever. An eye for an eye. That was what he wanted. He didn't want Lenny, he wanted Elly — Elly for his wife and kid. I told him he was crazy. That it wasn't the same. That taking out Elly wouldn't destroy Lenny. All it was was a way of committing suicide. If the police didn't get him, Lenny would. But he didn't hear me. So in the end I gave him an alternative. Something that would hit Lenny where it hurt but that wouldn't result in any funerals. And eventually he listened."

"Wait a minute. What are you saying? That you set Lenny up?"

If he heard my question, he behaved as if he hadn't. "I told him as much as he needed to know and let him get on with it. It wasn't my war. Not anymore. Then, out of the blue, you two turned up. What could I do? Send you away? Lenny would have smelled something. And I sure as hell couldn't tell you what was going on, however much I may have wanted to get Elly out of it. But then that day on the porch I got this real clear message beaming out from you. You didn't like Lenny any more than I did. And you'd come to take her home. So I gave you a few clues, as much as I dared. But I reckoned without Tyler. When he found out she was here he flipped. And when you and I ran into Nellie that day outside the feed store and word got back that I was hanging out with the ladies, he began to wonder whose side I was really on. I told him to cut it, that the last thing I could do was turn her away. But having her so near got him nervous. And hungry. He had set up a couple of guys

249

for a little surveillance — your camp stargazers — and now he gave 'em a pretty wide brief. They used it to have some fun."

"That's not the word I'd use to describe it."

"Maybe not," he said deliberately. "But that's all it was."

"What do you mean? I don't call a poisonous snake under my pillow fun."

"The snake wasn't poisonous. It was a rattler, all right, but its fangs had been removed. It was meant to scare you, not kill you."

I remembered again the lightning flash of the head. "Says who?"

"Your friends in the canyon. When I left you at the bar, I went and got Tyler out of bed, and together we paid them a little visit. They even showed me the box they bought it in. It came from a pet shop. Born and bred. When you pulled back the sheet, the little critter was probably more scared than you were."

"I doubt it," I said sourly.

"Well, whatever, they won't cause you any more trouble. They broke camp tonight. I watched them go. They won't be back."

So that was it, the whole story. All that fear and panic over a couple of bully boys and an emasculated snake. Full stop. The end. Except for the pages I wasn't allowed to read. Secret documents. It's a historian's job to uncover them.

"What about Lenny? What happens to him?"

He shook his head. The silence grew.

"Why won't you tell me?"

"Because you don't need to know. That was the deal, remember? It still is."

"Why? Because you've betrayed him?" I picked the cruelest word I could find, to goad him. He did not rise to it.

"It's none of your business. Your business is to take her home. Get on with it."

"Except it's not that easy, J.T. You were right. I can't simply tell her what you've told me. We both know what she'd do. March straight up to Lenny and demand to know if it was true. And where would you be then? She may want to leave him, but you know Lenny. Things happen only if he wants them to, wasn't that what you said? Well, according to Lenny he doesn't want to split up. In fact, according to him, he's out for a reconciliation. He's already arranged a trip for them to take together — a surprise second honeymoon. To England of all places. And when —"

"Wait a minute." This time I had touched

251

a nerve. His attention crackled across the table. "What did you say about England? What do you know about that?"

I explained. He never took his eyes off me.

"And did you?"

"Did I what?"

"Tell her about it?"

"No, I didn't. But not out of any favor to him. I thought if she knew it might soften her feelings toward him."

"My God, he doesn't miss a trick, does he?" But the words weren't really directed at me. I recognized admiration mixed in with the anger.

"You mean it isn't true?"

He looked up at me, as if he was almost surprised to find me still there. He frowned. "Do you think you can persuade her not to go with him — without making him suspicious, that is?"

I shook my head. "Not unless you tell me why. I'm not doing your dirty work until I know what it's about."

"Christ, you're stubborn." He growled in anger, slamming his fist down on the tabletop. The glass slab jumped, and a small avalanche of white crystals shimmered onto the wood. "I told you already, this isn't a game. Don't you understand? You can't know any more than you do. You know too much already. Catching Lenny is like trapping a fish. If he senses anything, anything at all, he'll be gone so fast you won't see him move. And if he goes, then Tyler's gonna be casting around for someone else to try his revenge fantasies on. You're a liability as it is. Got that?"

I stared at him. "Just why is she so important to you? How come you're willing to risk so much to get her out?"

He sighed angrily, as if it was a question he had already answered a hundred times before. But when he spoke his voice was quiet and patient, the adult to the child, making sure that this time she understood. "Because she just fell into it all, that's why. He never really told her the truth, and she believed the lies." He paused. "And because somewhere along the line I guess you get out what you put in. Sure I would like to have met her first. Maybe next time I will."

Love on the cocaine trail. True confession. I wondered if I believed it. In light of the facts, this didn't really sound like a love story.

"And maybe she's just an excuse for you to get back at Lenny?" I said quietly.

He looked at me steadily for a long time. "Sure it's about Lenny. I could say the same

thing about you. Lenny and Elly. You don't
like it any more than I do. I wonder why
not? What is it that hurts you? Makes you
risk so much to get her out? See, same question. I can't figure your fantasies any more
than you can figure mine. It doesn't matter.
It's not something I need to know. You keep
your secret. But you'd do well to remember
that you don't own her. Even if you once
did. She pulls people in different ways. You,
me, Lenny, we're all in her orbit. And the
fact is, she doesn't even know it. Strong
stars are like that. All heat and light and attraction, pumping out energy faster than
anything else in the sky. Until, that is, they
burn themselves out. She's got no protection against herself. That's how come
Lenny can fuck her over. He's too rich for
her, too similar. He speeds up the process of
her own destruction. And everyone else's.
Do you know what happens when a star
goes critical? It starts to scorch its own satel-
lites. Then finally it collapses in on itself,
pulling everything with it. Black holes. Attraction and destruction. A law of the universe. It applies to all things."

He looked down at the mound of cocaine
in front of him. Moma Coca: glitter in the
galaxy, her own force of nature. How many
had she energized and then devoured? The

sermon was over. The Gospel According to J.T. We fell silent. Outside the animals were getting restless. Tomorrow had arrived. I didn't feel ready for it. Traditionally after the bedtime story comes sleep. I needed to dream some of it out.

"You should get some rest," he said, uncrossing his legs and standing up, the bones in his ankles cracking in protest. Unfolded again, his size surprised me. I got up to face him.

"I'll drive you home," he said.

"No. I'll walk. I need the fresh air."

He didn't argue. On the front porch it was glorious summer, hot even in the early morning. "You going to be all right?" he asked, as if the thought had only just struck him.

I nodded, refusing to consider the question, and made my way across the deck onto the earth below. When I reached the vegetable patch, I turned back. He was still standing there, watching me, but somehow he seemed smaller than before.

"One thing, J.T. How long have I got?"

He shook his head, and I think he may have frowned. "I dunno. But not long." He stopped, and I began to turn away. "Marla," his voice brought me back. "Look after yourself, OK?"

It was the first time he had called me by my name. It felt almost improper. I raised a hand in salute and headed off into the morning sun.

Twelve

The house was without reptiles. I lay down to doze and fell into a fast-running sleep, a conveyor belt of images, insistent and confused. When I woke I could remember nothing, save a rasping sense of urgency and exhaustion, as if I had spent the hours in endless flight. It was almost noon. The midday heat was pressing down on the landscape, flattening the shadows, squeezing out the air. I sat and watched the grass grow. The screech of the telephone was like shattered glass. On the other end of the line, Elly had become a city girl again, bright and busy. Or maybe she just sounded that way, phoning from a room where she was not alone. She was sorry it was so late. They had talked most of the night and slept into morning. Had I been OK? Was J.T. back? Yes, she was fine, and no, she couldn't really talk now. There had been a change of plan. Would it be all right if I came up to the city? Lenny had to be there another day or so and then, well . . . she'd tell me when I arrived. It wasn't really telephone news. Could I bring our bags? Maybe J.T. could give me a lift — Lenny would like to see him anyway. Otherwise there was always the Greyhound.

Over the hill J.T. was already up, if indeed he had ever been asleep. The animals were fed, the garden watered, today's crops had been picked, and he was sitting out on the deck, busy doing nothing. He was not surprised to see me. I told him about the phone call. He already knew. He had spoken to Lenny and agreed to meet. Old friends, remember, touching base. We would drive into town together. The news struck ice into my soul. I conjured up an image of the four of us, sitting over cocktails in some desperate plastic decor, making conversation. Except I couldn't imagine what we would say. For the first time I began to understand the burden of knowledge.

"It's no big deal," he said sharply. "Ritual, that's all. You don't even have to be there. Go shopping or something."

Back at the house I rang and left a message at the hotel, then packed our bags quickly, careless of snakes and things that go bump in the night. I left the house without sentiment or sense of occasion. There was too much ahead to waste emotion on what was past. The canyon rustled in the heat, benign and empty. Too late. When I reached the brow of the hill, the truck was waiting.

We climbed down to sea level and traveled north, hugging the coast road, the ocean smashing in over rocks beside us. We drove fast and kept our own counsel. The intimacy of the dawn confession had faded with the day. But the silence was not uncomfortable, simply pragmatic. We were supposed to be strangers still. It would not do to arrive chattering like magpies. We spent the time rehearsing our separate performances. An hour and a half later, the road ran out of scenery and we found ourselves cruising urban sprawl, ahead of us a concrete runway taking off into the maze of freeways that fed into the city. J.T. drove them like a cabdriver. Back at ground level, San Francisco welcomed us, but the sharp angles hit hard after the rolling empty countryside. Paving stones over grass. It all seemed unnatural. Downtown shone, as if the place was cleaned daily, a great dusting cloth run over the mirrored skyscrapers and business blocks. And in the middle of it all the Hyatt Hotel, a monument to the marriage of art and commercialism, its huge glass frontage opening onto waterfalls and jungles which framed reception desks and coffee shops. We did not fit in. At the desk I brushed up my accent and was accepted as an English eccentric, while J.T. stood by the bags, untidying the foyer with his sandaled feet and denim shirt, a rural blot on the urban landscape. It did not seem to worry him. I wondered what camouflage he had used in the Hiltons of South America. Presumably he had once practiced the art of fitting in. The man at the desk handed me the phone. Lenny answered. Maple syrup politeness: great to hear my voice; I sounded suntanned; they would be down soon.

We stood and watched the glass lifts glide up and down through the foliage in time to an invisible string orchestra. Out of the third space shuttle burst Elly, small and eager. Behind her Lenny was more laconic, confidence emblazoned in neon across those high cheekbones. Where would he be without his bone structure?

She got to me first. Over her shoulder I watched Lenny's face as, in the same instant, he welcomed me and located J.T., lurking like some discordant Godard extra in the corner of the frame. I was trying to look in all directions at once. The two men greeted each other with a wrist grip. Then Lenny smashed his old colleague on the

shoulder. He grinned, and J.T. came peril-
ously close to a smile. We were watching a
ritual, the accepted ceremony of greeting
between North American males.

"I swear to God you look more like a ref-
ugee from *The Waltons* every time I see
you, *amigo*." Lenny's voice was loud
enough for an audience. J.T. mumbled
something I didn't catch. It made Lenny
laugh. "So, you've been hanging around
with the *señoritas,* eh?" This time he turned
to me. "What did you make of him, Marla? I
bet you know now how the West was won."

I gave him a substandard smile that was
meant to say nothing at all. I felt Elly slip
her arm through mine. The division of the
sexes. Was this where the ladies went shopping?

". . . in the wilderness?" I caught the end
of another conversational sally. Lenny
made a face and feigned a punch to the
chest. J.T. parried it. A few heads turned. It
was appalling. Amateur dramatics. Surely
even a stranger would have smelled the mistrust between them. How did they used to
be together? Somehow I got the impression
that it had always been Lenny who had tried
just a little too hard. Or was I overcompen-
sating, seeing what I wanted to see? I
glanced at Elly. But the ghosts were not vis-

ible to her. For the first time I looked closely at her face. She looked tired but not tense. Maybe it had been a night of home truths for us all.

"Come on, break it up, you guys. We've got better things to do than stand around in the lobby watching you two slug it out. I want to show Marla her room. Which bar are you going to drink in?"

Lenny looked at J.T., then back at us. "The Tudor room, don't you think? We want him to feel really at home. Take your time, ladies. We'll see you there."

At the reception desk I filled in my registration card: "Marla Masterson, academic and private detective." Did I look like someone carrying secrets? If so then Elly didn't seem to notice.

Room 1064 turned out to be a small apartment with a peach bathroom en suite, filled with beauty preparations. The bellboy palmed the dollar bills Elly slipped him and faded smoothly into the hall. Behind closed doors we faced each other. She bounced herself on the bed, pushing the springs with her hands in salesmanlike enthusiasm. "You like . . . ?" She waved extravagantly around the room.

"It's hideous," I said warmly.

"Great. I knew you'd get off on it."

It was good news, I could feel it in the air. I let her get there in her own time.

"Well?" she said, smiling.

"Well what?"

"Well . . . I told him."

Gently now, Marla. No celebrating before the chimes of the clock. "And . . . ?"

"And I won," she said softly. "The battle's over. Elly Cameron is an independent operator again."

I allowed myself the pleasure of sitting down. The armchair was soft and velvety. I wondered if they kept champagne in the fridge. I think I was smiling.

"Don't you want to know what happened?"

Every detail, I thought. "Yes," I said.

"God, I'm not even sure I know myself. But I'll tell you one thing, Marla. Something had changed, right from the first moment we met at the airport. I don't know what it was, and I don't even know if I can describe it, but it was like we were more careful with each other, not taking anything for granted, more separate, more like friends than lovers. He asked me how I was, and I told him I was feeling good and that I had something to tell him. And he said — I remember his exact words because they seemed so formal — 'Well, Elly, what a co-

263

incidence, because I too have things to say to you.' So we drove into town, to this quiet funky French restaurant where we sat and drank fancy wine and decided to part."

"Just like that?"

"Yep, just like that. Incredible, eh? The joint, civilized decision. Or that's how it felt. I did most of the talking. At least to begin with. Christ, I had my heart in my mouth for the first few moments — literally, it felt — I could hardly get the words out. But the longer I spoke, the more confident I got. You'd have been proud of me, Marla. I told him everything, just as told you, only a little shorter and maybe a little sweeter. But the truth. I said I thought we were no good for each other anymore. That we pushed each other's buttons. That loving him had got me caught up in his shadow until I didn't know who I was anymore. And that even though I wasn't sure where I was going, I knew it had to be away from him. And when I finished I felt OK. No, that's not true. I felt more than OK — I felt great. As if I'd been walking round with this bloody great steel band clamped to my head, and now someone had released me. All I had to do was walk away from it. I had made the right decision. I knew it."

Her eyes were shining.

"What did he say?" I still couldn't quite visualize it, this torrent of words falling at the feet of His Serene Majesty. Compassion in the face of revolution. Something didn't fit.

"At first nothing. Scared the shit out of me, facing this great yawning silence. I kept waiting for the anger to break. But then he smiled, took my hand over the table, and said, 'You sound like someone I met once in Colombia.' " She winced.

Good old Lenny, I thought. Big city snake charmer.

"And then he told me he thought I *was* right and it was time for both of us to let go. And of course once he started talking, it was clear he knew it too. He said a lot of things that made sense. About the catch-22 we lived. How my independence had attracted him; how he'd gone out of his way to undermine it; but how when he succeeded it wasn't attractive anymore. God, he knew it all. We both knew it all." A shadow passed over her face. "It's just we couldn't do anything about it."

"Wait a minute, I don't understand. Are you telling me that Lenny had come all this way to say exactly the same thing to you?" In the pursuit of pleasure one should never forget the quest for truth. It made no sense.

Where were all those promises of soft summer reconciliations amid heather and history now? Or had they always been just an elaborate lie to explain a plane he should never have been on?

"No," she said with a sigh. "That's the whole point. He had come to say something quite different. He had come bearing gifts. But when he heard what I had to say, he knew it would be no good . . . that it was already too late." She stopped and swallowed, frowning at the carpet.

"What gifts, Elly?" I prompted after a while. "What did he offer you?"

"England," she said almost angrily. "Can you believe it, he offered me England. Home, a trip, a way of repairing the damage. The grand tour, beginning in the Highlands and heading south for tea with a few of the family. All a big surprise. He was going to spring it on me, just get me to an airport and, hey presto, flourish the tickets. But he got cold feet. Thought it might be too much of a shock. So he came to tell me, prepare me. And do you know what he asked? If I hadn't perhaps guessed already. Guessed! Christ, how could I have guessed? It was the last thing I could ever have imagined."

"And did you tell him that?"

She nodded hard but said nothing. I

looked at her face, the trembling lower lip. Of course the idea had captivated her. Of course she had loved him for it. I had done the right thing in not telling her, even if it had been for the wrong reasons. I watched her fighting back the tears. "Oh shit, I'm sorry," she said fiercely. "I did this last night — sat dripping salt into my lemon sorbet, mourning lost chances." She wiped her hand roughly across her eyes. For as long as I could remember Elly had never carried handkerchiefs. The Hyatt, however, like the Boy Scout movement, was always prepared. From the peach bathroom I plucked a handful of peach tissues. She blew her nose noisily, like a child, then mangled the remains of the tissue in her hands as she spoke.

"There was nothing more to say. We drank our wine and left. We'd eaten so little that even the chef came out to ask whether the food had been all right. Then we took a cab back here and went to bed." She paused. I did not ask for details. Then she said, wearily, "And it was then, in the *omnes anima tristus* bit, that he asked me to go with him anyway. For old times' sake. A way of saying good-bye. 'Use it as a ticket home,' he said. 'You take the single, I'll have the return.' "

I stared at a small smudge of mascara just under her left eye. A few more tears would wash it away. I waited and wondered what she was going to say next, whether if and when the earth moves it really can take with it a woman's common sense and resolve.

She shook her head. "He made it sound so easy. But it was just a fairy tale. A magician's last trick. I knew that really. I told him that I already had my ticket home, via Paris with you. After that I had no plans, and could make no promises. Not anymore."

"Well done," I said softly. "How did he take it?"

She shrugged. "One hundred percent in character. Gold-plated Lenny. Said he understood, but that he would probably go anyway. He had always wanted to see Scotland, and there was a friend of a friend . . . the possibility of setting up another store in London —" She broke off with a sharp little laugh. "My God, I should have known. Always a subtext to everything. I suppose it was reassuring to discover that under all the sweet-talk Lenny was still Lenny. So we left it at that. The star-crossed lovers fell asleep for almost the last time. In the morning I called you, and here we are — two single women, footloose and fancy-free with Gay Paree on our social horizon. What could be simpler than that?"

What indeed? Elly had made her decision and taken control of her life. Mission accomplished. Nothing else mattered. There were no longer any secrets to conceal. What Lenny did now was his own business. Not hers, not mine. An eye for an eye. One thing was sure. There would be no grouse chasing in the Scottish Highlands for him. I was glad not to know the details. What wasn't known couldn't be withheld.

"How do you feel?"

She grimaced. "It's a bit like pulling teeth — I think I'm still under the anesthetic." She screwed up what remained of the tissue and lobbed it at the wastepaper basket. It missed.

"So, what now?"

"I've got one last obligation. I have to go back and sort out the store. I owe him that much. It won't take me long. Four or five days, then Indigo can take over till he decides what to do. But you don't have to come. You could go straight to Paris. Or check out a little more of America. I'm sorry, it hasn't exactly been the greatest of vacations. You could always stay here. Soak up some sun."

I smiled. "And what would I do, lying frying on a California beach on my own?"

269

"Oh, I don't know. Why don't you ask J.T. to join you?" she said, with admirably concealed mischief.

"Because two silent people do not a conversation make," I retorted just a little sharply, remembering the hours between four and six that morning. "What about Lenny? What are his plans?"

"He has some business here, then he'll come back to New York. I suppose we'll spend the last few days together. Maybe go up to Westchester. It sounds corny, but I'd like it to end well. But you know you're always welcome, I —"

"No. No thanks. There's someone I want to visit in Boston. I'll go there and join you later."

"You sure?"

"Yes, I'm sure." And I was. After all, I had won. I could afford to be generous.

Downstairs in the Tudor bar, wasp-waisted wenches in freely adapted Elizabethan costumes were revving up for the evening trade. But Lenny was drinking alone. J.T. had gone. I subdued a small flash of panic. Elly was upset. Lenny, I noticed, was interested in her distress. I kept my feelings on the matter strictly to myself.

"But I wanted to say good-bye," she said

with a hint of petulance.

"So wait till he gets home and call him." Lenny sounded almost amused.

"It's not the same." Pause. "Did you tell him?"

"Tell him what?"

"About us?"

"No. Why? Did you want him to know?"

"Oh . . . I don't know . . . ," she faltered. "I just thought. I mean we had some good times together, all of us. Maybe he'd like to know."

"Yeah, maybe he would."

It was not necessarily a sarcastic remark. I had been playing the wallflower, keeping my eyes fixed firmly on the fake oak table leg. Now I risked a glance upward. And ran straight into steel blue eyes. Without J.T.'s broad shoulders, the world seemed suddenly very full of Lenny.

"How about you, Marla?" He smiled. "Are you feeling deserted too?"

"Hardly." I said lightly. "He always made it clear his first priorities were his chickens."

"How right you are." That seemed to please him. "Well, ladies, since this is, in all manner of ways, an exceptional occasion, I'd say a celebration was called for. I suggest a stroll in the park — take in the evening air

271

— then perhaps a trip across the bay for a little Sausalito seafood. Unless, of course you two would prefer to dine alone?"

So Lenny had taken her leaving in his stride, had he? This time the razor edge broke through the skin of his charm. She felt it too. "Don't be ridiculous, Lenny. Of course we'll go together."

I shook my head. "Only on one condition."

That turned both heads in my direction. When I had my audience, I addressed him. "That I pay for the meal."

Elly winced. Lenny smiled. "Marla, I'd be delighted to be your guest."

We took a cab to the park. It was a balmy early twilight. For once there was no chill wind coming off the bay, and the gardens were still full of people. There had been some kind of concert or performance that afternoon, and the crowds had lingered on in the sunshine and flowers. There were a lot of bodies on show, most of them brown and many of them beautiful. As befits the city's reputation, the flesh exposed was more male than female. The pace was lazier than Polk Street, but it was still a parade-ground, a place to see and be seen. It was a strange experience, coming into a world where the roles were so suddenly and specifically reversed. Here the trade was exclusively male. Being with Lenny was a little like owning a prize racehorse at a track meeting; he turned heads as a matter of course. He seemed supremely unaware of it all. This cannot have been the first time he had tasted the triumph of his bisexual beauty, and he accepted it almost as his due. I admired his detachment, but found it despicable at the same time. There was something monstrous in his confidence.

Outside the park we stood waiting for a cab. On the notice board by the gates, a flurry of colorful posters announced forthcoming attractions. Elly stopped to read them.

"Hey, the Klondyke Klan," she exclaimed. "Didn't we see them once, Lenny? Weren't they the group from Oregon who all live together and train their kids to join the circus too?"

"Uh-huh." Lenny's response was casual, but the look he gave her was not. She was already talking to me. "Oh, you should have seen them, Marla. They were great. No animal acts or stuff like that. Just real circus skills. And they had this incredible finale, about twenty-five of them, all onstage, juggling to a speeded-up version of the Saber Dance. Brilliant. They were talking of doing a world tour, weren't they, Lenny? Did it ever come off?"

"I don't know," he said carelessly, as if he was thinking of something else entirely. Across the road a cab pulled up to let out a fare. I stepped out from the sidewalk, and we heard no more of the Klondyke Klan.

An hour later we sat looking out over a picture postcard of the Golden Gate at sunset. All that was missing was a dry-ice cloud to elevate it to heaven. I was unimpressed. There had been too many stupendous views recently. I was gorged on beauty and suffering panoramic indigestion. Maybe it would not be so bad to sit on top of a London bus and watch concrete streaked with bird shit. At least there you knew your enemies. Here there were snakes in every canyon. Even in the cities.

On the other hand, the meal was going well, despite the echoes of that first evening in the East, an occasion where the power structures had been so different. Then I had been the stranger, allowing myself to be wooed. This time I made the running, filling the air with chatter, because silence felt secretive and I wanted to make it clear I had nothing to hide. Lenny seemed content to let me control the show. I did the ordering and chose the wine and, when the waiter poured it into Lenny's glass to taste, he handed it back to me with exaggerated ceremony. Any tension that there was — and there was — could easily be explained by the circumstances.

For her main course Elly chose salad, declaring that after Nepenthe she associated lobster with bad dreams. The waiter presented her with a plate the size of a small tray and guided her toward a salad bar where someone had expended a good deal of energy doing extraordinary things with vegetables. Knowing Elly's appreciation of art, I knew she would take her time. For the first time since that morning in New York, Lenny and I were alone together. It was like the silence in the marriage ceremony when objections are called for — that dreadful compulsion to speak, combined with the terror of what you might say — "If anyone knows any reason . . ." Lenny did.

"Well, Marla. I think I should congratulate you."

Set poised to murder an oyster, I granted it a moment's reprieve as I looked up to meet his gaze. "On what?"

"Where do I begin? On Elly's spiritual recovery? On your keeping of my secret? Or, perhaps, on the guarding of your own?"

As I lifted the shell to my mouth, I could

have sworn I saw the oyster shiver. "My own?" I swallowed.

"I don't think I'd realized that you'd come to take her home."

I swallowed again. "I hadn't. It was her decision."

"Of course. And yet even when she made up her mind to go back with you, you were never tempted to tell her about my proposed trip?"

"You asked for my word, Lenny. And I gave it."

"Indeed you did. As an officer and a gentleman. Alas, neither of the descriptions does you full justice, Marla. You know, it really is a shame our acquaintance has been so brief. I would very much like to have gotten to know you better."

I didn't waste time trying to look flattered. "I'm not sure you would. I'm actually quite a dull person."

"That's not what J.T. says."

It was a remark designed to cause a reaction. I gave him the pleasure of one. Since he had to be lying, my consternation could give nothing away. "What does J.T. know? We hardly spoke more than a dozen words to each other."

He shrugged. "Well, you must have picked the right dozen. You should be flattered. He really hates most people, you know. Sometimes I think he doesn't even like me."

"Really," I said evenly. "But I thought you were good friends."

"Well . . ." He made a dismissive gesture. "Perhaps I'm just paranoid. It's only a feeling I get sometimes. That maybe we keep secrets from each other. But then I don't find that strange. I think there's probably quite a lot of ambiguity in friendship, wouldn't you agree?"

Come into my parlor, said the spider to the fly. Sod off, said the fly. "I wouldn't know. I suppose it depends on the friendship in question."

"Exactly," he said emphatically, as if it had been just the answer he was looking for. "Here comes Elly. Right on cue. You can always spot her in a restaurant. The smallest lady with the fullest plate. I'm going to miss her, you know. Although I daresay you find that hard to believe. Nevertheless, it's true."

Suffice it to say I was not moved. As confessions go, it was a little threadbare. He was not telling me how much he loved her. He was simply expressing regret at losing her. It was still about possession. Not the noblest of qualities.

She arrived back bearing a harvest in front

of her and, mistaking the tension for the one she had left behind, took it upon herself to spread a little sunshine. The rest of the evening went passing fair. I think what I loved most about her that night was her innocence. She truly believed that she had fought her battle and won. I don't think it ever occurred to her that Lenny had not conceded defeat. She had always been one for happy endings, and whatever wounds she had sustained over those last few years, it seemed that something of optimism and energy had remained. And so, when Lenny raised his glass across the table and announced with full pomp and circumstance — "To Paris" — she met his eyes and did not, I think, read the challenge in the toast. But then it was not meant for her.

Thirteen

If we had lain becalmed in California sunshine, now the wind was up. I woke early, disturbed by the hermetic silence of the sealed box, and decided on a preemptive strike with regard to the bill. It was ten to eight when I approached the desk. But I had been outmaneuvered. The room had been paid for in advance, my night bought for me. At the house phone Elly answered. Lenny was gone. A call had come just after dawn and he had slipped away, instructing her to apologize and to say he would see me in New York. What could be so urgent as to pull him out of bed at such an inhuman hour? Of course Elly didn't know. Why should she? He hadn't told her his business when they were together, why should he start now that they were apart?

I rode the glass casket up to the eleventh floor. Her door was unlocked, and breakfast was laid out on the table. She was standing by the window, staring out into a bright blue San Francisco morning, a woman alone.

279

Rejoicing or regretting? I didn't ask. Over hot rolls and coffee we made plans. A few local calls turned them into plane reservations, and then Elly picked up the phone one more time and asked the operator for an out-of-town number.

"Santa Cruz 6791, please — J.T.," she explained, her hand over the mouthpiece: "I just want to say good-bye."

6791 . . . 6791. I retreated to the bathroom to give her privacy and to scribble down a number which, with any luck, I would never need to dial. Through the half-closed door I heard chippings of conversation. J.T. did not appear to say much. I imagined him double-thinking every word, picking his way through meaning in search of unexploded mines. His reticence seemed to embarrass her, making her clumsy where, I suspect, she had rehearsed elegance. But the facts got out somehow. She had called to say good-bye. She was leaving, going to Paris with me, then back to England for a while. She had wanted to thank him, for hospitality provided and advice given. She was sorry they hadn't talked more. She hoped he understood. She also wanted to ask him a favor, however stupid it might sound. Would he look after Lenny for her?

In the bottom of my stomach something

twisted, a small but sour pain. Conscience lives not in the head but in the bowels. I caught sight of myself in the bathroom mirror. My skin and hair had ripened in the sun, but the large strong nose and big mouth remained the same, and under them the chin still announced truculence to the world. Unlike Ophelia, I was neither honest nor fair. It was not, however, the time to mourn lost virtues. Through the door I heard the ping of the receiver, and I strode back into the room. Elly looked a little crumpled sitting there but smiled as I came in.

"He sends you his regards. Said if you ever need any help with the sky at night to give him a call." She frowned. "Whatever that means."

"It means I told him once that I was interested in stargazing. Just a white lie in the cause of keeping the conversation going." I lied a darker shade of pale. "I'm surprised he remembered."

"Yeah, well, I always said you scored more of a hit than you realized." She stood up, brushing the crumbs from her skirt. At the same instant there was a tap on the door. Time to go. She picked up her jacket and looked at me. "Well — ready for the mysterious East?"

We said our good-byes under the soft hum of airport strip lighting. It was only a temporary separation, and we treated it lightly. Of course, we could have done it differently. We could have traveled back together and I could have gone on to Boston the next day. But we had decided against it. Or rather she had. Now that the going had begun, she wanted it done cleanly. She had started alone; that was how she would finish. I admired her certainty, but even so, as my plane circled over the Cape for our final descent into Boston, I couldn't help but wonder how it was for her, arriving back in New York for the very last time.

"Don't fret, Marla," she had said and smiled. "That apartment and I are used to our own company. We've shared a lot together. It'll do us good to have a couple of days alone to say good-bye. Cleansing rituals, that's all. But you're not excluded. You can come back anytime."

Nevertheless, I would give her the full five days. Boston would occupy me for that long, sightseeing and visiting. I had embellished the truth a little when I told Elly that there was a friend I had to see. Teresa Geldhorn was not exactly a friend, and I did not have to see her. On the other hand, she was pretty high up on my list of acquaintances, and there were always things to talk about. She had been eleven years older than I when I arrived at Cambridge, but she was already the best medieval historian of her generation and one of the university's toughest tutors. She was one of a new breed of women academics, feminist in word as well as action.

Before her had been generations of advance guard, women who protected themselves against discrimination by denying their femininity: J. D. Pendleton, D. S. Johnson, the list continues; pince-nez women, with flat shoes and brains filed like teeth, digging into the silt of lost history; omnivorous, with insatiable appetite for detail. She was different. The brain was just as sharp, but she refused to bury herself in excavation. She challenged the status quo and made it clear that hers were victories for gender as well as individual ego. The men, of course, were wonderfully threatened but could do nothing to undermine her.

Against the odds, she and I had got on. Maybe it was her need to be challenged, or maybe she had sensed in my isolation and belligerence a shadow of her younger self. Whatever the reason, she had taken me up as her good academic cause and, with a thoroughly unsentimental dedication, had set about fashioning my academic future, guiding and bullying me through tripos exams to research, and from research to teaching. Our relationship had never been anything but formal and academic. I knew nothing of her private life, and she knew nothing of mine. But still over the years we had kept in touch. A kind of politeness almost. And so, when she decided to take up the Harvard offer of a three-year teaching post, six months after I had been appointed to UC, I had been one of the people she had written to, extending a firm invitation to tea if ever I should be passing through. And, since I was, I called her and we agreed to meet.

Looking back now, I see that those Boston days were like the last days of summer, a time when everything is ripe and still, and yet you know it cannot last. I suppose I should have realized then that what was resolved could also be unresolved, but I was too busy enjoying the triumph of Elly's return. Boston joined in the celebrations. The city was at its best — hot, green, and glorious — with its wide tree-lined avenues and its brown sluggish river shining under a hazy sun. It reminded me of London, rather formal and not without pride. Not unlike Teresa herself. America, it seemed, had done nothing to pollute her Englishness. She lived, fittingly, in Cambridge, in a small but elegant brownstone house within walking distance of my hotel.

When I arrived there that first afternoon, punctual to the minute, I discovered it to be full of cats and bookshelves. She sat me down in an armchair in the study next to a window cull of birdsong, poured me a dry sherry from a cut-glass decanter, and asked me questions in her cool precise way, for all the world as if this were her room in Girton and wc wcrc meeting again after the long vacation. And watching her sitting there in her blue skirt and blouse, a single gold chain around her neck, and her hair cut short with flecks of gray, I wondered whether I wasn't looking at an image of myself ten years on, discussing academic futures with favorite pupils. Certainly I could do worse than this Olivia de Havilland self-containment; quiet pleasure amid the smell of paper and ink.

And then I wondered, not for the first time, if she ever lay in bed at night crippled by a sense of futility, or haunted by the specters of sexual frustration. I wondered about this while all the time we talked of other things — the comparative curiosity of American and English students, her latest published articles, my half-formed, unpublished ones. And if she was a little disappointed in the speed of my academic progress, she did not show it. Instead we mused over the problems of reconciling teaching with research, and she suggested a few people I might contact, publishers who might be interested in my work on the Lindisfarne monastery. And for a while she really did go some way to convincing me that this was it — the sunshine, the sherry, the study of the past, and her firm, poised grip on the world. But when at last I left her on that fourth and final evening, after a quiet simple supper, and we stood on her polished step, shaking slightly awkward hands under the glow of the streetlamp, I knew that the illusion went with her; that for me it could never be quite as whole or as satisfying. And I think she knew it too. And I wondered how much it mattered, or if perhaps she had a store of heirs apparent to carry on her good work.

Back in my elegant, expensive hotel, I fell asleep almost immediately. In fact, those nights in Boston I slept remarkably well, better than I had done for months. So, when Elly's phone call woke me the next morning, the sun was already high in the sky and I was prepared for anything.

". . . well, I was planning on taking the

train. Probably late afternoon. It would get me in around nine P.M. tonight. Why?"

"Could you make it a little earlier?"

"Yes, of course. Why?"

"Oh, nothing really. There's been a slight change in schedule. I wanted to tell you about it."

"What is it?" I sounded wonderfully unperturbed.

"I'll explain when I see you. It's not important. Do you want me to meet you at the station?"

"No," I heard myself say. "No. I'll find my own way. I'll be there as soon as I can."

And I was. Amtrak did not waste time, and I hit Grand Central Terminal when most people were leaving it. It was a good introduction back into New York; bedlam, with a thousand commuters pouring in through the barriers and flooding onto the trains. Another day of upward mobility. I was moving against the flow, but the pace was infectious. Outside I hailed a cab with what looked like a knife wound in the backseat. I sat and watched the meter move. There was no point in worrying about something before I knew what it was. I imagined Teresa Geldhorn pouring boiling water over Earl Grey tea leaves and getting stuck back into Capetian foreign policy.

There is much to be said for dead men, even if history discovers that not all of them told the truth.

Outside the apartment block, I held my finger on the bell. The intercom buzzed her voice down. It had broken glass in it. The door opened. I nodded to the porter. The lift was waiting. On the eighth floor so was she, a tight little smile on her face. I walked past her into a maelstrom, a chaos of furniture and wooden crates and, in the corner, two smart leather suitcases, all packed and ready to go. I turned.

"Lenny's father has had a heart attack," she announced quickly. "We heard last night. He took the last plane to Rhode Island. It sounds bad."

"How did he find out?" You see, even then something didn't quite fit.

"His mother called."

"But I thought you said they didn't keep in touch."

"They don't. But he'd given her this number. In case of emergencies. I suppose this qualified . . ." She trailed off.

"What will you do?" I asked, moving from fact to implication. "Do you want to stay until you know he's OK?" Forty-eight hours to D-Day. Another dozen or so couldn't matter.

She shook her head. "That's not the problem. We can still go, but . . ."

"But?"

"I have to go to London first."

Strange how you can go for months without hearing your own heartbeat, and then suddenly there it is, loud and insistent, like an amplified drum smashing against your rib cage. I realized I hadn't spoken. "London?"

"Lenny was due to leave tomorrow. I have to go in his place."

"Why?" I tasted dust in my mouth.

"Because there's someone he has to see. Apparently it's important. It can't wait."

"And what about Paris?" I think I may have raised my voice, but only to make it heard above my heartbeat. "You and I and Paris?"

"It doesn't change anything," she said quickly. "It's just a delay. Probably only a day or two. I'll still come to Paris, I promise you."

She smiled brightly, as if it was the simplest thing in the world. But it fooled neither of us. A small chasm had opened up between us. We both studied it with surprise. I said, "Elly, I don't understand. Why do you *have* to go? What's so important? Why can't you cancel it?"

And there was a pause, during which the ice cracked and the chasm widened. She looked at me, clear-eyed and certain. "Because I can't, that's why. And I can't explain it either, Marla. Believe me. It's just something I have to do for him. A favor. A way of saying good-bye, if you like."

I stared at her and felt a tightening in my gut. And I knew then that I had been neither as clever nor as blessed as I had thought. Because what Elly was saying was there was something she had not told me. I was not the only one with secrets. It was a shock well deserved. I had been so busy celebrating, I'd forgotten there was still a war on. Now, across the battlefield, Lenny's sword glinted in the sun. I stepped carefully.

"I thought you didn't approve anymore?" I said quietly.

She shook her head. "You don't understand. I know you're upset, and I can see why. It wasn't supposed to be like this. But I haven't changed my mind. It's no big deal, right? There's nothing to worry about. There never is with Lenny. I'm not doing anything illegal. It's just that I can't talk about it. And I do have to do it. I owe him one. Please don't make it any harder. I tell you, by the time you get to Paris and order the first espresso and croissant, I'll be on a plane to Charles de Gaulle. And real life starts then. All right?"

Here it was, my big moment. I heard my cue, watched the spotlight playing over the stage waiting to pick me up. I knew the speech, word-perfect — *No, Elly, it's not all right. Sit down, I have something to tell you. I have reason to believe that your lover has been set up and that he has moved you into the firing line.* Simple. So why couldn't I say it? Maybe I had waited too long. Or maybe I had just got used to the sound of my own silence. I opened my mouth. But nothing came out.

She smiled. "Come on, Marla. It's not the end of the world."

Oh, but it is, Elly. It is. "All right," I heard myself say. "So you have to go to London. I assume I can't come with you. But at least we could fly out on the same day. Share a taxi to the airport. Or is that forbidden?"

She laughed, and a little stream of anxiety flowed out of her and away. "Idiot . . . of course we can. Oh, thank you, Marla. I knew you'd understand."

"What are friends for?" I said weakly, but the weight on my heart didn't lift. I needed to get away from her, think things through. I looked around. "How long is all this going to take?"

"Not long. Lenny's letting the apartment for a while. I'm just casing up some of the valuables. I'm already packed." And she pointed to the two suitcases by the door. "Smart, eh?"

"Smart," I echoed. "I think I need a cup of tea. How about you?" I said with enormous casualness.

"You bet."

In the kitchen I stood over the kettle, watching to make sure it didn't boil. My head was thumping. What did it mean? Could it really be just a devastating coincidence, or was it more than that? The only person who might know the answer was three thousand miles away. I opened the fridge and reached down for the carton of milk. In an absence of mind, it slid smoothly through my fingers and onto the floor. I swore wearily.

"What is it?" she called through the opened door.

"I dropped the milk," I said, looking down as a river of white gulped its way across the tiles.

"Never mind, I'll have mine black."

I had to talk to J.T. But not here. My brain made a welcome return and took down the Out to Lunch sign. Not here. "It's all right, I'll go out and buy another pint. I want to get a newspaper anyway."

"The stall will be closed by now. Are you OK? You look a bit off-color."

"I'm fine. Sudden calcium deficiency, that's all. You need anything?"

"Blueberry cheesecake with fudge cream sauce and rum and pistachio ice cream."

"What?"

"Nothing. Just a fantasy. The milk will do."

Out on the street, I discovered I was shaking. What if J.T. wasn't there? What then? I ran most of the way to the corner deli. Like exercising in a sauna. People stared at me as if I were dangerous. I gave the woman at the counter a twenty-dollar note and asked for five dollars in change. Clutching a fistful of quarters, I went in search of a phone, then had to wait five minutes while an old man with liver-spotted hands shouted what sounded like Polish abuse to someone who presumably understood the language. He slammed down the phone and shuffled past me muttering. The number was dancing in my brain. I punched the digits fast. There was a pause. A cheery automatic voice told me to deposit four dollars and twenty cents in change. I stuffed in the quarters. Somewhere in the system an electronic brain counted the cash. And put me through. The number rang. If he was out feeding the animals, would he hear it above their cackles?

"Yep." A voice like a fingersnap.

"J.T.?"

"Who is this?"

"Marla. It's me, Marla. Calling from New York."

"What is it?" Instant attention.

"Lenny's father's had a heart attack. He was due to fly to London tomorrow. Elly is going in his place."

Silence. For so long I got cold feet. "J.T.?"

"I'm here. You didn't tell her?"

"No, I . . . there was no point. She was leaving him anyway. It seemed better to —"

"Well, it's too late now. If she changes her mind at the last minute, he'll know why."

Another silence. I was suddenly tired of all the things I didn't need to know. "What's happening, J.T.? You have to tell me."

I heard him make a sharp clicking noise in his throat, a kind of angry impatience. But he talked. "OK. Now listen to me. In the bag she's taking to London are four sets of juggling balls, regular circus equipment, right? Each ball is maybe the size of a fist, covered in soft leather and pretty weighty. Four sets. That's twenty balls in all. You have to take them out. Got that?"

Now he said it, I realized I had probably known all along. Funny how everything has a point. I remembered back to a poster outside Golden Gate Park and Lenny's sharp look as Elly chattered magpielike of things she knew nothing about. Of course, a little knowledge is a dangerous thing. I still knew everything and nothing. On the other end of the line, J.T. was talking.

". . . Marla, have you got that?"

"Yes, I got it. What shall I do with them?"

"Suit yourself. I don't want to know."

Message understood. I was behind enemy lines, and HQ had no more advice to give. Some have greatness thrust upon them. It appeared to be my turn.

"What about Lenny? What happens when he finds out?"

Three thousand miles away, I thought I heard him smile. "Oh, Lenny. I would say he already knows."

"What does that mean?"

"Nothing. Don't worry about Lenny. Leave him to me. Where did you say he was supposed to be now?"

"Rhode Island. He went last night. He's with his mother."

"Like hell he is." The laugh was loud and mirthless. "Lenny's mother is in a Boston

295

cemetery and has been for the last six years. And if his father really had had a heart attack, Lenny would be out celebrating."

The case for the prosecution rested. There was no more to be said. Thanks for the information, J.T. Remember me to the chickens.

"Marla?"

I brought the receiver back to my ear.

"Put it somewhere no one else can find it, all right? It's your insurance as well as hers."

Sure thing, J.T. Thanks for nothing. I put my finger down on the cradle switch and held it there. Men. Who could ever depend on them?

"Hey yoon lady. You finish wid the phone?" Polish brown spots was back, no doubt with a few insults he'd forgotten. I handed him the receiver and walked home. I was halfway up in the lift when I realized I'd never picked up the paper from the counter. When I finally got in through the front door, I was shiny with sweat. Elly looked up from a half-full packing case.

"What took you so long? Did they send you out to milk the cow?"

I shook my head, gulping in air to disguise my panting. "No, I went for a walk."

"In this weather? You could die of dehydration. You didn't get a paper?"

I stared down at the carton of milk. ". . . er . . . no, I couldn't find a stall."

"Here, give me the milk. Now sit down. You look terrible. I'll make the tea."

I did as I was told, squatting glumly on the edge of a chair filled with books. And as I perched there, in a kind of daze, my eyes alighted on the two smart leather suitcases by the door. And so I made my plan.

The first part was easy. After the packing was done, she took a shower. I didn't need to suggest that. As the bathroom door closed behind her, I hit the living room. The suitcases were locked. Naturally. I checked the desk drawers and all available surfaces for keys. No sign. I tried the bedroom. Dressing table, coat pocket. Nothing. They had to be in her bag. I fumbled around and pulled out a large leather satchel from under the bedclothes. Inside was a microcosm of Elly's life: colorful and cluttered. I kept my eye on the bathroom door as I dug through loose change, spare Tampaxes, handfuls of pens, and crumpled bits of paper. And finally a bunch of keys. My hand closed over them, and I lifted them out and turned them over in my palm. There they were — two small shiny metal creatures. It would take no time at all to slip them off the ring and into my pocket. From behind the bathroom door, I heard the shower switch off. No time was exactly what I had. I dropped the other keys back and returned the bag to the chaos of the unmade bed. Seconds later, as Elly emerged, dripping onto the carpet, I was standing in the doorway, a casual visitor who just happened to be passing.

"I've decided," she said, shaking her hair like a dog. "We're going out for the evening. If there's any news, Lenny will call later. We deserve a last supper."

I've always wondered how Judas felt, sitting there knocking back the bread and the wine, listening to the speeches, knowing what he knew. Who knows? Maybe he genuinely thought it was all for the best, that it was just a flash in the pan and everyone would thank him in the end. Poor old Judas. History really had it in for him.

As for Elly and me, well, we did our best given the circumstances. But the circumstances prevailed. We were fighting too many things. The statements of leaving were everywhere: the last walk across a certain intersection, the smell of an all-night bakery, the final meal in a city that had once been home. There were so many black holes between us, the things we couldn't or wouldn't talk about, and it seemed to take all our energy avoiding them. So many times I almost told her. So many times when the conversation lay fallow and my imagination ran riot through customs halls and circuses. But I didn't know where to begin. Or worse, where the beginning would end. I suppose I was afraid of what I would unleash, afraid of losing her so soon after I had won her back. Or maybe it was pride. That I should be the one to save her. I have thought about it all until I can think no more. Only the facts remain. And the fact is I did not tell her. Instead, when the pauses grew into silence, I plugged them with inconsequential chatter of Boston, of Paris, and of the London to come. And although it did not really help, it served to keep my mind off other things. Such as smuggling and burglary.

It was almost midnight when we got home. The apartment was cool and empty. I remembered that very first evening, when we had talked through the night. Not now. Now we were exhausted and the world was full of things that couldn't be said.

"God, Marla, I'm out of it." She propped herself against the wall and yawned. "What do you say to an early night?"

"You don't want a nightcap?" I did. Very much. She must have registered my need.

She pulled herself up and smiled. "Sure. What's it to be. Scotch?"

I shook my head. "I'll get it," I said firmly. "This time you sit down."

In the kitchen I practiced white magic. Into a tall glass I tipped the fifteen milligrams of crushed Valium, pulverized with loving care. Then a spoonful of coffee and sugar, and a hefty slug of whiskey followed by a river of boiling water. And finally some cream, sliding over the back of the spoon onto the surface like a white oil slick. A garnish of cinnamon to confuse the taste and it was done.

She was duly impressed by the offering. "You have to drink it all." I presented it with both hands, like a loving cup. "It brings good luck on the eve of a journey."

"Bullshit," she retorted affectionately, settling herself in a chair and cradling the glass. "Since when did you know anything about folklore?"

"You're talking to a professional historian here, remember? The Ionan monks used to drink this every night before retiring. Just in case there should be a journey of the soul in front of them."

"Your nose is growing longer, Marla. Drinking coffee ten centuries before it was discovered?"

"Very good. I was sure you wouldn't spot it."

"Yeah, well, I'm not as green as I'm cabbage-looking."

Once upon a time, in school playgrounds, that had been one of our stock-in-trade phrases. On that last New York night, the memory hurt. I raised my glass. "Here's to you, Elly."

"To both of us." She took a long sip. "Oooh, what a strange selection of tastes. What's in this?"

Adder's fork and blind worm's sting. "Cinnamon, sugar, and a considerable amount of whiskey — to counteract the effects of the caffeine. It's designed to make you sleep."

"Yeah, into the middle of next week." She took another slug. "And where will we be by then, I wonder?"

"Sitting sipping Chablis on the banks of the Seine?"

She smiled, but I could tell the image didn't take. The air-conditioning buzzed angrily, its mood as volatile as ours. She was sad. After a while it seemed cruel not to help.

"It might not be that bad," I said limply. "You might even find you enjoy it."

"Life without Lenny, you mean?"

301

Life with me, I thought, but said nothing.

She looked across at me. "You never really liked him, did you, Marla?"

There were already too many lies to add another. "He hurt you," I said quietly. "Why should I like him?"

She sighed. "I suppose it was my fault. I gave him such a lousy press. But it wasn't that simple. He really isn't as black as I painted him. Honestly."

"Is that why you're going to London for him?"

She looked, I thought, troubled. "Yes, maybe. That and other reasons." I waited, but she didn't elaborate. Instead she turned her attention to the drink and took three or four sips, as if all the time she was thinking of something else. I watched the liquid disappear. "I wonder how his father is," she said at last.

. . . Lenny would be out on the town celebrating. . . . J.T.'s words screeched in my head, separating us even further. "Was Lenny very upset when he heard?"

"You know, he was, actually. It surprised me how much. He couldn't even talk to me to begin with. After he put down the phone, he walked straight past me onto the balcony. Stayed there for a long time. When I went out to him, he turned on me, as if there was a kind of violence in the pain. I don't know what she said to him, but it certainly got through."

I wondered who "she" had been. And more to the point, exactly what it was she had said. I made one last clumsy lunge toward her.

"Come with me to Paris tomorrow, Elly. Leave him to do his own business."

"Marla, let it be." And this time there was steel in it. "You've helped me as much as you can. Now let me end it my way. This one is between him and me."

I retreated into silence and studied the inside of my glass. She watched me. After a while I heard her getting up. She came over and squatted beside me. Then she put her arms around me and held me tight. It was an act of symmetry, a mirror image of that first night, when I had tried to hug the hurt out of her. We both remembered it. I stayed still in her arms.

"I'm sorry. It isn't meant to exclude you. It's just something I have to do, that's all. It'll soon be over. Listen, I'm going to crash out now. The world is full of ghosts for me tonight. I can't fight them. They'll be gone in the morning. Sleep well. And thank you, Marla. For everything. I'll do the same for you one day."

You already have, Elly. Don't you know that? She would forgive me when she knew. Surely. Just as I would have forgiven her. It was all done out of love, after all.

I don't remember how long I sat there after she left. All I know is that when I finally got up and went to my room, the clock read 2:40 A.M. I sat and watched the hands complete another half circle. Her bedroom door was ajar. I entered quietly. She was lying curled on her stomach, one arm flung across the bed, as if feeling out for another body. Her clothes were strewn in a small heap on the chair, the bag on the floor beside them. "Elly," I whispered. Then again more loudly. She slept like the dead. I picked up the bag and went out.

In the living room I allowed myself the luxury of a little light. The lamp shot yellow streams across the floorboards. The suitcases were heavy as I dragged them into the middle of the room. The keys slid in, new and eager, and the locks snapped smartly open. I lifted the first lid. A mound of clothes sighed upward, on the top a flash of purple, the summer dress Elly had worn the day we had gone to Carmel. I slid my hands in and under, feeling my way through layers of cloth. I took my time. I was methodical and precise, investing the process with a kind of ritual, which, after all, it was — a separation of good from evil, a further act of white magic.

The first bag yielded no secrets. I repacked it with equal care. Then turned to the second. It didn't take long. They were at the bottom, to one side, stashed neatly in two plastic bags and wedged in with underwear and socks. I lifted the bags out, then removed the balls one by one, until next to me on the floor a row of twenty dark leather lumps sat in silent ceremony, unperturbed, it seemed, by their change of destiny. I counted them twice, then repacked the second case, locked them both, and returned them to their sentry positions by the door. In the center of the room, the balls were caught in the light. I was reminded of a poem about apples drying in an autumn attic — golden sunshine and old newspapers. Very English. Yet another memento from school days: poetry anthologies consumed in boring literature lessons, Elly and I above it all, reading Eliot on Saturday afternoons. It was, you might say, satisfactory.

What had she and Lenny forged that could be put against such intimacies? How dare he think he could even try? Somewhere outside in the city, a siren whooped and wailed. It broke the spell. Out through French windows I recalled that first night visitation, lean limbs and shining hair, the world in the palm of his hand. I picked up the balls and put them back in their plastic bags. In my room I buried them at the bottom of my hand luggage, hidden deep under the bed. Then I returned the keys to Elly's satchel and deposited it in her room again. I stood and watched her for a while. She looked lovely, like the Elly I remembered from years before, eyelashes like dark fringes on her cheeks, her eyelids flickering with dream images. Were we walking together through Paris boulevards, or was she fleeing shadows in an English customs hall? There are some places you cannot follow people, however much you love them.

Back in my own room, I lay down and closed my eyes. I had no intention of sleeping. Dawn arrived just after 4:00 A.M. I watched the light change from ink blue to gray, and from there into a gauzy soft mauve. From a tree somewhere down the street, a band of Manhattan sparrows let rip with a hymn to morning. Someone once told me that the dawn chorus is one long wave of sound, which begins in the far north, where the light comes first, and sweeps down over the world like a kind of bush telegraph until, presumably, it hits water or the equator. I wondered about Santa Cruz, and Rhode Island, or wherever he was supposed to be. Was anyone listening there?

Five slid into six, slid into seven and then eight. Just before nine I got up and went into the kitchen to make tea. Then I took a shower. All these things I did deliberately, making no attempt to disguise the noise. Still Elly slept on. At ten I made a cup of strong coffee and woke her. She opened her eyes and groaned as she pulled herself up on the pillows.

"Jesus." She pressed her fists against her eyes and blinked slowly. "What did we drink last night? I feel like someone dropped a ton of bricks on me. What's the time?"

"After ten."

"Shit, we'd better get moving."

I was grateful for the sense of urgency. It blocked up the day and kept us in motion. The London flight was at 8:30 P.M., the Paris one an hour later. We booked a cab for 6:00 P.M. Before that there were cases to be labeled, phone calls to be made, bank accounts to be closed and charge cards canceled; the systematic unplugging of one life in preparation for connection into another. If any of it disturbed her, she didn't let it show. There was a kind of courage to her that day, as if the vulnerability of the night before had been stored away with the packing cases and now there was just the present to be getting on with. She was bright and busy, and in the whole day there was only one moment when the world shook.

It came midafternoon, as we were waiting for the man from the apartment agency to come and pick up a set of keys. Just as the doorbell rang so did the telephone. Lenny. Or maybe even J.T.? Either way my fingers itched to pick it up. But it was not my job — my job was to answer the doorbell and make small talk with a man with glasses while Elly took the call in her bedroom. And when she finally emerged, her face grave, it was still my job to keep the conversation going until business had been concluded and the door closed behind him.

"Lenny," she said frowning. "It looks as if his father's going to pull through. If things stabilize within the next twenty-four hours, he'll try to make it to England. He sounded funny. A long way away." She smiled wryly. "He asked to be remembered to you."

Remembered. I liked that one. Did he really think I'd forgotten? I nodded sympathetically, and the angel of death moved on. Time was running short. Elly went off to change. I kept myself amused with Lenny's library, picking out a few slim volumes from the packing cases. Plane reading. Mementos in lieu of a lock of hair.

Six-fifteen P.M. The cab was late, and she was standing by the window peering down into the street, tapping a neat impatient foot on the wooden floor. Elly Cameron, newly designed for departure. I had got over the shock of the transformation. She was dressed in dollar bills: the linen suit had money in every seam, cool and warm, smart and casual. Top to toe, the image coalesced, from the matching court shoes to the hair carefully flicked back and lightly sprayed into place. *E* for elegance. But not for Elly. She looked, I realized later, like Lenny's girl.

God knows what the cabdriver made of the two of us: this pert, polished little figure with her lumpen proletariat companion clutching a large canvas bag to her chest. Luckily, he had his own problems. Twenty minutes late and the New York rush hour to contend with. The first half hour was horrendous. The traffic moved so slowly that Elly's anxiety became contagious as she sat forward in her seat, nervously playing with her small gold watch while the minutes ticked away. But she was meant to catch the plane, and once we had crossed the bridge the road opened up and the driver put his foot down. We reached JFK with almost too much time to spare.

In the BA terminal, we parted company briefly, separate trolleys to separate destinations. My flight had not yet opened, so I stuffed my bags into a twenty-four-hour locker, rattling the door to make sure the lock had taken. At the ticket counter, Elly had graduated to the top of the queue and was communing with the check-in agent, her neat little head bent to catch a question, smiling back an answer, clearly enjoying herself. I watched. Now it was begun, I realized the script suited her. There was an energy field around her, the right kind of nerves. It struck me that I was witnessing a performance which had been given before. Now, when it was too late, I began to understand some of the attraction between them. She bent down and heaved the two suitcases onto the scales. The man slapped labels on them and they were gone, chugging their way along the conveyor belt toward the hole at the end, through which they would fall into the airport underworld, to reemerge halfway across the world, spewed out onto another revolving belt. But that was something I would not think of now.

When she joined me, there was half an hour to kill. We wandered around the building, making airport small talk, saying nothing at all, sitting in plastic scooped seats rechecking timetables and telephone numbers. At last the Tannoy boomed instructions for her departure. We both stood up immediately. She caught me in a clumsy bear hug, then pushed me away. I did not watch her go.

Back at the locker, I retrieved the canvas holdall and deposited another quarter to keep watch over the rest of my luggage. Together the holdall and I paid a visit to the ladies' loo. Once safely ensconced in a cubicle, door locked and Muzak seeping all around, I sat down and put my mind to the question of what was to come.

The logic of events, as far as it went, was incontrovertible. For reasons which it was not in my power to know, Lenny had been traveling to London with four sets of juggling balls. Originally, in theory at least, those balls would have been just what they claimed to be, circus paraphernalia, filled with beans, sawdust, or whatever. They would not have been filled with cocaine. Lenny didn't take those kinds of risks. Wasn't that what Elly had told me? So somehow, somewhere, someone had made the substitution. How, where, and who were not my immediate business. What to do with them was.

However much Lenny did or did not know, he had learned enough to realize that it was not safe for him to travel with them. That surely had been the news which had come through to him by telephone two days ago, in the person of his "mother's" voice. What that voice must also have intimated was that someone had betrayed him, and that that someone was close to home. Why else would he possibly have asked Elly to go in his place? But how, if that was the case, could he possibly have interpreted her acceptance? If indeed she had known, agreeing to go would have been suicide. It didn't make sense. But there was no time to waste over questions I couldn't answer. Back to the facts. Lenny had passed the buck to Elly; I had taken it from her. Whatever went down in the Heathrow customs hall tomorrow, she would walk away from it. Which left me.

I lifted out one of the balls from the plastic bag. It sat in my hand, firm, full, and heavy. The leather was soft and malleable, the stitching fine, the deception high class. It would not have taken much to slide a penknife in through the side and disembowel them one by one, dig out the tightly packed bags of cocaine, slit them open, and watch while the snowstorm tumbled into the toilet bowl. Like tearing up fifty-pound notes and setting fire to them, the idea was seductive, satisfying, thrilling. Why not destroy them? Whoever had planted the coke must have assumed they would never see it again. Customs officers are not in the habit of returning contraband. No, it had been meant as a sacrifice, a small price to pay for the pleasure of Lenny's downfall. Ah, but there was the rub. If I did indeed flush it away into the New York sewage system, I also flushed away any other chance of his destruction. How that chance might come about was something else I couldn't answer. But for now it was enough to know that it existed.

One further question remained. If it couldn't be got rid of, where could it be kept? It could hardly stay in an airport locker. Twenty-four hours and it would be dug out by a security officer. Lenny's flat was all locked up and in the hands of an agent, and J.T. would, I knew, not thank me for mailing it registered post to Santa Cruz. When it came down to it, there was only one thing to do. And I had, of course, known it all along. It had simply been a question of dismissing all other alternatives.

I got up from the seat, packed the ball carefully into the bag, flushed the loo, and went out to the washbasins. On a side wall was a full-length mirror. I turned to face it. Canvas holdall in hand, I considered what I saw. A large, plain woman in a somewhat crumpled trouser suit. Square face, unnaturally aged in the strip lighting, but otherwise remarkable only in its ordinariness. A face in the crowd, one you would not look at twice. Certainly not the face of someone with the flair or the chutzpah to earn her living by smuggling drugs. I was Ms. Ordinary, Ms. Awkward, Ms. Uncharismatic. I had led a dull life, and it showed. ENGLISH ACADEMIC CAUGHT WITH KILO OF COCAINE — the headline was not written for me. No way. I was just one of a few hundred tourists coming in from New York. Not an incriminating passport stamp to be seen. What would be the logic of carrying this particular illicit cargo on such a route? What I knew about smuggling could be written on the back of a razor blade, but I knew enough to know this was not the kind of haul you built empires on. The profit margin made no sense. Unless, of course, someone knew. Or had been told. But what they "knew" in London, they didn't know in Paris.

I stood to attention, and my reflection smartened up. It was simple. If I wanted to destroy Lenny, I had to have the power to do it. And the power, to coin a phrase, lay in Lenny's balls. I smiled at the image of the criminal I was about to become and marched out into the airport compound.

I rescued my luggage and set off for the check-in desk. I had not gone more than thirty yards when I spotted her, hunched into her plastic seat, smooth black head bowed over a copy of *Vogue*. There was something about that head that brought back Iowa City. I stopped right in front of her.

"Indigo," I said, because there really was absolutely nothing to lose. "What are you doing here?"

To be fair, I'm not sure that even Meryl Streep would have got away with it totally — and Indigo had been resting for a while now. She made a valiant stab at Complete Surprise but missed by the best part of a mile. By the time the eyes had settled back into Friendly Innocence, I knew that I had been watched.

"Oh . . . oh, hi there. God, I jumped right out of my skin. Wow, this is a coincidence . . . it's . . . er . . . oh, forgive me, I—"

"Marla. Elly's friend. We met at the shop

315

a couple of weeks ago."

Light dawned in Technicolor. "Oh, oh yeah, now I remember. Marla. How are you?"

"Spiffing," I said. "How about yourself?"

"Oh, fine . . . fine."

"What are you doing here?"

"Here? I'm — I'm meeting my mother."

"Really, how interesting. Where's she been?"

She was so nearly on cue. Someone else would not have noticed the shimmer of a pause. "Paris. Paris, France. Among other places. She's been doing a trip. Europe."

"How adventurous. Is she with your father?"

"No. No. She's with a group. A package."

"How lovely for her." It may sound cruel, but just for those few moments I was having fun, watching her jump through the hoops. "How long will she be staying in New York?"

"Oh, she's just passing through. Connecting planes . . ."

"Back to Iowa City?"

"What? Oh, yeah, back to Iowa City. Hey, you got a good memory. Imagine you remembering that. What about you?"

"Morocco." I smiled. "I'm beginning a trip to Africa."

"Africa . . . but I thought —"

"You thought I was going to France, right? Well I was, but I changed my mind. I just saw Elly off on the flight to Zurich."

"Zurich?" She paused for a second. I didn't stop smiling. Somewhere in midair I felt her complete a somersault. "But I thought she was going to Paris with you?"

No, Indigo was not as green as she was cabbage-looking. Elly had not told her about London. It was supposed to be a secret. It was therefore important that she remember not to know.

"Another change of plan," I said gaily. "We'll meet later. In Tangier. Have you ever been there? It's a wonderful city. Full of pirates and adventurers, smugglers and spies. You'd love it. Well, I must be off now. Who's minding the store, by the way?"

"It's closed," she said, this time without fluster. "It's nearly eight o'clock."

"Of course, how silly of me. Well, I do hope your mother had a good trip in Europe."

"Thank you. And you take care. Sounds like a dangerous place you're going to."

"I'll remember that. Oh." I turned back. "Remember me to Lenny, won't you? I was sorry to hear about his father."

"Yes," she said, staring unashamedly at

317

me now. "It was terrible news."

Straight from the horse's mouth. That much I was sure of now. I smiled once more and headed off down the concourse, feeling her eyes stapled to my back. When I reached the check-in desk, I risked a look back. But Indigo was gone. No doubt checking nonexistent timetables to Morocco. Tall stories. All of them. In answer to my question, the girl punched up Arrivals on her computer screen and confirmed that the last flight from Paris had come in two hours before. I hadn't needed to ask. All the way to JFK just to watch her mother change planes? Bullshit, to use Elly's phrase. Maybe she just had mothers on the brain. Which particular voice had she used to fool Elly? And who had given her the information? Mystery Number 435.

I picked up my boarding pass and beloved canvas bag and made my way to the departure lounge.

Fourteen

"Mesdames et messieurs. Nous commençons notre descente vers Paris . . ."

Beneath us the Seine ran like silver thread through the French countryside. I snapped on my seat belt. The boy next to me was twitching to the sound of a Walkman, head back, eyes half closed, a look midway between pain and ecstasy on his face. A cruising stewardess tapped him smartly on the shoulder and pointed to his belt. Over his head we exchanged small smiles of adult exasperation. I was doing just fine, conformity personified. Paris grew larger and more inviting.

Processed through glass tubes and moving walkways, I placed myself behind the inevitable flock of French girls, small boned and fresh skinned, with firm little Gallic noses and clothes which looked as if someone had spent the entire journey pressing them. They sailed through the French Passports Only gate in a flurry of pouts and smiles. I took my place in the EC line, large and English despite my ancestry. The immigration officer studied my mug shot, bored already.

"Quelle est la durée de votre séjour en France, madame?"

"Quelques jours seulement. Je vais render visite à ma grandmère."

"Bien. Merci, madame. Suivant."

My canvas bag and I sauntered through, officially accepted. At the baggage reclaim I was joined by my vibrating travel companion. Together we watched as the baggage belt slid by, smooth and empty. My eyes itched from lack of sleep, but I wasn't tired. On the contrary, I had never been so wide awake in my life. I felt as if I were plugged into some mainline current, which kept me sharp and fizzing. In front of us the belt stopped, then juddered back into life again, as the hole at the back began belching out an unsightly procession of battered belongings, including, eventually, mine. I waited until it reached me, then heaved it onto my trolley, wedging the canvas bag behind it and laying my jacket on the top. I was maneuvering myself away from the belt when someone pushed past me; Willy Walkman, still wired up, a rucksack bouncing off his back and music seeping out of his headphones into the air. I quickened my step, and we approached the exit together. Ahead of us the great divide. *Rouge* and *Vert*. I never faltered, simply pulled down the left hand of the trolley and headed for freedom. In the green corridor, a scattering of customs men in shirtsleeves stood lounging against benches, surveying the scene. I walked. Not too fast and not too slow. The surroundings ceased to exist. Ahead of me, through the exit, I saw decades of student essays and gas bills, television licenses and Foyles's book sales. Nowhere could I find any trace of the inside of a French jail. I was three-quarters of the way to the future when the voice said, *"Un moment, s'il vous plaît."*

I turned my head to see a gray-haired officer heading straight for me. I stopped, my heart making a sudden desperate bid for freedom out through my rib cage. *"Excusez-moi, madame,"* he said, pushing in front of me and grabbing for the boy with the rucksack, who of course could not hear a word through the throb of New Wave. An excellent choice, officer. The triumph of the bourgeoisie. My heart fell back into place. I tightened my grip on the trolley and walked on. Out through the doors, a sea of faces focused on me, a second of intense concentration lest I should be their loved one. But there was no one there for me. A man carrying a sign which read MADAME JONES smiled hopefully. Oh no, sir. You must be mistaken. I am Marla Masterson, history academic and international cocaine smuggler. You are looking for someone much more ordinary. Triumph got me as far as the taxi rank. A car drew up, and I poured myself into it.

The journey was quicker than usual. August in Paris and the city was empty. The café owner at the corner of rue Jean-Goujon had watched me grow up over annual holidays. He was only too happy to change a traveler's check so I could pay the taxi driver. He also let me use the phone. The Heathrow Hotel gave the impression of efficiency. Yes, they had a reservation for Eleanor Cameron. But no, Miss Cameron had not checked in yet. She had left only an hour before me. There could be a million reasons why she had not arrived yet. A million reasons. And none of them illegal. No message. I would call again.

Four doors down the rue Jean-Goujon, I pressed the bell to Apartment 3. Upstairs I imagined Gem's hand fluttering to the lace curtain, then ordering Elaine down to open the door. When she saw me, her face lit up.

"*Marla . . . quelle surprise*. We had no idea. You 'ave told 'er you were coming?"

I put my finger to my lips. "It's an impulse visit, Elaine. I've come for lunch. How is she?"

She stuck out her bottom lip and shrugged her shoulders. Funny how the French make their bodies so articulate. This gesture said, "Oh, you know Germaine. The same as always."

I picked up my case and followed her neat little figure up the stairs, catching in her wake a stream of muttered complaints. ". . . yesterday she accuse me of stealing 'er little ivory elephant. Ze one from Bangalore. Poouf . . . so stupid. It was there all the time. On the mantelpiece. You speak to her, Marla. I tell her . . . I will not stand for this. I will leave. *Immédiatement*."

Elaine had been leaving "*immédiatement*" for the best part of thirty years: from the day, in fact, she had first moved in. "Companion for widowed army officer's wife, newly arrived from India." She had taken one look at Gem and they had known it would be an adoring hatred, a battle to the bitter end. Elaine might have looked fragile, but she was ten years younger than Gem and tough as old boots. She gave as good as she got.

Through the doorway of the apartment, I saw Gem's silhouette in the front room, head peering forward out of the armchair, her stick legs stretched out on a stool in front of her like some aging bird at rest. As a child I used to think of her as an ostrich. Now, with her long slender neck turned to wrinkles and the cloud of white hair, she looked even more the part. Germaine Lemans was one of those women for whom the word *indomitable* had been invented. She had lived the first fifty years of her life in India, and had never reconciled herself to the newfangled ideals of independence and equality. In 1947, when the colonel died, she had packed up her wealth and come to Paris, where she set herself up as a piano teacher — another family talent I had not inherited. But she couldn't stand the majority of her pupils (*"ils sont complètement bêtes"*), and for much of the last thirty-four years she had done nothing. I could no longer remember the last time I had seen her out of the apartment. She was eighty-four years old, but when she chose she had the brain of a woman half her age. It was as well not to underestimate her.

"Marrrlaa." She twirled my name off her tongue, endowing it with an exoticism which its owner did not possess. *"Pourquoi tu ne m'as pas dir, mauvaise enfante."*

I approached and kissed the parchment skin of her cheek, then sat myself next to her, digging out from my bag the California crystal I had bought for her and holding it up against the window till the sun flickered a hundred colors around the room. She clapped her hands like a child, then forgot it instantly.

"You look tired," she said, this time in English, which was not as perfect as her French. "You are unwell? What is wrong with you?"

I explained the all-night flight, carefully introducing Elly and the possibility of her arrival.

"But of course I remember her. Such a sweet girl. So dainty." Gem had always despaired of my big bones, which she saw as some kind of genetic betrayal. "Well, I will not ask 'ow long you will stay. Young people can never answer this question. We shall take it one pace at a time. But now you must change your *vêtements.* We will take an early lunch, and you have been traveling too long in one garment. *Entiens?*"

My grandmother was one of the original exponents of the clean underwear theory. I have no doubt that when Germaine is told she is going to die, her last act will be to change her clothes. And the Grim Reaper will just have to wait for her. In this case, though, she was right. As I stood up, I too could smell the dried sweat on me, evidence of an adrenaline turned sour.

In the spare room, I did what I had come for and stashed away the treasure. In the top of the wardrobe, at the back of the cupboards, there was a small cubbyhole, the place where as a child I had hidden plates of food stolen from the kitchen for solitary midnight feasts. It had been a precarious business then, constructing a pile of books on top of a chair in order to reach. Now I could do it on tiptoe. The place was thick with dust. Nothing had been put there for years. I shoved the plastic bags right to the back, till they were lost in darkness. The only person in the world who knew where to find them was me. Then I showered, changed my clothes, and called London. It was midday, and she still had not checked in. This time I left my name. "Tell her Marla called. Ask her to ring me. The minute she arrives."

It was around this time that my invincibility began to desert me, to be replaced by a creeping, corrosive fear. Lunch was traditionally served on trays in the living room, each one accompanied by its own set of engraved condiments and a small carafe of wine. The first half glass made me drowsy, and I dropped the saltcellar. Germaine watched me, hawk-eyed, her small silver knife darting in and out of the fish carcass. The conversation followed accepted lines. She asked me questions and I sidestepped them. She had been waiting for ten years now to hear me announce my marriage, and her patience was beginning to wear thin. So was mine. I sat listening for the phone. Why hadn't she called? Something had gone wrong. The Regency clock chimed 1:00 P.M. I used the excuse of clearing away the first course to closet myself in the study.

This time the receptionist had a different tale. Miss Cameron had booked in half an hour before. Yes, she had got my message. But she had also left strict instructions not to be disturbed. By anyone. But this was an emergency. The woman hummed and hawed. A matter of life and death. She asked for my name and told me to hold the line. Two minutes later the answer came through. Miss Cameron did not want to speak to me. I put down the phone to find that my hand was shaking. Elly wouldn't speak to me. My sense of triumph exploded, launching slivers of fear like shrapnel into my brain. Behind me I heard the door to the study open and Germaine's voice crack the air.

"Marla. *Qu'est-ce que tu fais? Le repas n'est pas fini. Viens immédiatement.*" Mealtimes were sacrosanct. Even my grandfather had been pukka enough to wait until after supper to die.

I turned. She must have seen it in my face. *"Quoi! Tu es malade?"*

I shook my head. "Grandmère, I have to leave. Forgive me. I have to go to London."

"What, now?"

"Yes, now."

We stood for a moment in the darkened room, shutters drawn to protect the brocade against the sunlight, a place of childhood memory and security. And I felt, just for that instant, an absurd desire to tell her, everything, all of it, as if her instinct for survival might somehow allow her to comprehend something that her upbringing couldn't. But the moment passed. I went to her and put out my hand. She took it almost angrily, squeezing it hard between her bony fingers and making a small, clicking sound with her tongue. Then she said, "You always were a most peculiar child. Always too much silence. Too much" — she gestured to her head — "too much living here. It was not good. You and this Elly —" She broke off. "So, you must go. Something so important you cannot finish your *repas*. So go. But you remember. I, Germaine Lemans, am old, but not stupid. *Faites attention,* Marla. You are sometimes very careless with your life. It will bring damage. *Bien . . .* go."

She dropped my hand and made a small shooing gesture. In the doorway I turned and spoke to her back. "Grandmère, there is one thing you could do for me." She did not move. "If Elly calls, tell her I'm coming."

Where there had been triumph there was now only terror. In London it was raining. A soft summer rain, which hung so low over the city that as we finally broke cloud the runway pushed up to meet us. I was sick of airplanes, and sick of airports. Any glamour had long since seeped away. On the flight I could hardly keep my eyes open. Elly wouldn't talk to me. The weight of my exhaustion seemed suddenly insupportable. It was only anxiety which kept me upright. We came into Terminal 2. A different customs hall from the one she would have passed through. I had to force myself not to run through it. Outside there was a queue for taxis. I stood in the rain and waited. The driver was disappointed by the closeness of the fare and left me to wait while he applied for a reentry ticket. I sat in the back with the proverbial rat gnawing at my entrails. The Heathrow Hotel took ten minutes along a rain-soaked dual carriageway. It was a ghastly affair, sitting like some Battlestar Galactica in the middle of nowhere, a large circle of boxes, Elly in one of them. At the reception desk I asked for her room number.

"Three-twelve. But . . ."

"She's expecting me," I said, and if I had been at the receiving end of my voice, I would not have argued either.

At the door I knocked. Loudly. "Elly. It's me, Marla."

No answer. "Elly, let me in." Silence. An absurd scene flashed through my mind: me, shoulder to the door, splintering collarbone against wood to gain entry into an empty room with the French windows open . . . but my mind refused at the last fence of fantasy. I was about to start kicking when I heard a small noise from behind the door. Then a click as the lock turned. I stood still and waited. But nothing happened. I put out my hand, turned the handle, and went in.

The room was in shadow. She was sitting in a chair by the window, looking out onto a slate gray sky. I was reminded of Gem's daily vigil. When one has finished living, all one can do is sit and watch. I willed her to turn around, to say something, anything, but she seemed oblivious of my presence. I walked to the end of the bed and sat down, studying her profile in silhouette. We sat in silence. It seemed like forever.

"Hello, Marla," she said at last, quietly. "How was your flight?"

The sound of a stranger. I felt my heart pound with fear. "Elly, what happened?"

"I would have thought you already knew. Wasn't that why you took them out of my luggage?" Now she turned to face me, and now I was stung by the whiplash in her voice. "It was you, Marla, wasn't it?"

No time for half-truths now. I took a breath. "Yes. It was me."

"How did you find out?"

"J.T. I called him that last afternoon in New York, and he told me."

She nodded slowly, as if the movement caused her pain. "What did you do with them?"

"They're safe. Safe and nearby. Elly, for God's sake tell me what happened."

"What do you think?" she said sharply. "You want the whole story or just edited highlights? They searched me. They searched everyone. Three hundred people.

X-rays, the lot." She paused, frowning hard, back in a crowded customs hall with a suitcase full of cocaine. "And they knew just what they were looking for. Oh yes. The woman two places in front of me was carrying a child with a bag full of toys. When they found a set of rubber balls, they had her in the back room so fast it made you eyes water. I realized then it had to be a setup. And that I had to be carrying more than sawdust.

"Funny. I'd always thought I'd be OK when it came down to it. That the adrenaline would get me through. But I was so frightened I was nearly sick. I could hardly keep my hand still to unlock the cases. And all the time I kept seeing Lenny's face, smiling me good-bye. The end of an affair. My God . . . I couldn't believe it. Not even Lenny . . . I stood there waiting for them to find it. Waiting for his hand to close over the plastic bag. Except, of course, it never did. He went through both cases, smiled at me, then asked me if I'd mind repacking them myself to save time and moved on to the next one. And I knew then it had to be you. I had checked the bags after Lenny left. No one else had been near them. No one else knew. You had been so strange that night. Suddenly it all made sense. Except for one thing." She broke off with a harsh little laugh. "If you had taken them, that meant you knew what was really inside. And if you knew, then why the hell hadn't you told me?"

I stared at her, face white and drawn, eyes lost in shadow. I imagined her last four hours, caught in a web of unknowing, with no one left to trust. And I realized then that knowing the truth and suppressing it does not make it go away but may, in some cases, make it even more terrible. We had been friends for eighteen years. She was the most important person in my life, and I had hurt her. I reached out from the bed and put my hand on her knee. My fingers rested there uselessly, the extent of my physical courage. I had one defense. And I knew it would not be enough.

"Elly, I was only trying to protect you."

"Protect me! Christ almighty, Marla, protect me from what?" And now came the anger. Anger and pain, a great rushing wind of it, filling the room like howl round. "What am I, some piece of porcelain too fragile to be told the truth? J.T., Lenny. Now you. How come nobody tells me what's going on? Fuck it, for the last year I've been trying to reestablish control. Take back the part of me that's mine. How can I do that when everybody around me is making my decisions for me? Treating me like a child. For better or worse, this is my life. How can I live it if I'm not in control of it? God, Marla, you of all people should have understood that. There are some things you can't do for people. However much you love them. I asked for your help, Marla. I didn't ask you to do it for me. No one can do that. Don't you understand? You should have told me. I should have known."

She broke off with a kind of moan, pulling herself out of the chair and away from me. But the room was too small for her furious energy, and after a few moments prowling she pushed herself into a corner, arms huddled around her body, eyes down. And all this time I sat paralyzed, waiting for the storm to pass. I had no memory of such ferocity in her. Or if I did, it had never been directed at me. Outside the rain blurred everything. What could I say which would bring back the love? I had done it all for her. Just as she had once done it for me. But how to tell her? It was my turn to speak. But not without sanction. I looked up at her, and across the room our eyes met. And she smiled, a weary, desperate little pucker of skin, no pleasure in it. But it was a kind of welcome.

"Elly," I said. "There's more that you should know."

She closed her eyes and sighed. "So tell me."

And so it came flooding out, all of it, from that first vision of male beauty in the Club Class of a jumbo jet to the last telephone call on a Manhattan pavement. From Lenny's first deception to Indigo's last. I spared her nothing. Not even a mother and child at the bottom of a Santa Cruz canyon. Surely now she would understand why some of it had been so hard to tell. Surely now she might forgive.

And in the silence that followed she stared at me, dry-eyed and still. And when at last her voice came out of the shadows, it was quieter, in sorrow rather than in anger. "Oh, Marla. Why didn't you tell me?"

"Because I was afraid you'd go to Lenny," I said, emboldened by her kindness, and because there was nothing left to lose. "And that he would lie to you and you would believe his lies. Because you needed to."

"And is that why you believed J.T.?"

It was said so softly that I had to strain to hear the words. And even then I didn't — or couldn't — grasp the implication behind them.

"Elly, haven't you heard what I said? He

335

set you up. Don't you understand? The cocaine was meant for him. And when he found out about it, he passed it on to you. He knew that you'd be caught."

"No, he didn't." And this time her voice was loud and clear. "He knew I'd be saved."

"Elly, listen to me. Look at the facts —"

"I said he *knew,* Marla."

"Knew what?"

"He knew that you'd take them out."

"Don't be ridiculous. How could he 'know' that?"

In answer she smiled grimly and walked over to the bedside table. From the top drawer she drew out an envelope and handed it to me.

"When I cleared Customs, I found this on the message board at Heathrow. We had agreed that if he needed to get in touch with me, that was how he would do it. Tradition. Read it, Marla."

I withdrew a sheet of paper. A British Airways message. On it were written the words "Don't fret. Marla has your luggage. You have her to thank for carrying it."

I stared down at it, and my brain whirled. Lenny trapped like a fish on a hook, wriggling to get free. I made a clumsy lunge through the water.

"Elly, how do you know this is from

Lenny? If it's a tradition, then why shouldn't someone else have known about it? Why can't it be from J.T.? He was the only one I told. He knew I'd saved you. It could be from him."

The little smile was still there, sadder now than tears. "Look at the envelope, Marla."

I picked it up from the bed. On the front the words *Pamela Richardson*. "A joke," she explained. "Heroine and author. We always did it. A different one each time. We decided on it just before he left. No one else knew the name. It was his message. It came from him."

"But how could . . ."

"I don't know. That's one of the things I have to find out."

No. I refused to accept the words. "It doesn't change anything, Elly. Think about the past, about what he's done. The woman in California. Indigo. Think about them."

"I don't know anything about the woman in California," she said harshly, as if to dismiss the subject. "But Indigo —" She gave a sharp little laugh. "Oh, Indigo I knew all about. How could I not? You've met her. You know what she's like. She's had the hots for Lenny ever since she first set eyes on him. It was no secret. They had even got it on while I was in Hawaii. He told me when I got back. But he also told me it wasn't important. And he told me she knew nothing. I believed him. Maybe I was wrong. But she would have done anything for him. Believe me, if Lenny had told her to go to the airport and check our destinations, she would have done it, no questions asked."

"Elly." I couldn't bear it. This dreadful doomed revisionism. "Listen to what you're saying. The man lied to her. He lied to you. How can you believe a word he says?"

"He's not the only person who has lied to me, Marla," she said softly, and if it was intended to wound it succeeded. She sounded so certain, so worldly-wise. So she had known about Indigo all along. Yet I hadn't even noticed. "You live too much in here" — Germaine's words echoed in my head. "You are sometimes very careless with your life." Mine and other people's. How could I have been so wrong? I could not believe it.

"He wants to see me," she said quietly. "I think I owe him that much."

"No." And the word spat across the room.

"Marla, listen to me. It isn't your fault. I know that. But you have to understand that this is my story and you can't finish it for me. You, J.T., anyone. I need to know the truth. I'm not naïve. I know what he's done to me. All the pain and the dishonesties. But I also know that he didn't set me up. I owe him the chance of an explanation."

Like rain on a watercolor, the picture of our promised future began to drain away. Lazy French days of sunshine, the new life in London, time spent doing nothing, all of it blurring into itself, leaving nothing but a few rain-washed smears.

"But —"

"I know what you're going to say, but I don't want to hear it. He has been nearly two years of my life. I've loved him more than I loved anyone, and I have to know for sure what the lies were. I deserve that much. And anyway," she added, this time more gently, "I owe him one."

I felt a kind of physical pain, somewhere deep inside my bowels. Conscience again? "Elly, you don't owe him anything," I said, horrified.

She looked at me with a sort of tenderness. "Did anyone stop you as you went through Customs this morning, Marla? You knew that someone had set him up. He knew that you knew. Yet you said nothing. You didn't lift a finger to save him. It would have taken only one phone call to the Paris Customs to make you quits. But he didn't do it. He saved you. That's why I have to see him."

Just like that. From horns to halo. I had lost her. I knew it then, and it hurt so much it took my breath away. The world went black, and for a moment I seemed to be falling through space. Even the room had lost its definition. When I heard my voice, it came from a long way away.

"Where is he?"

"In a hotel. In Scotland. That much at least was true."

"When will you go?"

"I don't know. When I feel ready."

I rallied for one last stand. "Let me come with you."

She shook her head. "No, I think you should go home now. I won't do anything without telling you. I promise. But I think we both need some time alone." She waited, then said again softly, "Go home, Marla. You look exhausted. You need to sleep. It will be all right. I'll call you later, I promise."

The room began to slide again. "Let me stay with you, Elly. I won't disturb you or try to persuade you." I could feel a wave of panic building. It came from a long way away, down through many years, back to a time when each tomorrow seemed an unbearable prospect and when I had begun to realize that she was the only one who mattered. Maybe the panic touched her too, because she leaned over and put an arm around me, laid a hand on my head. We sat for a while in silence. Mother and child. It had happened before.

"I'll call you a cab," she said at last. "You mustn't worry, Marla. Nothing will happen to either of us. I know what I'm doing. Go home and sleep. I'll talk to you tonight."

And because it hurt so much, I pulled away from her and clothed myself in adulthood. I stood up and fumbled for my bag. "All right, Elly. You do it your way. But remember that I warned you."

Home. Gray skies over Haverstock Hill, an afternoon turning to evening with no change in the light. Up the stairs a musty, dusty little flat with five letters on the doorstep and a triumphant total of three messages on the answering machine. The fruits of two weeks' absence. I could not bring myself to listen to them. I made black coffee to keep myself awake and lay on the sofa wondering when she would call. I thought about ringing California but had no idea what I would say. In the heavy gray of an English evening, everything seemed so far away. I would close my eyes to stop them hurting. But I would not sleep. The coffee would keep me awake, and even if I did doze off, the telephone would wake me. That is the last thought I remember.

The phone did not wake me; neither did the dawn. I suppose if I hadn't been so stupid with tiredness I would have realized — realized that I had left the answering machine on, so that when the call came the machine would take it on the first ring and Elly would talk onto a piece of tape. But I didn't realize. If you believe in fate, then that was what it was. I have not yet made up my mind on this. When I woke, it came with a rush. Outside it was brighter. At first I thought the storm had simply passed into a glow of evening. When it finally hit me that I might in fact have slept through a night and a day, I was mad with shock. On the hall table the telephone sat quietly. Beneath it a little red light flashed a fourth message. I whirled it back. A man's voice was talking about double glazing. Then the bleep. Then Elly, curious and tired.

"Marla, where are you? It's eight o'clock. Listen, I have to talk to you, tell you what's happening. Are you there . . . ?" Pause. Then, "I'm taking the night train to Scotland. Lenny will meet me in Inverness, then

342

we'll drive together to the hotel. I know this news is going to hurt you. I'm sorry. But please understand. I have to do it. See him, talk to him. And I have to do it alone. The hotel is the Metropole. In a place called Inverlochy. On the west coast, not far from Ullapool. Telephone number: Inverlochy seven-four-eight-nine. But please don't call it. Not until I ring you, all right? God, I wish I could hear your voice. I so wanted to talk. Tell you I'm sorry. We were both so tired and strung out. I didn't mean to be angry. I just felt so out of control. But it wasn't your fault. I should never have got you into all this in the first place. That's why I have to resolve it alone. You do understand that, don't you? I love you, and I'll see you soon."

Sooner than you think. I picked up the phone. The man whose job it is to tell the time told me it was 7:56 P.M., precisely. British Rail took longer to answer, but I still made the night train. It never occurred to me to call first. Elly had told me herself. I owed Lenny. Whether it was an apology or an attack would become plain in due course. But whichever it was, I would deliver it in person. And I would not leave him alone with her.

The train was fully booked, with no sleeping berths. But then I wasn't sleepy. I sat through an endless night watching fields flash by, ghostly under a half-moon. And in the small hours I was joined by J.T., conjured up as an ally and traveling companion. Why not? In a symmetrical universe he would have been here anyway, the fourth star in this doomed little cluster. And with him came his words: "She's got no protection against herself. That's how come Lenny can fuck her over. He speeds up the process of her own destruction . . . Get her out . . . before it's too late."

And, just as in childhood the train wheels had always sung the chorus, now the smooth electric rumblings echoed his exhortation.

I'm coming, Elly. I'm coming.

PART THREE

. . . and nothing but the truth?

Fifteen

The Inverlochy Metropole was not hard to find once you had found Inverlochy. God knows how Lenny had come to pick this particular spot. Maybe somebody from the Scottish Tourist Board was involved in payola. At a rough guess, the Metropole had last been fashionable (and full) around the time of the Festival of Britain. It was perched on the edge of the coast in crumbling dignity, looking out over a dark gray sea furrowed with waves. Summer, it seemed, had not yet reached this far north, if indeed it ever did. Even from a distance the place reeked of Daphne du Maurier. Probably the only trade it got now were old ladies who had fallen into a habit of holidays, and the occasional television crew filming yet another period serial. I parked the hired car carefully in an empty courtyard. Our relationship had cautiously improved over the sixty miles or so from Inverness, but we were not yet on speeding terms.

Inside the Metropole, the girl at the desk was the only new thing since the fifties, young and fresh, with peaches-and-cream skin and nut brown hair, which waved unfashionably but exuberantly around her face. The kind of hair which, no doubt, she tugged and ironed into temporary obedience, not yet understanding that its very nonconformity made her spectacular. She smiled me welcome, and it was clear from her bright eyes that nothing really painful had ever happened to her, nor did she believe it ever would. She reminded me of someone I had once known.

"Gud afternoon. Can I help you?" The voice danced. Obviously she liked her work, liked the sensation of being an adult when she was still so close to a child. I realized with alarm that she made me want to cry. I was not as in control as I had thought. I took a hold on myself.

"Yes, I'm looking for a couple who are staying here. He's American, she's English. She would have arrived some time yesterday."

"Oh, yes, the American gentleman." She smiled, and I read in her eyes fantasies of lovers to come. "He met her off the train. They arrived in the afternoon. They're in Room Twenty-five."

So, they had spent the night together after all. Like Bothwell and Mary Queen of Scots. Elly did not mind the smell of blood on his hands. Romantic fiction. It hurt like hell. I took a breath.

"Would you call them for me?"

"Och, no, they're no in now. They're out sightseeing. The gentleman asked me to mark out some places of interest on his map. They left a couple of hours ago."

My stomach felt funny. But then I hadn't eaten for a long time.

"If you'd like to wait for them, there's a wee lounge across the hall. But I doubt they'll be back before afternoon. They took a long list of places and brochures, and they didna make reservations for tea."

Her words gave me time to think. I turned back to the bright, eager face. "I wonder, do you have a room?"

"Aye yes. You'll be wanting a single? There's a lovely room on the third floor with a view of the sea. Number Twenty-two. It's just a few doors down from your friends."

"Fine. I'll take it."

"Do you no want to see it first?" It was part of the game: the appraisal before the acceptance. You could see she enjoyed it.

"No, no, I'm sure it's lovely. Can you tell

me which way they went, so I can try to catch them up?"

She frowned slightly. Things were not going entirely according to protocol. "I'm a close friend," I added quickly. "And I have some rather important news for them."

"Oh, I see. Well, I could point you out the same route I showed the gentleman."

"You didn't speak to the lady?"

"No, no, she didna come down for breakfast, took tea in her room. I talked to the gentleman, and then they left about an hour later."

How did she look? How were they together? Had they been quarreling? Were her eyes swollen? This girl had probably noticed nothing. Just a good-looking couple, the man doing the organizing, the woman following on behind. Just as it should be.

I bought a map, and she set to work, drawing a thick pencil line across from Inverlochy through the peninsula below, snaking round lochs and across marshland down into Ullapool, then out to the east, taking in part of the road to Inverness, and from there looping up and back toward home.

"Actually, the gentleman was very interested in this piece of countryside. The castle by Loch Assynt. It's the place where the

Earl of Montrose was imprisoned on his way down to Edinburgh to stand trial. He was executed later for high treason. Really, there's no much there anymore, it's all ruins. But he seemed very keen to see it nevertheless."

I nodded. "I think he has an interest in history." I imagined Lenny standing over the young girl, watching her, smiling, eyes concentrating on every word. No wonder she couldn't remember much about Elly.

"Could they have reached there by now?"

"Oh, it would depend on which way they went. I suggested they take it in on their way back, after Ullapool and the Measach Falls. In which case you might well wait for them there."

"How long will it take to get there?"

"Och, it's no that far. Maybe fifteen, twenty minutes, though the road's no wonderful, and it's worse if it rains."

I shot a look out through the doors. The wind was rolling in heavy clouds, bellies full of Scottish winter. I folded up the map and thanked her. I'm almost there, Elly.

The road was clear for the first few miles. The scenery, had I been in the mood to look, was devastating; vast spongy carpets of dark heathers and moss, broken by

351

mounds of rock which looked as if they had been folded on top of one another; granite layer cake. A little way out the road branched. I took the instructed fork. It was my belief he would have made for the castle first. After so many years, to walk the same stones as Montrose would surely be too much of a temptation. Maybe they would be there still, battling out their own history amid the ruins of someone else's. I was no longer thinking about what we should say, or what would be demanded of me. That would be answered soon enough. I put my foot down, pulled out, and passed a caravan chugging its painful way up a steep gradient. The clouds had kept pace with the car, and a slow, fine drizzle was now beginning to fall. The loch and the castle when I came upon them seemed rather an anticlimax. The land was flat and crumpled, the water cold-black, and the ruins themselves small and scattered. I parked the car and walked quickly out toward the spit of land on which there had once been a fortress.

The rain was so soft I could hardly feel it falling, but tiny beads of water hovered on the weave of my jacket and clung like spray to the strands of my hair. There was no one there. I could see that even from the car. But somehow I felt the need to check, or maybe just to be where they had been. I clambered up one of the remnants of a wall. There was moss growing everywhere, and sheep droppings among the boulders. The only part of the castle which retained any semblance of architecture was one of the towers, part of which stood up, stern and silent against brooding skies. Montrose's view must have been one of unbroken desolation, a long, bleak horizon of water against looming dark hills in the distance. He probably knew it was over by this time. That he had fought and lost for the last time, and that his nobility would not save his skin.

To the left, by the banks of the loch, stood the remains of an old manor house, burned to the ground in the eighteenth century the girl had said. Maybe in the evening the daughter of the house would have walked to the water's edge and looked across at the castle. Montrose had a reputation for charming the ladies. Perhaps she had dreamed of rescue and redemption in his arms. A potent fantasy, whichever age you lived in. For others, that is. I went and stood where I imagined she might have done, but I couldn't be sure. The sense of stillness might just have come from the landscape, not from the people who had lived in it. I couldn't even feel the imprint of Elly. Yet if they had been there, surely some shiver of atmosphere would have remained? I turned and made my way back to the car. The rain, I think, had stopped.

The next point on the map was Ullapool, and then the Measach Falls. If they had taken the suggested road, maybe we would now meet en route. The weather continued to be capricious, occasional sun bursting through cloud, splashing pools of golden light onto the hills. According to the map, the falls were some distance away. Cars passed me, and I caught flashes of faces. The road rolled on through marsh and moss, empty even of sheep. Ullapool came as welcome relief, a busy, pretty little seaport. Maybe they had stopped here for lunch. From a side street a police car zipped out in front of me, siren blasting, a sight unusual enough to stop a few passersby on the pavement.

Out of town, the road was better and I pushed on faster. So fast that I missed the turning. The signpost was small and badly weatherworn and, according to the mileometer, still over a mile away. It took me another three to become suspicious. When I stopped by the roadside and approached a man cutting hedgerows, he redirected me as if it was something of a regular occurrence.

How much time did I waste which might have been saved? It is not a bearable question. The car park, when I eventually found it, was a leveled stretch of gravel with just two cars on it. Hardly a popular tourist spot. On the other hand, the map showed two entrances. Maybe the coaches came from the other side. What had the girl said? That you had to take a path and follow it for about a quarter of a mile. It was, she had assured me, worth the walk. Part of the Corrieshalloch Gorge, and one of the finest canyons in Scotland. The falls had a drop of over 150 feet to the river below. Even the suspension bridge was memorable, built by the man who had owned the land before bequeathing it to the National Trust for Scotland.

The path was well trodden. It had been a wet summer, and the ground had turned to mud. Not like the California earth. I imagined J.T. in front of me, goat-dancing his way through the puddles, graceful despite his size. One canyon leads to another. I quickened my step. The path divided: to the right a sign for the viewing platform, to the left the falls themselves. I took the right. That way at least I would be able to spot anybody on the bridge. The platform when I reached it was a primitive affair, a little verandah built like a cage, jutting out over the side of the gorge. I was alone there. Scotland was beginning to feel distinctly underpopulated.

I stepped into the cage. Heights do not bother me, and this was a beauty. I was standing perched out over a drop so steep and so sheer that looking down brought a rushing sensation of swirling air plunging into darkness. The girl had been right. The Corrieshalloch Gorge was spectacular, a vast great crack in the earth's crust into which millions of tons of ice had poured, eating like acid into the granite. Below, through the spray, the rivet ran like a ribbon of white foam, while above, the walls of the canyon were a dark wild green, covered in moss and lichen, softening the roar of the water. I had miscalculated. The falls were further than I'd imagined, maybe as much as a quarter of a mile away up the gorge. A vertical sheet of foam, too distant to be real. The bridge across was thin and wiry, just a few silver lines against the horizon. With eyes screwed up, I could just make out figures on it. Two of them. A man and a woman maybe. Elly and Lenny, awed by the magnificence. I was suddenly sure it was them. I had taken the wrong turning.

I walked fast back along the path, and the

roar got louder as I went, a rushing, wailing sound that vibrated the air and shivered the ground beneath. What would I say to them? Our first words of greeting? My gut began to stretch taut. The track veered right, and I walked straight into a barrier slung by chains across two trees. FALLS CLOSED UNTIL FURTHER NOTICE. Perhaps they had approached by the other path. If I went all the way back and round, I would surely miss them. I clambered over the sign and continued. The sound of the water grew deafening. Fifty yards on, I came upon it — a sudden clearing with a view straight to the bridge and on either side the edge of a treacherous cliff, fenced off by long rope railings.

The first thing I looked for were the two figures, revealed now as men in blue trousers and shirtsleeves. Both of them. I registered officials. National Trust officers perhaps, inspecting. They were near the other side of the bridge now, looking into the gorge below, concentrating hard. So hard that they didn't spot me. I took a few steps out onto the wooden slats. The bridge swayed ever so slightly under my feet. It was then that I recognized the uniforms. The two figures were policemen. I took another step and missed my footing, grabbing hold of the railing to right myself. The movement made them look up. I noticed behind them other men in among the trees at the top of the gorge, one of them with a length of rope. In front of me a figure was approaching, his hand held out to stop me.

"I'm sorry, madam. But the bridge is closed. Did you no see the sign?"

"What seems to be the trouble, Officer?" I heard my words plucked out of a subconscious made up from television clichés.

"There's been an accident. So if I could ask you to —"

"What kind of accident?" Much louder now than the water's roar, my voice demanded attention.

He looked at me strangely. "Someone has had a fall. Now please, madam . . ."

I must have tried to get past him, because I have a recollection of the bridge swaying violently, and the fear in his voice as he grabbed hold of me and called to his companion for help. Somehow they must have got me to the side, because the next thing I remember is sitting on a bench, my head pushing down in between my knees. I opened my eyes, but the ground would not stay still. I was falling through black holes, and the water was still rushing. I knew, you see, even then I knew. Somewhere inside, I think I had known all along. I spoke, and my voice boomed through the caverns of my head. "I'm here to meet a friend, Officer. A girl, about thirty years old with short dark hair. Her name is Eleanor Cameron. She was traveling with an American. Have you see them?"

And as I opened my eyes, his face told me what his mouth could not. After that I remember nothing but a long wailing scream, which penetrated deep into the sound of the water. And then the black hole returned.

Sixteen

In the hotel lobby, the peach-skinned princess was still on duty. Her eyes grew wide with pity as she watched me walk toward the desk. Outside the main doors, the police car which had brought me home was heading through the gates, back to the glacial gorge where they were, even now, lowering men and harnesses down the cliffs in search of the body.

I had been processed through a Dr. Finlay's casebook of care and attention. I had dreamt that Elly was dead on foaming rock. When I had woken in someone's living room to find the dream a reality, the earth's crust had split open to swallow me again. Tea had been administered by a kindly practitioner, who had urged tears as a release from my deathly silence, then offered sedatives to numb the pain. But I would have none of him. Lenny had sat there before me, sitting in dishonest sorrow, sipping comfort and gulping pills. He would be sleeping now. Sweet dreams, Lenny. May you wake up screaming and sweating. "Stricken with grief." That had been the doctor's phrase. The very words had made me laugh out loud. And so my comforter had grown fearful for me and left me alone. Even the police had been careful. "At this stage, Miss Masterson, we'd just like you to help us check a few facts. If you'd be kind enough. Is this Eleanor Cameron . . . ?" The picture from her wallet. Elly at twenty-eight, taken in a photographic booth at Goodge Street Station, eyes popping wide, like those of a rabbit caught in the head-lights. We had laughed about it at the time. Yes, this was Elly Cameron. How long had I known her? When did I last see her? Could I give details of next of kin? They asked for facts; I gave them facts. They did not seem interested in opinions. I withheld mine. Until I had seen Lenny.

"Oh, he's in his room, sleeping. He left instructions to wake him in time for supper."

That's right, Lenny. Don't miss a meal for her. "Does he know I'm here?"

"Oh yes, indeed. He seems very relieved. Wanted me to tell you he would see you later." She was nervous with me, her soft little face filled with compassion, trying so hard to be kind and understanding, not to intrude. But she was hard-pressed to hide the other feelings, the sense of excitement and curiosity at being so close to such drama, such tragedy. She was looking intently at me, as if trying to locate my sorrow. But I had nothing to show. Unlike Lenny.

I took my key and turned to go.

"Can I get anything sent up to you? Tea or something?"

I shook my head. I was suddenly tired of seeing her. What was it Elly had said that first night about watching soft-skinned youth and envying it its possibilities? Elly need not have worried. She would never grow old. I picked up my trusty canvas bag and dragged my feet upstairs.

Three hours later I came down. No doubt you'd like to know what happened in the time in between. What I did, what I thought . . . how I felt. Well, first I ran a bath, and stood for a long time looking out of the balcony window onto the beach below. Stood so long in fact that the bath overflowed and I had to pull out the plug and let in more cold before I could stand the temperature. I lay soaking for a while, but the heat made me dizzy. So I got out, wrapped myself in a towel, and lay down on the bed. I stayed there for a while, listening to the sound of the sea. Then I got up and dressed slowly — clean underwear for Gem's sake, and a short-sleeved shapeless black dress perfect for graduations and college functions. And on my feet walking shoes because I had no others. I dried my hair with the now wet towel and brushed my teeth. I did not look in a mirror. Then, when the hands of my watch read twenty past eight, I opened my door onto an empty hall and walked down to the dining room.

That much is easy. That much I can tell you. What I cannot tell you is what I thought or felt during that time. Because I cannot remember. No, that is not strictly true. I do remember feeling something. But it was not to do with Elly. Don't get me wrong. I would have cried for her if I could, wept my life away. But I could not even bring myself to picture her face. There were no tears to be had. No wall of sorrow to be kept at bay. All there was was the familiar void and, at the center of it, a small hard nut of emotion, hot and cold at the same time. Hatred. I hung on to it because it was the only thing I could feel that would not destroy me, and because it proved I was capable of feeling. So I nursed it and let it grow. In retrospect, it seems to me that those hours were a kind of suspended animation, preparation for what was to come, a meditation on war. Whatever it was, by the time I left the room I was ready.

The reception desk was empty. Thank God. From behind a pair of heavy swing doors came a delicate percussion of china and cutlery. I pushed my way in. The room was filled with echoes of Terence Rattigan, an atmosphere of genteel aging caught between the folds of heavy velvet curtains and under napkins on starched white tablecloths, each with its set of silver condiments, candleholder, and single flower vase. All this I took in slowly, a wide-angle shot, unhurried and cool. In an alcove on the left sat a couple from *Separate Tables*, thin lipped, the woman lifting a soupspoon to her mouth with exaggerated precision. A few tables along another aging marriage; then, nearer to the door, a family with two adolescent children, surly and uncomfortable in their dining clothes, obviously wishing they were somewhere else. No one was speaking. And there, to the right, at a table in a window bay, was Lenny, sitting staring at the door.

I stood for a while, savoring the moment. Then, with deliberate ceremony, walked toward him. It seemed to take me an age to reach the table. A figure approached halfway through my journey, a middle-aged man in a white jacket, the maître d', smiling, diverting me politely to another part of the room, away from the tragedy-stricken guest. Scandal, like bushfire, travels fast. He realized, a little too late for elegance, that I was in fact the other "bereaved" character in the drama, and the gesture of deflection turned into one of welcome. He reached the table before me and pulled away the chair, deftly scooping it back under me. Then, being good at his job, he disappeared.

I raised my eyes to look at Lenny. He was sitting absolutely still, one sculptured hand resting on the white tablecloth, the other in his lap. The skin, usually so smooth ironed and flawless, was puffy and a little crumpled, especially around the eyes. Anyone not knowing him better might have thought they were seeing the aftermath of tears. Even the steel-chip dazzle had gone from the eyes, replaced by a dullness which might have been born of a sedative hangover. As I say, a stranger could have read sorrow. But then I wasn't a stranger. And I had anticipated authenticity. It would have been the least he could do.

"Hello, Marla." The voice was heavy. Even the body — that triumphant, self-confident torso — seemed laden and sagging. Full marks for trying, Lenny. I said nothing.

Let him sweat. "You've seen the police? You know what happened?" Once again the same lifeless tone.

I counted the pulse beats in the back of my neck. I had intended to nod my head. But when it came to it, I did not seem able to move. That tiny pinprick of emotion which I had nurtured so carefully was threatening to overwhelm me. I swallowed and clasped my hands together hard to avoid any unauthorized trembling.

"Marla . . ." He leaned forward slightly, as if in preparation for intimacy, then seemed to change his mind. He studied the tablecloth, frowning, then looked back up at me. The tragedian following stage directions. I got bored with waiting. Over his shoulder I watched as the waiter hovered in an agony of indecision. Should he do his job or wait for us, lost souls, to ask for help? I focused back on Lenny's face. Slow hand clapping from the audience. "We never really did get to know each other, did we, Marla?" he said, smiling. "We still connect only through Elly."

At the corner of his eye, I spotted a tiny shimmering of water. I had one clear thought, lit up in neon capitals in my brain. If he cries, I swear I'll pick up my fork and ram it into his chest. The violence of the image caught me off guard. I had not intended to be so near the edge. I pulled myself back, and my voice, when it emerged, was admirable, ice-cold and even.

"What happened on the bridge, Lenny?"

He stared at me, and the little droplet of water trembled. Trembled and shone, but did not fall. You bastard, I thought. With all your skill you can't even squeeze out one whole tear for her.

"Marla, I know what you must be feeling. I understand —"

"No you don't," I said quickly. "And I think this fiasco would be less painful if you stopped pretending that you did. In fact, I'd appreciate it if you'd cut the 'charm' altogether. Because it makes me want to throw up."

To his credit, his gaze never wavered once; the eyes stayed stapled to mine, unblinking and steady. "What did you tell the police, Marla?" And there was, I believe, just a touch of muscle to be heard this time.

"Just about as much of the truth as you did." I was definitely feeling better. "So you've got nothing to worry about."

He sat back and regarded me with something near to confusion. Then he lifted his left hand a little and shot a half look over his shoulder. The waiter who had been standing to attention by the sweets trolley flung himself toward the table, menus in hand. He muttered a good evening into his bow tie and handed me a leather-bound volume.

"Actually, if you don't mind, I don't think we're ready to order yet," I said loudly.

The waiter shot me a look of horror, then turned to Lenny with a plea for guidance.

"We'll take a bottle of wine." Lenny's voice was quiet, but designed to be heard. "White, I think. Maybe a Chablis or an Entre-Deux-Mers. What do you think, Marla?" He looked at me but gave me no time to answer. "And we'd like two plates of smoked salmon, and bread. As soon as possible, please." He flashed a smile at the waiter, who nodded gratefully. Male collusion in the face of female emotion. If I said any more it would only reinforce the impression of me as distraught and potentially out of control. Lenny, it seemed, was attempting to reestablish himself. I bided my time. The waiter scuttled for home.

"I think we should wait until the food comes, don't you?" Lenny said evenly. "If we start to talk now, the waiter will only interrupt us."

Welcome back, Lenny. I preferred this version. It was more real. I turned and looked out of the window. It was almost night. No policemen had come to bundle us into waiting cars. That surely meant they had not found her yet. And if not yet, then we would have to wait till morning. Morning. A whole night on the rocks. But I would not think of that now, or the sorrow of it would turn me stupid and he would get the better of me.

In the kitchen, they busted a gut to please the bereaved. The salmon arrived minutes later, gleaming pink strips of it, with little wedges of lemon decorating each plate and a mound of thinly sliced brown bread. The candle between us flickered as Lenny unfurled his napkin. Silver. Salmon. Wine. It was like some dreadful travesty of a lovers' meal. The waiter presented the Entre-Deux-Mers, uncorked it, and poured a little into Lenny's glass. He picked it up and handed it to me. Memories are made of this. I took it and, with deliberate ceremony, poured it slowly over my plate of salmon. The waiter stiffened. Lenny smiled.

"That's fine," he said, nodding. The waiter poured two full glasses, carefully avoiding my eyes, then put the bottle in the ice bucket and made a run for home. I pushed away my plate and sat back in my chair. Lenny took a sip of wine and peeled off a strip of salmon. He ate it slowly, watching me. Then he said, "So, you want to know what happened. But you know already. Surely you made your decisions a long time ago, Marla. Nothing I say now will change your mind."

He was growing more like Lenny with every second. It was like watching someone change size: Alice eating the cake in order to get through the door. I took the key off the table. In this fairy tale, no one was leaving.

"Why don't you tell me anyway?" I said. "I enjoy stories."

"Oh, you really do hate me, don't you, Marla? I think even I underestimated how much. So — you want to know. Even though you won't believe me. Well, maybe that doesn't matter. But let me say one thing. The reason you won't believe me is that you can't possibly afford to. You do know that, don't you? You simply can't take that risk. Because, of course, if you did, you'd have no one to blame. And no one to hate. And you need both of those things much more than you need the truth. Isn't that right?"

I felt like yawning, a great, ostentatious yawn, huge and ugly, like a scream from a Francis Bacon painting. But instead I kept my mouth tight shut, teeth clamped together until my jaw ached. I would say nothing. I would not join in his games.

He waited awhile, then said quietly, "The fact is I don't know what happened. I swear that's the truth. We had crossed the bridge and were about to head back to the car when Elly decided to walk down to the edge of the gorge. That's all I know. The ground was wet, she was wearing those damn stupid plastic sandals of hers. They had no grip. The railing was rotten . . . when she slipped it couldn't hold her weight. It couldn't save her. And neither could I . . . I was walking away. All I heard was the scream . . ." He broke off, and his face was white, drained of blood. "There's no more to tell. That's it."

I nodded. "Don't give it another thought, Lenny. It could have happened to anyone. I wonder, have you called Indigo yet? Maybe the wine should have been champagne."

It was beneath the belt, but that was my intention. I wanted him to get mad, to lose control, to give himself away. He didn't rise to it. I pushed further. "And that's really all you have to say, is it, Lenny?"

"Oh no, Marla. That's nothing. Nothing at all. But it's all you want to hear." This time the trail of fuel ignited. "Elly was right. There's no point in telling you the whole truth. It would destroy you to have to hear it. So why don't we stop playing games, huh? Why don't you just go to the police? Tell them your sordid little tale. Blow it all sky-high. You've got the dynamite strapped all over your body. Just light the fuse. That way we all go up, and the truth gets buried forever with the bodies. Then you'll never have to hear it. Just as well, huh? Because how could you bear it? Cover your ears against it, Marla. It would microwave your brain. My God, J.T. must have seen you coming. The original innocent. His lucky day. Drink your wine, Marla, and let's do it. Call those quaint Scottish policemen and tell them a story that'll burn their ears off. Get it over with now."

He was standing up, pulling away his chair, the last few words public knowledge. From the back room the maître d' burst forth, almost rupturing himself to get to us. Across the room, the thin-lipped couple paused over their sorbets. The woman turned, pale blue permed head snapping to attention at the possibility of the socially outrageous.

"Sir, can I be of assistance?" The maître d' like a guardsman.

"Yes. The lady would like to make a phone call."

The maître d' looked toward me. I

avoided his eyes and said nothing.

"Madam . . . I'm afraid we have no facilities in the dining room — if you'd care to accompany me to the main desk, or perhaps give me the number . . ." His voice drained away. I sat serenely, contemplating the tablecloth. I felt an exchange of looks between him and Lenny. From a table by the door, someone giggled and was fiercely hushed. The room vibrated with tension. Then Lenny said softly, "I'm sorry to have troubled you. Madam seems to have changed her mind. Perhaps you could bring her a glass of water."

The assembled company let out the breath they had been holding while the maître d' brought a jug of water, then made for the sanctuary of the kitchen. Behind closed doors you could feel people listening. Lenny sat down.

"Very good," I said after a while, still in communion with the tablecloth. "So, what do you want?"

"To tell the truth," he said quietly. "But only if you are willing to hear it."

This time I looked up. Across the table I saw a good-looking man with a kind of anger in his eyes. I noticed furrows I had not seen before. A sallowness of the skin. For the first time I could imagine a Lenny who was not forever young and invincible. I felt for the nugget of strength inside me. I had tended it well. It was still there, hard and sure. I was safe.

"All right," I said. "You've made your point. I'm listening."

"Good." He picked up his glass and sipped it. Then pushed it to one side. And this, for what it is worth, is what he told me. I gave him — and so will give you — the courtesy of no interruption.

"I had been waiting to meet you, Marla. Elly had told me so much about you. You had been painted in such bright colors — as one of nature's originals, not quite of this world. She had told me how you had grown up together. How hard it was for you, how brilliant you were, brilliant and strange. Oh, I had quite a picture of you: a kind of modern-day Virginia Woolf, too sensitive for the sun, needing the shade of others to nurture you and let you flower. It appealed to me. I have always had a certain admiration for English eccentrics. A product of my New England upbringing — the indoctrination that we are closer in spirit to Europe than to the barbarian Midwest. And Elly made such a case for you. I think even then she was trying to assuage her guilt at having

374

left you. I never did penetrate the mystery of your friendship. You were Elly's secret, and she was proud of you. So, you see, when we finally met, you were quite a disappointment. Not so much strange as impenetrable. All granite and ice, with your English nose in the air. We were fated to be enemies, it seems. Well, I guess she had made it sound pretty bad, huh? Which it was, but not entirely in the way she thought. Don't worry, Marla, I'm not about to dazzle you with revisionism or turn myself into some misunderstood, much-maligned victim. Nothing so crass. I'm just looking to set the record straight.

"Yes, there was trouble between us. Some of it was a result of the job. She had found it very exciting in the beginning. Of course, everyone does. But when you come down to it, a job is just a job. Except for the few high moments, the rest is just real life. And that's what she wasn't prepared for — the real life in the middle, the times when there was nothing to do, when you got up, ate, lived a little, and then went back to bed. The hibernation months — being rather than doing. She found that very hard. Maybe you recognize that in her. Anyway, it got worse, and when she started making demands, I began backing off. I'm not particularly good at being private with people. Maybe you've noticed that too. On the other hand, I still loved her. Ah . . . now that hurts, doesn't it, Marla? I can feel it in you. Well, there's nothing I can do to ease your pain. I'm sorry. You're going to have to bite on it. I loved her, but I didn't totally trust her. That make it any better?

"To be fair, I didn't single her out that way. I don't totally trust anyone. I never have. That particular personality defect predates my professional life. I had a somewhat eccentric childhood, a lot of money making up for a lack of attention. If we had the time, we could discuss it, but we don't. So let's just say I kept some of my defenses up. You know the chronology as well as I do. She got higher and less in control, and I didn't help her. Unforgivable behavior, huh, Marla? Except there are some things you don't know. Because this is where our 'love story' comes in. And where the versions of the truth begin to differ.

"Let's talk about California, Marla — J.T., the fourth character in this domestic drama. Let's talk about him, the things he told you, the things you believed. Such an important part he played in all of this. He should be here now, don't you agree, completing the circle?

"So, what exactly did you learn under the stars in his mountain retreat? Well, let me see if I can guess. That he and I met in Colombia in '76, when he was the initiate and I was the novice. That we hit it off together; he broke bread with me, taught me some ground rules, and set me off on the road. All this is true, give or take a little goodwill. So how did it go then? No doubt be described to you how I became full of hubris, grew careless, and how I almost fell. Almost, because — of course — he came to my rescue. And how, following that near tragedy, we agreed to disentangle ourselves professionally but stayed good friends. Then he decided to retire, hit a streak of bad luck, found himself in danger, and I stepped in with a little homicide to repay the debt. But that my methods offended his implacable sense of morality, so when my wickedness was discovered, he could do no less than stand by and watch me get my just deserts. Have I got it more or less correct, Marla? Yes, I think I have. And you believed him. Oh, I can understand that. It must have been music to your ears. There it was, the justification for what you already felt, the reason for saving Elly from this murdering fiend.

"That is what you believe. I know nothing

I can say will shake that conviction, but you won't mind if I waste your time with an alternative version. I'll make it brief. The truth is I did not become careless, or greedy. The truth is I was set up. Not obviously, or unsubtly, but set up all the same. And, just to complicate matters, I was set up by the man who saved me. A lesson. From the master to the pupil, the pupil who was learning too fast and daring to presume to show it. That straightened me out. It took me a while to recover my name, and my confidence. And to find out the truth. Our relationship cooled, although we stayed drinking companions. Then came the bust, about which you know most of the facts but not who was behind them. Who, for instance, really paid the man from the East to tamper with a certain brake cable.

"It was, of course, the same man who stood to gain from the silence of the river. The same man who could finally use the evidence to point the finger at someone else, someone he had framed once before. However, since these are exactly the kinds of things you don't want to hear, I won't bother pursuing them. But the truth is there, should you care to look at it.

"So, where did Elly and I fit into all of this? Well, as you know — and I have to hand it to you, Marla, for an English academic you have become very well versed in the intricacies of the narcotics underworld — Tyler got out of jail around the time Elly and I were in Colombia for the second trip, when things were beginning to splinter between us. The trip was bad enough. But when we got home I discovered that we were being watched. With Tyler a free man, it made me nervous. If he was really dumb enough to believe that I had killed his wife, then he might also be dumb enough to try for poetic revenge. It would have been easier to tell Elly the whole story, only by then she was in no fit state to listen. Five miles high and suffering from vertigo. The only thing to do was get her out of it. If Tyler could be made to believe that she'd left me, then maybe he'd leave her alone. It was obvious we were near some kind of bust-up anyway. I simply did nothing to stop it. As I'm sure she told you. It was a little brutal, I grant you, but I had no choice. With Elly out of the way, I could get on with watching the watchers.

"It was then, about a month later, I heard that Elly was in California. Now, this is where your imagination comes in, Marla. I want you to do the impossible. Try to put yourself in my position. What was I to

379

think? On the one hand, why shouldn't she go there? She thought J.T. and I were friends. If she needed to talk, then J.T. was a logical choice of confidant. But I have told you I have a suspicious nature. I owe my life to it. She had left New York hating me. There were other reasons she could have chosen California. And there were other stories J.T. could have told her, certain fairy tales — of which you know him to be a connoisseur. She was in exactly the frame of mind where she might have believed them. So they talked, and then, as you know, she came home, walked back into my life and said not a word about where she had been. J.T. had sworn her to secrecy. We both know that now. But not then. Then all I saw were the facts. Elly had spent time with a man who had tried to destroy me, and she had kept the visit a secret. I did not feel reassured. Yet here she was arriving home revitalized, determined that, if only I would give up the profession, we could have a future together. What if she knew something I didn't? How could I trust her? She was claiming love, but there was a kind of tension about her, as if she didn't quite believe the script either.

"Well, we agreed to try again. But you can see now it was doomed. California was like a

380

glass wall between us. I couldn't forget it, and I couldn't disregard it either. The irony was that I too had given some thought to winding it up. Against the odds, I had missed her, and she could have been a reason for finding something else to do with my life. Aaah, I feel another rage growing in you, Marla. My admission of vulnerability seems to disgust you. It clouds the picture, and we wouldn't want any gray areas in a story which is so beautifully black-and-white, would we?

"Back to the facts. I let it be known that I was taking temporary retirement. To quieten her, and to force them — whoever they were — to tempt me back. It didn't take long. A month or so later I was approached by two English 'businessmen.' They needed my help, they said. They were running a small, successful organization, but their connections were Asian rather than South American — trading in hash. They could see the writing on the wall — it wasn't hard; people were lining up to read it. America's coke market was reaching saturation point. With thirty-five billion dollars going up people's noses every year, it was already the biggest business in the U.S. behind the auto industry. And every step outside the law. You could see the problem.

It was becoming too big to be tolerated. But while America was closing up, Europe was still wide open. The appetite had been created, all that was needed was increased supplies. I had built up a reputation. They came to me for a feasibility study, a few schemes and the odd trial run. And they were willing to pay for it. A lot of money, too much to refuse. Too much altogether, all things considered, which made it even more interesting. I said yes. And began my research.

"I won't bore you with my scholarship. It was a simple question of routes and cargos. Rumor had it that Spain was the best port of entry, but I wasn't sure. Concerned parties were putting a good deal of pressure on Spanish authorities to get their act together. In the old days Ireland had been the golden trail, sliding it in through Shannon. The amounts of hash spirited through had become folklore. The obvious holes had been plugged, of course, but sometimes it pays to be old-fashioned, to go to the one place no one expects you to. So I decided to look into resurrecting old glories. I took a trip to Britain to check locations, and I ended up in London. It was then that I had another idea — about Elly and me. I will not insult you by pretending it was entirely philanthropic. I still didn't know for sure which side she was on. And by now I was certain that the whole deal was some kind of a setup. I just didn't know how. The trip would be the test. If she really knew nothing, she would come with me. If not — well, I would deal with that if and when it happened. But whatever my motives, the trip at least was real. And the very glorious Inverlochy Metropole was part of it. You can check. All arrangements made at the tourist office in London, signed, sealed, and dated. You know the date. It was the day before your flight to New York.

"From now on the story is your history too. I told you the truth about the plane. I wasn't due to fly British Airways at all. I arrived at Heathrow — a little late, I admit — to find myself a victim of an overzealous booking computer. It didn't matter to me which airline I flew. Not then, at least. I even walked behind you into the departure lounge. You don't remember that, do you? I was struck by your hair. The extraordinary color of it. A corn harvest. I remember wondering if you might be an example of the 'buxom English wench.' Aaah, I seem fated to upset you. Elly warned me you were sensitive about your appearance. Should I call the waiter for the telephone? How come you're so clever and so stupid, Marla? Even about yourself? Whoever told you you were ugly? Don't spit at me. I thought then, and I think now, that you are an immensely striking woman. I did not set out to be your enemy. Remember that. That was entirely your decision. Like it or not, that is what I think of you. But we will not mention it again.

"So, coincidence brings us together, and we travel across the Atlantic on the same plane. We walk through the same terminal together, and here at last you catch me in my first lie. *Mea culpa,* Marla, *mea maxima culpa.* Yes, I did see Elly on the other side of the barrier, and yes, I did watch the two of you meet. There was no danger of my being spotted. You only had eyes for each other. I knew then that you must be Marla. And I knew also, of course, that I was not expected on that plane. So I decided on a little detour before arriving home. And where did I go? I can hear the question clicking away in that admirable brain of yours. Well, you already know, don't you? Who was my ally in all of this? Which other poor dumb female did I exploit? Yes. I went to Indigo.

"Poor Indigo . . . Tangier! — you should have been ashamed of yourself. She had to find a map to check the continent. The spirit is willing, but the brain is weak. And, since she has introduced herself into the story, I might as well answer your questions about her. What do you need to know? That I met her while Elly was away, and that we 'paddled palms' together. I was, of course, everything she'd ever dreamt of, everything she thought New York could give her — a patron for her art. But you overestimated her, Marla. She was what she appeared. No more, no less. When Elly came back, I told her what had happened and I told Indigo it was over. But it seemed cruel just to slam the door in her face. So I suggested a little work at the store.

"Ah, I see you don't believe me. Well, in this case you're right. Well caught. But it's only a ten percent lie. Indigo needed the job, and she was good at it. Even Elly agreed. But yes, she was more than just a salesgirl. She was also a way of watching Elly. Just in case. I told her nothing. Or nothing of the truth anyway. I suggested marital difficulties and the need to know for sure. She was very good. Watched and reported and never demanded payment. So, it was to her apartment that I went that night. And it was on my instructions that she had a gas leak the next morning. Remember? The leak that meant Elly had to go to the store, leaving you and me alone in the apartment, giving us a chance to meet and see if you remembered me. Or at least that was the plan. Unfortunately, something went wrong. I got a phone call from the English connection. They needed to talk, urgently. I left you sleeping, which meant there could be no intimate meeting between us. Instead we would face each other publicly.

"And so to that evening. I wonder if your memories are as vivid as mine. From the moment I saw you, sitting at the cocktail bar, I knew you had come to do me damage. I don't think you know just how honest a person you are, Marla. How the truth shines out through that marble skin of yours. I almost didn't even bother asking you for your silence. It seemed so impossible that you'd give it. So you'll understand why, when you agreed, I — I of the suspicious nature — had to assume a degree of dissembling, to assume that you would not necessarily keep your word. You will, I think, be able to imagine my distress when, on that very night, Elly informed me that you were going to California. I must admit, I almost told her then. All of it, the whole thing. She seemed so obviously innocent. How could she do something so potentially incriminating? But I said nothing. How many times have there been in this whole affair when someone had the chance to stop it? Huh, Marla? How many times did you almost tell the truth? It doesn't bear thinking about, does it?

"So, you and Elly went behind enemy lines. Meanwhile, back home I got on with the job in hand. The trial run was set up. I wonder how much you need to know. The circus was hardly an original idea. In the past the international music business had been the goose that laid the golden egg: world tours with customs clearance winging half tons of hash stashed in cavernous speaker cabinets around the globe. It seems incredible now that the authorities took so long to bust it. But in principle it was a sound idea: legitimate groups who moved around the world carrying significant amounts of luggage with them. The Klondyke Circus Klan may have begun as 'alternative' entertainment, but they had broken into the international circuit and were even respectable enough to warrant sponsors. They also took a lot of equipment with them, and I had a contact backstage. They were the perfect guinea pig: coming from South America, booked in through Shannon for the Dublin Theatre Festival.

"I kept the scale of the thing modest. I was more interested in seeing how the connections held together. The juggling balls were a gift from heaven. As Elly was so eager to describe (you will understand now my consternation at her interest that day in San Francisco), the Klondykes specialized in spectacular finales, juggling symphonies where the whole company joined in. They carried a very large stock of balls. The perfect cargo. Substitute two or three dozen, get them into Shannon and across to the mainland through a Customs more interested in guns than in drugs, and you were home and dry. It was all arranged. All that was needed was for a couple of dozen balls to be made in Dublin and substituted when they arrived. I would be in London to talk expansion and profits. Nothing could go wrong. And if it did, I was nowhere to be found. If they were planning to set me up, then something had to change. It did.

"You and Elly had been in California for four days when I got the call. Klondyke had come through Shannon, no problem. But the man in Dublin paid to substitute the balls hadn't. His work wasn't good enough. My contact insisted it would be spotted. Since I was going to London anyway, would I take another set with me? It stank right from the beginning. Either J.T. had lost his touch or they hadn't let him in on the details. On the other hand, if I had suspected nothing, then there would be nothing to suspect. Mistakes do sometimes happen, even in the best-run deals. I made it clear how much I deplored the inefficiency but agreed to do it. They were offering to deliver the cargo to New York. I told them I would pick it up in person. That way I got a chance to see the three of you together. And to talk to Elly. Now I knew how and where the setup was to take place. If she was in any way involved, then so would she. She would, at the very least, know what to avoid. And top of the list would be a trip to London with me.

"Looking back, I guess I was prepared for everything but what happened. She threw me, right from the moment we met. You had done one hell of a job, Marla. I always meant to congratulate you on it. Elly was glowing, charged with a confidence and energy I hadn't seen in her for ages. She was fabulous that night. So much so that I began to mourn what I had lost. And what you had won. It was over. Simple as that. Except was it? You see, if she really knew nothing about my future, then her timing was one hell of a coincidence. And there had, you will agree, been altogether too many coincidences by now. So I decided to try out the English trip anyway. Just to see what kind of look came into her eyes.

"She hadn't known. I would bet my life on it. Sure, she had a talent for dissembling. But not to that degree. She knew nothing. I swear it. In fact, she was so innocent she almost came with me. Maybe you don't know that. And you probably don't want to hear it, but it's true. In fact, if it hadn't been for your trip to Paris, I think she would have given in and joined me. Your trip to Paris . . . now that interested me, Marla. What was your motive? You knew about London. You could have let her come home that way. Were you so frightened that I would charm her back? Or maybe there was another reason. Maybe you knew something about London that I didn't. Impossible. You and J.T. as confidantes? It didn't fit. Surely this time I was just being paranoid.

"I discarded the possibility. Until you arrived. And Marla, you were a giveaway. Try as you might, you could not disguise your triumph. Success was oozing out of you. Pleasure at my failure. But there was still no proof. It might still have been just coincidence. Then, early next morning, I got a phone call. A little Santa Cruz bird had seen J.T. in the company of a certain large blond woman. He had left her for a couple of hours in a bar in the middle of the night. Don't look so surprised, Marla. Watching is part of the game. All kinds of people are paid to do it. Now, what was I to make of that? On the one hand, your rounded English vowels told me that you and J.T. had spoken less than a dozen words to each other. On the other, I had this story of a night spent in each other's company. You'll forgive me if I assumed the affair was platonic. In which case, what else could you and J.T. possibly have in common — except perhaps Elly's welfare?

"I could still have been wrong. There was one way to find out. Elly was so anxious about my father's 'illness' that she even shed her own tears. Of course she'd go in my place. She knew enough about the business to know there are some arrangements that can't be changed. I told her there was no danger, and she believed me. I even packed her suitcases for her. I told her nothing. I couldn't. Anything I said would have led back to you, and I wanted to watch you for myself. Through Indigo's eyes.

"Your visit to the pay phone told me everything I needed to know. I knew you very well by then. You may not have wanted us to be friends, Marla, but you couldn't stop me worming my way inside your brain and bugging your thoughts. I knew you would call J.T., and I knew what he would tell you. I also knew that you would save her. My only concern was that, in order to do so, you might be tempted to tell her the whole story, then and there. But I banked on the fact that you would want her out of America first, away from my clutches. You had proved good at keeping secrets. I was sure this one could be kept for one more day.

"The rest you know. Or rather you think you know. Because there is one thing left to say, although you are not going to want to hear it. Because in all of this rotten little tale there is only one thing you did wrong, one miscalculation that you made all the way through, right to the bitter end. What happened when you told her, Marla? How much did she hate me then? Oh yes, she was angry. I had lied to and deceived her — believe me, she made that plain when I saw her. But she did see me. It was important enough for her to come and meet me face-to-face. She owed me that much. Why? Didn't you ask yourself that question? Well, the answer is, Marla, that she loved me. And that despite all the shit, there was still something left between us. Something that had to be sorted out. And that's what you can't stand, isn't it? You never could. Right from the beginning you could not accept that there had been something between her and me which was as powerful as the relationship between the two of you. It hurt so much that you simply refused to acknowledge it. That refusal blinded your judgment all along. And that refusal meant that in the end she had to come to me to find out the whole truth.

"And I told her. That afternoon when I picked her up from the train. We drove back here and walked along the beach, walked and talked for hours. Just like you and I now. I told her everything, exactly as I have told you. But the difference was that she believed me. Believed me enough for her to spend the night with me and for us to go out together this morning. To walk together to the falls. What did you think, Marla? That I dragged her screaming from the car and flung her over the edge to stop her from talking? What would be the point of that? And even you, I'm afraid, won't be able to prove it. Alas, there are witnesses to our mutual goodwill. The waitress in the restaurant where we lunched in Ullapool, the girl at the reception desk, the couple we passed on our way across the bridge. All these people, if asked, would talk of a kind of togetherness between us, an ease. I don't want to hurt you more than necessary, Marla. I am not saying that we were reconciled. We were not. There was no future for us. We were both aware of that. There had been too many lies and too much pain. She had been hurt almost beyond healing. Certainly it was over. But with sadness rather than violence.

"And so we return to your original question. What happened this afternoon at the Measach Falls? There is more if you want to hear it. I could tell you for instance that we were talking about you as we crossed the bridge. About why it was you hadn't told her, why you had been so eager to see me damned; eager enough to accept J.T.'s story without thinking to question it. You see, I was not the only one to have hurt her, Marla. She had expected more from you. I was only a lover, but you were a friend. You were sacrosanct, and your lies had damaged her. When we reached the end of the bridge, she fell silent and would not accept my comfort. I thought she needed to be alone. I left her there and started to walk back toward the car. But I remembered she had the keys. I retraced my steps, and that was when I saw her, by the edge of the gorge. There was something in the way she was standing that chilled me. I called out her name. She turned, and it was then that her foot seemed to slip. She lost her balance and fell sideways. It happened so quickly.

"The next thing I remember is her hitting the railing, the post ripping out of the ground and her body going with it. That's when she screamed. I ran to the edge. I even tried to climb down, but the ground was covered in thorns and thistles, and below was a sheer drop — I couldn't even see the bottom. I lay there, hollering her name into the canyon, screeching till the echo hurt my ears. The two people we'd passed on the bridge must have heard my screams. They came running back. It was they who pulled me back from the edge and ran for help. I knew it was too late. We all did. No one could have survived that fall. No one. Not even Elly. Elly . . . the rest you know. That's it. There's nothing left to tell. You have it all, Marla. The truth, the whole truth, and nothing but the truth . . ."

So help you God. The dining room of the Inverlochy Metropole had frozen in time. The tables were empty, and the candle had long since burned out. The silence after his words stretched back and forward into in-

395

finity, I could feel his eyes boring into my brain.

"It's your choice, Marla," he said softly. "Am I really the villain of this piece, paranoid enough to kill twice to ensure silence? Or am I too one of the victims, despised, mistrusted, and framed by those who envied my success . . . envied me Elly. All I —"

But I was not listening. I was looking at his arms resting on the tablecloth and noticing for the first time a crisscross of cuts and scratches which, like stigmata, seemed to have miraculously appeared during the telling of the story. There they were — Exhibit Number 3. Lenny's arms as proof that he had tried to save her. Another vision appeared to me. Of her nails clutching at his flesh as they clung together on the edge before the final swift push sent her spinning down through the crack in the earth's crust. The two images, angel and devil, blurred into one. I returned to the marks on his arms, which had begun to pulsate in front of my eyes. I saw maggots and squirming yellow grubs nosing their way out from the wounds, watched bulges of skin erupting into small volcanoes of pus. I dragged my eyes from the sight. The room rotated on its axis. Welcome to the void.

"Marla." His voice licked its way over my neck, making me shiver with its tenderness. "I know how hard this is for you. But we can't bring her back. All we can do is to let her death make peace between us. I think she would have wanted that."

It was so overwhelmingly tempting, this prospect of forgiving and forgetting. The future ahead of me stretched bleak and empty, so utterly lonely that it seemed unbearable not to be able to share it.

For what it is worth, I had believed Lenny. Just as I had believed J.T. All good stories deserve to be believed, and his had been a cracker, complex, compulsive, consistent, cajoling, filling in the silences that other versions could not reach. So it must have sounded to Elly, and so she must have been charmed again. And yet. And yet . . . what is any good story but a kind of fiction? The spinnings of a fertile brain. How credible it sounds is not the point. The point is that in order to write history you have to choose. When all the source material has been uncovered, that is the historian's job. And I had already made my choice. Although each of the stories may have fitted the facts, only one fitted my feelings. Lenny and I would always be separated by a gorge filled with the sound of rushing water and the corpse of a woman on the rocks. One woman or two, it hardly mattered, so long as one of them was Elly. After all the lies — whoever they belonged to — only the facts remained. Fallen or pushed — and there was, despite his innuendo, no other possible alternative — it made no difference. The line of her life had led through Lenny to death. There could be no forgetting or forgiving that.

Now, at last, I could look at him. The face had recovered some of its former sleekness. The eyes were sharp again, and the skin had regained its color. This was a man flushed with the pleasure of performance.

"You look sick with tiredness, Marla. Why don't you go to bed? There's no need to say anything. I just wanted you to listen, and for that I'm grateful. Everything else can wait till morning."

I opened my eyes into the sunshine of his smile. Brotherly love. He was, once again, invincible. Everything else could wait till morning. What else was there?

"You're right," I said thickly. "I do need sleep. Good night, Lenny. I'll see you tomorrow."

I began the Long March. From the table across the room, through the heavy swing door out to the reception desk, and up interminable stairs to a dimly lit corridor to Room 22.

I locked the door behind me and lay down on the bed without bothering to remove my clothes. Sleep, near to instant unconsciousness, rushed up to greet me. As I gave myself up to it I heard Lenny's words — "Everything else can wait till morning." And in a corner of my mind I saw a dark cubbyhole at the top of a Paris cupboard. Five kilos of high-grade cocaine. Of course. Out of Lenny's two lovers, only one was dead. There was, for him, comfort in sorrow. Tomorrow. It could wait until tomorrow.

Seventeen

It was early that morning they found her.

I woke at 5:00 A.M., as if by alarm, to find the pain lying in wait for me, an ambush on the edge of sleep. It descended like a physical attack, a poisonous cloud of despair, the weight of it pinning me to the bed, making it hard for me to breathe. I struggled against it, driven by an even greater fear of paralysis, of being discovered hours later by some scuttling maid or, even worse, by the dapper figure of a morning Lenny.

I heaved myself off the bed and into the bathroom, where I put my head under the cold tap. The shock stunned me into a few precious moments of alertness. I used them to change my clothes and get myself out of the room before the walls began closing in.

Downstairs, the dawn had made little impression on the nooks and crannies of the mahogany reception room. The front doors were locked. I pushed my way through the heavy fire doors into the bar, where stale beer and cigar smoke lingered in the air.

The French windows had a key in them. I turned it and was released into a gray morning and a long slope of lawn down to steps onto the beach.

My feet crunched shingle. Out at sea a wind was driving long white furrows into the shore. The air was sharp with the taste of salt. I walked down toward the water, feet slipping on wet pebbles, dragging my sorrow with me. At the edge, where the waves sighed over the stones, I stopped, then walked a little more. I felt the cold of the sea on the soles of my feet. Then the water crept up over my ankles, curious and playful. In my head, a percussion of blood beating in tune with the waves. I took a few more steps. To the right a piece of driftwood pounded onto the beach, dumped by a rush of surf. I thought of a body, pulling sluggishly in shallow water, facedown, the fabric of a skirt billowing free. On the feet a flash of white plastic. Then I saw a second corpse, larger than the first, fair hair matted and dark with water, limbs bloated, while small fishes darted in and out from under the face, a meal already in progress. Together we gorged, they and I, on images of death and oblivion. The water sucked at my trouser legs, reaching greedily for my knees.

I had begun to cry, although I do not remember when. The horizon blurred with the rain of my tears, and the images washed away. The blur turned to blindness, closing up my eyes and clogging my nostrils. Elly. The loss of her blotted out the whole world, an abstract force, so much itself, so selfish that it brooked no competition. I became aware of a sudden relief, as if the real pain had come from resistance. She had been part of me: part of me was dead. I heard round me a kind of wailing, my own voice like the roar of the sea. The water clutched at my thighs. It seemed it would go on for-ever, this drowning. How long had it taken her? Would I feel the same instant of extinc-tion now, if I opened my arms and lungs to the sea? It seemed so close, so easy. But something inside me held on and would not be released. A symbolic death mine, nothing more. And so, eventually, like water after high tide, the sorrow and the tears began to recede and I pulled myself back from the ocean.

When it was past, I examined myself for damage. I found I was squatting in the surf, my chest pressing close to my knees, arms locked around my body. A vise grip. So tight I could feel a pain in my ribs, cutting out the chill of the water. I uncurled a little and felt the wind tugging at my skin, drying salt on salt, spray upon tears. I was quieter, more real. After a while I looked down at my watch. Seven-twenty A.M. I had been at sea for hours.

I stood up slowly, unlocking my arms and lifting them above my head. My body felt light, like in that children's game where someone pushes down on your head, then suddenly releases you. I stood on tiptoe and stretched and stretched until my muscles sang. I pushed my head down onto my chest and felt rivulets of strain running down through my shoulders. Then I lifted my head and let it fall backward until all I could see was the sky, the world upside down. My body had been clamped shut for so long holding in the pain. Even in sleep I had been rigid. Now at last, in this early morning with the world deserted, now I could let go. I began to do a few simple exercises, stretching, flexing, pushing into the wind, taking long deep breaths until my heart was beating hollow in my chest and the blood pumped at the sides of my temples. I became almost lightheaded. I, me, Marla, was feeling these things. My muscles, my limbs, my rib cage expanding and contracting, breathing in my life. I could mourn Elly forever. I could love her as hopelessly as you can love only the dead. But I was still me, still here now, alive — and she was not. I could not share her death, not even by experiencing my own. I could not black myself out for her. The realization of that swept over me like a last unbearable wave of pain, but I held my ground, and in its wake it brought unexpected comfort.

I stood for a while getting my breath back, letting my body settle. Then I turned back toward the land. Beneath me the gray-and-white façade of the hotel sat, brooding and stained by salt winds, its curtained windows like closed eyelids overlooking the sea. All, that is, but one. Because there, in the middle of the third floor, out on a stone and iron balcony, stood Lenny, immobile, watching, trespassing on my sorrow.

I whipped away from him, feeling like some child caught in forbidden games in a dark corner. I had no way of knowing how long he had been there, or how much of my catharsis he had witnessed, but the idea of his cold observation drove me mad with panic. And there was something else; even over the distance it was impossible to mistake its meaning. Animosity, like electricity, pulsating across the sands. In that second of silent communication there was more truth than in all his worries of the night before. The knowledge was like chain mail; it must be worn next to my skin always. That way there could be no surprise attacks. I turned back, but he was gone, curtains drawn again. I made my way up the beach to the hotel. In the dining room, breakfast was being served. The day had begun.

I was sitting over cold coffee when the police officer arrived. I knew immediately why he had come. Lenny was waiting in the lobby, smart trousers and lamb's-wool sweater, new and blue as his eyes. The policeman watched us greet each other: half smiles, a quick hand on my shoulder. Collusion. Comfort exchanged. Ours was a private battle. In public we would appear friends.

The morgue was in Ullapool, the best part of an hour's drive from the hotel. They had taken the body there early this morning, after it had been carried up from the gorge, found at first light half a mile downstream. That much we were told. We asked no further questions. In the back of the white car we sat together in mutual neutrality, both of us conserving our energy for what was to come. Around us stretched miles and miles of purple heather. We were driving the same road I had traveled yesterday. Yesterday by this . . . But I would not think of that. Ullapool, the policeman told us in a vain attempt to lighten the silence in the car, was one of the Highlands' more interesting towns. Founded by the British as a seaport in the early eighteenth century, it had become an important embarkation point for thousands of emigrants, survivors of the highland clearances, heading for America. The ships had been run by men out to make a fast buck, and they had packed the people like rats belowdecks. It was a dark memory for Ullapool and for the whole of Scotland. Nowadays the place had happier associations. Hands across the sea. The port was used by Russian trawler fleets, and it was not such a strange sight to come across Scots and Russian fishermen drinking in the same bar. No cold war here, although of course once in a while someone would drink too much and have to be "looked after" for the night.

He chattered on, encouraged by the odd prompting from Lenny. Strangely enough, the horror stories were not upsetting. Sometimes stories are the only things you can listen to. Interesting, I thought, how quickly history becomes stories rather than reality, one step already from the truth. Was that how Elly's death would be? Another small piece of Ullapool history to be related to next year's visitors as a modern-day tragedy.

The police station was a large granite house constructed to withstand the weather, with the surreal addition of a palm tree outside, tethered to the ground by a ship's hawser, testament to a warm gulf stream in a cold climate. The morgue was a makeshift affair hidden away in the bowels of the building. The sergeant at the desk seemed familiar, yesterday's gentle questioner. I studied his face as we shook hands, noticing a small scar over the left eye. Given the sleepy nature of the town, I couldn't help thinking this must be a leftover from some childhood bicycle accident rather than the trophy of gangland warfare. On the other hand . . . a vodka bottle smashed in drunken Cossack fury? Anything to keep my mind off the task in hand. His manner was friendly, the Scottish caress softening the bald horror of his words.

"What we are looking for is positive identification that the body is that of Eleanor Cameron." We were not to be too upset, he added. Although the body had been badly battered by the fall, it had not suffered the ravages of time in the water. To my unspoken question he went on to say that though there had been no postmortem as yet, it seemed certain that death had been instantaneous. Her neck had been broken by the fall. He had talked our way down the corridor, and we were now standing by the door. Were we ready, he asked. I nodded, and Lenny put a hand on my arm. I did not look at him.

The door opened onto a small room, obviously some kind of doctor's surgery converted for the occasion, all white with scrubbed surfaces and a sink, the smell of hospitals and public baths. In the center was a trolley. On it a body covered by a white cloth. I could make out the shape of small sharp toes, but there was no label hanging out from under the feet, as in the movies. I had hoped to be protected by the familiarity of such images of other people's deaths, people whom I didn't know or care about. But when it came down to it they were, indeed, just make-believe, and here in front of me was the real thing, seen for the first time. I walked to the head of the trolley, taking the lead because I could not bear to stand and watch. The policeman marked my step. At the top he stood by me, ready. I nodded, and he pulled back the sheet. I steeled myself and looked down. Elly.

I don't know what I had expected: crushed bone and open flesh, a scream of death amid cruel lacerations. But it was not like that. Yes, she was damaged. There was a long gash along her left temple, and puffing and bruising on the left cheek, but it was not unbearable. On the contrary, her skin had a smooth, almost waxy quality to it, and whatever fear there may have been in the eyes, they were closed now. Her very fragility was lovely. She looked almost peaceful, as if death had resolved the pain and the conflict. Elly in marble. It suited her. I put out a hand but withdrew it again quickly. Cold flesh would destroy the illusion. And it was just an illusion. I stepped away, making room for Lenny. The policeman was watching me. "Yes," I said. "That is Elly Cameron." I began to walk toward the door. Behind me I heard a sharp, theatrical intake of breath from Lenny. And I tasted bile in my stomach.

Afterward, over the inevitable cup of institutionalized tea, there was more to be said. Separate statements, just for the record. And a few leading questions. What could I tell them about Elly's state of mind? Was she at all depressed, in any kind of trouble, perhaps? Any reason why she might think of . . . ? No. None. None at all. I would not even hear the word spoken. What poisonous seeds had Lenny planted in their little brains? Ridiculous. Not her. Not Elly. What about Lenny then? How long had I known him? Had there to my knowledge been any problems between them? Once again it was casually put. And casually answered. No, nothing I could think of. What else could I say? Oh yes, I knew the other story by heart, but even if I told them, they would never catch him. Not Lenny. He would squirm and charm his way off their hook, leaving me in his place, dangling on the skewer of my violent jealousies and previous unstable mental history. What was it J.T. had said about trapping Lenny? No, the Ullapool police force were not the right fishermen. This one needed larger bait.

It didn't take long. They were easily satisfied. A holiday tragedy. They had seen it all before. The only really controversial thing about it was the rottenness of the wooden post that had torn out of the ground under her weight. That would make the local news for a season or two, agitation on the borough council. Everything else was technical. Contact had been made with the Cameron family in the Sudan. It was not clear whether Mr. Cameron himself would be able to get away, but his wife was taking the first plane out and should be with them in forty-eight hours. It was to be expected. Patrick Cameron had been too busy for his daughter's life. Why should he find time for her death? Dorothy would sweep in, stricken with grief and immaculately groomed. That she had hardly seen her daughter in the last nine years would be irrelevant. She had given up on Elly a long time ago, unable to bear the fact that her only child refused to live life the way her mother had planned it. Elly's death would return her to the fold. "A desperate tragedy . . . such a waste . . . my daughter, who would, if she had lived . . ." et cetera, et cetera. Dorothy would mourn the Elly she had always wanted, not the Elly she had had. And any aggression toward Lenny, the man who had stood by and watched her daughter fall, would undergo a sea change when faced by the power of his Princeton manners and his upwardly mobile charm. The apartment, the house, the chain of stores, it would all be Mozart to her ears. In her mind Dorothy would make a company director of him, endowing her daughter with a posthumous respectability. Let Lenny stay and meet her, hold her hand and listen to her revisionist memories. Their stories would soothe each other.

It was lunchtime back at the hotel. The thought of yet another meal together was more than I could stomach. But there was still unfinished business. Lenny was mind reading.

"How about a walk on the beach, Marla? Get some fresh air after the car?" It was, in the circumstances, an offer I could not refuse.

The tide was out now. Shingle petered out into sand, grubby and gray, decorated with crisscross patterns of seagull prints and wormholes. There were mounds of fresh seaweed strewn over the shore, pulpy and wet. That, and the gusting wind pushing off the sea, made it the perfect British landscape, sand in the eyes and skins tinged blue with the cold: childhood without rose-colored spectacles. I pulled my jacket around me. What, I wondered, would an East Coast American make of it all? If indeed he was from the East Coast. It seemed to me the more I learned about Lenny, the less I knew who he really was. Still, after all this time, the single consistent fact about him was his charm, and that was the one quality which could not be believed. We walked on in silence, our feet making small sucking noises on the wet sand. He was waiting for me to speak. He could wait for the rest of his life. After a mile or so we came upon an upturned fishing boat halfway up the beach. I directed my feet toward it. Clusters of barnacles clung to its hull. I picked a smooth patch and leaned back against it. On this rock will I build my church. It was time to talk.

"Well, Marla," he said at last.

"Well what?"

"I was wondering what your silence meant."

I shrugged. "Maybe it means there's nothing more to say."

"Is that right? Nothing more. No thoughts, no questions about last night?"

"No." I said. "None."

"So, you believed me?"

I scuffed sand with my foot. I would not lie to him. At least not on this. "I said nothing to the police, Lenny. Isn't that enough?"

"Is it all you're willing to give?"

"It's all that I have," I said bluntly. "Her death takes everything but that."

He looked at me for a moment, then nodded. "Then I accept it. And I'm grateful to you for not lying to me."

"What would be the point? As you yourself said, it's over now. I don't mean to be rude, Lenny, but I don't see what else we have to talk about."

"Don't you, Marla?" He frowned. "Don't you really? I would have thought you had realized the kind of danger you were in."

I had made a mistake. It was not just his charm that was consistent. It was also his unpredictability. Inside me a small depth charge was released. "Tell me," I said.

"It's very simple. You have something that doesn't belong to you. Sooner or later the people who own it are going to want it back. And then they'll come looking for you." He paused to let the words sink in. "I must admit, Marla, I underestimated you. I never thought you'd do it. Take it away from Elly, yes, but not bring it with you. I figured you'd leave it in New York somewhere. Stash it in the apartment maybe — which is why I made the place unavailable. I didn't relish a sudden police visit the day after you'd left. Or send it back where it came from, mail J.T. a ticket for some left luggage somewhere. I tell you, I was pretty impressed when Elly told me you'd carried it with you.

"Now I understand that this isn't the perfect time to talk about it. But believe me there isn't going to be a better one. And if we don't talk, then it may be too late. God damn it, Marla, I'm not ready to identify a second English corpse."

It was a speech designed to cause panic. I swallowed. "Are you trying to frighten me, Lenny?"

"No. But I am trying to explain to you that business is business. Especially in this profession. And that what may be over for you isn't over for everyone. What did you imagine, Marla? That they'd just let you walk away with the best part of five kilos of high-grade cocaine? Because at a rough guess that's how much you've got stashed away in those precious little balls. Purchase price maybe fifty-five, sixty thousand dollars. Street price? Well, I don't know exact going rates in England, but let's say five, maybe six times as much. At a conservative estimate, let's call it three hundred thousand dollars. Certainly, you'll agree, enough to put me away for a satisfying number of years. Especially here and now. This was a professional operation, remember. They'd done their homework. Picked their customs post with care. Your Iron Lady has been pushing for stiffer penalties for years. With a lot of success. Things have gotten much tougher here. No one gets the benefit of the doubt anymore, even first offenders. I should be flattered they went to so much trouble. Spent so much money on me. They could have gotten a hit man cheaper. Then at least they would have gotten value for money. This way they don't have the money or the satisfaction. Now I suppose they could just write it off to experience. But I wouldn't if I were them. All it needs is for J.T. to whisper your name and my bet is, when they find out Elly is dead, they'll come looking for you. And I don't see them leaving without what they came for."

Behind his head a streak of blue sky was sandwiched between rain clouds. Silver linings. Important to keep looking for them. It was my turn to speak. It would be dishonest to say I was not frightened. But I was not going to show it. Not to him. "So, what should I do, Lenny? What would you do in my place?"

"That's a tough one, Marla. I suppose it depends on what you want. If I were you . . . ? Well, I guess it might go through my head that I could use the spoils to get back at those I thought were responsible. Me, for example. Yeah, if I were you I might consider that as a course of action. But I would discard it pretty quickly. It's a house of cards, Marla. The whole thing. Pull one out and they all come tumbling down. On you as well as me. You've been honest with me. Now I'll do you the same courtesy. If you ever tried to use the cocaine to undermine me in any way whatsoever, I wouldn't hesitate to incriminate others. You and Elly.

And that would destroy us all. But then, of course, you know that. Which is why you won't do it. So, what other options are open to you? Well, you could try selling it yourself. I wouldn't advise it though. You're a clever woman, Marla, but I have to tell you you wouldn't make it as a dealer. The first whiff of business and they'd be down on you so hard you wouldn't know what hit you. Of course, you could always just invite them in, offer it back to them. That's a possibility. Although I should warn you you'd be a lousy insurance risk for a long time to come. In this business tidiness is next to godliness, and you'd be one hell of an eyesore. So, what does that leave us with? Well, you can always get rid of it. Destroy it. In fact, that might even be the morally correct thing to do. But I can't see you doing it. It would achieve nothing. And anyway, somehow I don't figure you for a moralist. You have too much imagination for that."

"So, what's left? Well, as it happens I do have a suggestion. I expect you knew I would. You see, when I asked Elly to take that flight for me, she didn't agree to do it totally for love. Neither did I ask her to. I offered her money. I hope that doesn't shock you. After all, it was only fair. I owed her. Not just for the shop but for other things, other favors done. You may think me a bastard, Marla, and you may be right, but among my many faults meanness is not high on the list. When you have as much money as I do it would be an ungracious, not to say dangerous, failing. I offered her a share of my profits. And the profits, had the deal gone through, were high. I told her I would give her thirty thousand dollars. Not a fortune, I admit, but enough to ease her passage home. Thirty thousand to carry a set of juggling balls across the Atlantic. Except, of course, she never took them. You did. So, by rights, the money belongs to you anyway. Part of the deal.

"What I am suggesting, Marla, is that I buy them from you. No bribery, just business. I, you see, could find a use for them. Revenge, as you well know, is not a pleasure limited to one party only. I am not offering you charity. I'm simply offering you what you have earned. As for me — well, I'd be getting them cheap. Half the market price. Then when they come looking for you, you can simply tell them the truth. They will, I promise, believe you. But I'll promise you something else. If you agree to the arrangement, I will make sure they never come for you at all. Ever. That's part of the deal. On that you have my word. And then it really will be over. You and I need never see each other again. I figure Elly would have approved of it too. You were more her next of kin than I was. If it had been her money, it would be yours now. So what do you say, Marla? I didn't want it to be like this. And I know that money won't, can't ease your sorrow. But it might save you from other kinds of pain. Well . . . do you want some time to think it over?"

But I had already done my thinking. Thirty thousand dollars. The amount it took to buy my silence, to pay for Elly's death. Except it wasn't that simple. There were set rates for such things. Payments for death. Blood money. And I knew all of them. *Wergeld*. One of the foundation stones of Anglo-Saxon justice. If you killed a man, you paid a tithe to his kinfolk. The law upheld it. "You were more her next of kin than I." As kin I could demand the going rate. People were valued according to their status. Serf, freeman, noble. There were documents to prove it. As much as twelve shillings for a noble, a fortune befitting their importance. Translate that into contemporary wealth and thirty thousand was an insult. Elly was worth much more than Lenny could ever pay. And there were other rules. If you didn't have the money or if, for instance, you tried to deny your guilt, then there were alternative forms of justice. I knew the laws. Who better to enforce them? And what of my own safety? What of his stories of vengeful visitations? Well, there were only two people in the world who knew what I had in my possession. Lenny and J.T. Would J.T. tell and allow me to be destroyed, or would he perhaps stay silent and use the knowledge to spin another web to catch his prey? If the cocaine was missing, why shouldn't they assume it was in Lenny's hands rather than mine? J.T. and Lenny. Once again I was faced with the choice of villain and hero. Black and white. Or maybe it was more a choice of shades of gray. It didn't matter anymore. I had decided. I took a breath, mighty and strong. Beowulf approaching Grendel — "from whose eyes there came a weird light." Strange I hadn't noticed the resemblance before.

"Lenny, I don't know how to tell you this. But there isn't anything to discuss. I would love to take your money. Elly's inheritance. But I can't. Because I don't have anything to sell."

His face didn't change. I looked into the same expression of sympathetic patience. Even the voice was still persuasive. "I don't understand. What do you mean?"

"I mean I don't have your cocaine. I never did. Or at least only for a couple of hours. You were right to underestimate me. I don't have that kind of courage. I destroyed it."

"When?" Now it began to show. A tight, icy word, its buttocks pinned together.

"Right after I saw Elly off on her plane. I went straight to the nearest airport loo and flushed the whole lot down the toilet."

A flurry of sand danced its way across Lenny's feet, across his pale cream Italian shoes, luscious and expensive. Behind him the sliver of blue sky had been squashed by thickening cloud. Unless the wind changed, it would rain soon. All this I noticed in the split second it took Lenny to respond. And he was, I must tell you, a little less serene now. We were getting through to something. And it felt like anger.

"I think you'd better tell me more, Marla. Explain to me exactly how you did it."

I felt my throat constrict, and my voice when it came was a little thinner, a little more anxious. Lenny had boasted that he had X-ray vision of my soul. And certainly he had proved himself adept at lie detecting. But lies sometimes cause the same tremors as guilt and fear. Even Lenny might be hard-pressed to recognize the difference.

Everyone else had told their stories. Now it was my turn. Short but sweet. "You know it anyway. Indigo was there. She must have told you. From her seat she had a perfect view of the loo door. She could tell you when I went in. And how long I spent there. You of all people, Lenny, must know that I am hardly one of the world's vainest women. I'm not in the habit of wasting time in ladies' powder rooms. I went through the door, locked myself into one of the cubicles, took out the balls, and split them open one by one . . ."

"What did you use to cut the leather?"

"A Swiss Army knife. I've had it for years. Normally I keep it in my suitcase, but I had transferred it to my handbag that morning." I paused, in case of further questions, but he said nothing. He was looking at me very hard. "Inside the balls were plastic bags, tightly packed. I pulled them out. It wasn't hard. Then I broke them open and emptied the contents down the loo. I flushed the toilet twice to make sure it was all gone, wiped off any powder I had spilled with a tissue, flushed that away too, then packed the empty leather containers into the bottom of my holdall."

The need to convince brought pictures to my mind, giving substance to the fiction. I watched myself, hands shaking slightly, digging my way through the soft leather, scooping out the bags, and staring in awful fascination as the stream of crystalline powder tumbled into the water and sank slowly to the bottom. Afterward, as I stood by the washbasin, my face looked one hundred years old in the strip lighting. A mixture of triumph and fear. After all, I had almost done it.

"I left the cubicle, washed my face and hands, brushed my hair, and went out, pushing the plastic bags into the tampon incinerator. Oh, and one more thing. I threw away the Swiss Army knife just before I went through the departure gates. I was worried they might find it in the security check and confiscate it as an offensive weapon. I suspect Indigo might have missed that little detail in her report. She was awfully busy checking timetables to Zurich."

"And how long did you say all of this took you?" He ignored the jibe.

I thought fast. "Not long. Ten, maybe fifteen minutes at most." Assuming Indigo could read a watch, we could not be so far out in our estimations. In which case it would at least give him pause for thought.

"What did you do with the leather casings?" He didn't miss a trick.

423

"Dumped them in three different litter bins in Charles de Gaulle airport. I had time to spare, waiting for Elly to arrive at her hotel. There was no point in going into Paris. I knew I would have to go to London. As soon as the receptionist told me she'd checked in, I took the first plane to Heathrow. The rest you know from her."

I felt a spot of rain on my hand. Not the fine Scottish drizzle of yesterday, misting the landscape, but a fat, heavy droplet. We would get wet. Lenny was still looking at me, not a trace of emotion on his face. He doesn't believe me, I thought. But he can't know for sure.

"If it makes you feel any better, you were right," I said quietly. "It had nothing to do with morality. I just wasn't willing to risk getting busted for you. Maybe because your fear quota is so small, you assume the same in others. That was never my kind of bravery. Elly's perhaps, but not mine. I would have taken your money, Lenny. With pleasure. I'm sorry I can't."

"Oh, don't be sorry, Marla. I don't blame you. I just don't know whether I believe you."

"Why should you doubt me?" Good return. Calm and steady.

"Because we're both historians, Marla.

And we both know the tricks of our trade. Don't you remember our first real conversation? The problems of fact and fiction. Do you ever believe anything until it's proved? Either by fact or by corroboration through at least one other source. So, you see, I do have a problem. Because the only other source I have is contradictory. It's very simple, Marla. You tell me one thing. Elly told me another. You say you destroyed the balls. She said you brought them with you. 'They're safe. Safe and nearby.' Those, according to Elly, were your very words. You were obviously lying to one of us. And somehow I don't think it was her."

In my mind church bells of victory chimed. I had won. If that was the only thing Lenny knew, then he knew nothing. I laughed, hoping that it sounded incredulous. "Oh, Lenny, you didn't expect me to tell Elly the truth about it, did you? Last night you accused me of making mistakes, of underestimating the power of your relationship. I hadn't realized, you said, that she would come to you to find out the final truth. You almost got it right. I did underestimate it. At first. But not by then. By then she'd made it clear exactly how much you meant to her. Even I could see that. I told her I still had the cocaine because I thought she — we — might need protecting against you. I knew you would be angry. And I thought the cocaine might be a kind of revenge for you. After all, you were in my brain, weren't you? Didn't it ever occur to you that I had crawled into yours too?

"Yes, I expected you to want it. And if you thought I had it, then you would have to bargain with me. With us. And whatever you felt, that meant you couldn't hurt her . . ." I hit the last words harder than I had intended. We both registered the splinters in my voice. But I couldn't stop now. The story wasn't finished. "The cocaine was my guarantee that you would look after her. It didn't work out that way. But at least I tried. I told Elly a lie because I knew she would repeat that lie to you. And I knew you'd believe her. And that way I could be sure of her safety. All right? Makes sense, doesn't it? So don't make me out to be more stupid than I am, Lenny. That would be your mistake."

The rain was falling harder now. But neither of us moved. He shook his head. "You still think I killed her, don't you?" And his voice was hushed.

"Well, didn't you?" I heard the words coming out of my mouth. I had not given permission for their release. Somewhere inside my head there had been a revolution, and the extremists had taken over. So be it. You can't stand in the way of history. I blinked the rain out of my eyes. Behind his frozen gaze something stirred. He made a small gesture of hopelessness with his hands.

"I can't talk to you, Marla. You're a madwoman. You're so eaten up with hating me that you can't see straight. Or maybe it's not just me. Maybe it's all men. I don't know."

"Don't be coy, Lenny. Why don't you just come out and say it? You'd really like to cast me as the raving lesbian, wouldn't you? Loathing anyone who dared to touch her, punishing them in any way I could. It would make the story so simple. Well, I hate to disappoint you, but it's a little more complex than that."

I felt my voice break. Damn and blast. I did not want it to be like this. Not with him. I turned away. All I could see was rain.

"Look at me." And his voice was so quiet I could hardly hear it. Sorrow or fury? "Look at me." This time I felt raw nerves. I looked.

"I'll say this one more time and one more time only. I did not kill her. Sure, I was in part responsible for her death. But then so were we all. You as well as J.T. Every single act that led her to the edge of that ravine in some way killed her. And if we were to be honest, then you figured pretty large in that action. Do you understand that, Marla? If there is blame, we all share it. You are as guilty as I am. But the difference is that I'll get over it. And you never will. There'll always be another Elly for me. To soothe the ache if not to heal it. Somebody willing to love me. But what about you, Marla? Who's waiting for you?

"And I'll tell you something else. You'd better not be lying about the cocaine. Because if I find out — and I will find out — and if I'm the man you think I am, then what's another body more or less? Didn't Elly tell me how you once made a suicide attempt? What's on your medical record now? Unstable personality. You were devastated by her death. Everyone knows that. Sorrow sometimes drives people to desperate ends. Like walking into the sea, perhaps? I'd be very careful if I were you, Marla. Not believing me makes your life very dangerous."

He took a step forward. A bolt of panic ran through me. Surely not even Lenny could afford a trail of bodies in his wake? I stuffed my hands into my jacket pockets to stop them shaking. The world was dark in his shadow. "I'm going back to the hotel," I said in a loud voice. "Let me pass."

For a moment he didn't move. Then, with a slight smile, as if my fear amused him, he stepped to one side. I walked past him, heart thumping, eyes straight ahead. I was facing into the rain, water driving against me, soaking my clothes and plastering my hair close to my head. Above me the sky groaned thunder. It was Lenny's storm: his black magic. I did not look back. Only when I had reached the protection of the hotel on my left did I turn. He was nowhere to be seen. I went in through the French windows, past an astonished waiter drying glasses behind the bar. In my room I called the Ullapool police. Did they need me for anything further? No, I was free to go. I took a shower and dressed quickly, stuffing the wet clothes in my bag. At reception I avoided the eye of the youth princess as I paid my bill. As she bent down to find me a piece of writing paper, I saw that Lenny's key was no longer on its hook. At the desk I composed a hurried note to Dorothy: a stupid scrawled message of condolence explaining that I had to be back in London to mark exam papers, but I would call her from there. I gave it to the girl and left.

The drive to Inverness took hours, crawling behind caravans, through horizontal rain, I just made the 7:30 night train. Once again there was no sleep. Only this time the words wrapped round the wheels of the train were Lenny's.

It was early morning when I arrived home, humping my bag up the hill from the tube. The trees along Parkson Road were ragged with late summer growth, the houses neat and brightly painted: a little like toy town after the Scottish wilds. The scale was comforting. Lace curtains and milk bills. I was glad to be back. Too tired to worry. Too tired to notice. Not as I came through the main door of the house, nor as I climbed the stairs. Even as I fumbled for the right keys, there was safety in the musty smell of the stair carpet. It was not until I put out a hand toward the lock and felt the door swing open in front of me, inviting me into the devastation of what had once been my home, that I understood how naïve I had been, and how, when someone wants something badly enough, there are all manner of ways in which they can go out to get it.

He, or rather they — for this had to be the work of more than one pair of malicious hands — had done an expert job. In the living room the sofa and chair had been disemboweled, their guts scattered over upturned tables and piles of books. In the bedroom every drawer and cupboard had been emptied, my filing cabinet dismantled. The kitchen was even worse. Systematic destruction. Anything large enough to have contained the cocaine had been overturned or smashed. Had they seriously believed I would have hidden it in the sugar jar? A kind of paralysis descended. In the living room I sat heavily on what remained of a chair, trying to adjust to the scope of the violence around me. Burglary as violation. The stubborn courage which had fueled my Scottish lies seemed in danger of deserting me now.

"You'd better not be lying about the cocaine. Because if I find out — and I will find out . . ." Had he already known then that the cupboard was bare, or had this been the result of last night's work? A quick job for the boys as I sat watching the moon from an Intercity sleeper. Maybe he had even expected me to be here. That last idea made my flesh crawl. Then I thought of something that made me feel even worse. The telephone was buried under the wreckage, the receiver off the hook, but the whining sound told me it was still connected. Eventually the dialing tone returned. I punched the buttons too fast, and the number didn't connect. I made myself do it again, more slowly. It rang. I imagined it sitting on the little Queen Anne table next to the armchair.

" 'Ello." A woman's voice, high and singing like a bird trill.

"Gem?" Alive and well and living in Paris. *"Qui est-il?"*

"It's me, Marla." I think I was laughing. I must have sounded like a lunatic. "Are you all right, *Grandmère?*"

"All right? *Bien sûr.* I am all right. *Qu'est-ce que tu penses?* Elaine has poisoned me? Where are you, Marla? You sound very strange. You said . . ."

She jabbered on, talking, as always, too loudly, as if she could never quite believe that the mouthpiece wasn't really a megaphone. No, there had been no visitors. No one came to visit such an old lady. Even her own family. My cousin Etienne had called to say . . . I stopped listening, and the wave of paranoia began to recede. "Safe and nearby." Those had been the words I had used to Elly. To Lenny I had sworn I'd never left Charles de Gaulle Airport. Two lies might surely make a truth. Why should he bother Gem? He knew nothing of her, not even her name. I interrupted the lava flow of words gently. There was someone at the door. I would have to go, but I would ring again soon.

It was only as I untangled the cord to put the phone back on the hall table that I noticed the answering machine. It was lying on the floor, its working days over. But whoever had smashed it had not been interested in its contents. The tape was still there. I prized it out of the machine and carried it back into the bedroom. Amid the mountain of papers that used to be in my filing cabinet, I found a small tape recorder which I used to record lecture notes. Too small to contain drugs, it had been left intact. I slid the tape in and wound it back. Elly's voice jumped into the room, giving me again the address of the Inverlochy hotel. I listened in a kind of horror. A pause. Then a bleep. Nothing. Another bleep. Then, incredibly, Elly's voice again — but different, tired and still. "I think you'd better come, Marla. As soon as you can. And bring the luggage with you. He wants it." Silence.

I grabbed the machine and whirled back the tape. Again the bleep, again her voice in my hands, flat and subdued. "I think you'd better come, Marla. As soon as you can." And frightened? Was that the shadow I could hear stalking the words? There was something hollow inside her. Where had she been when she made that call? In her room

433

with Lenny sitting over her? Or at the reception desk, a secret hurried call . . . or in the lobby of an Ullapool restaurant while Lenny paid the bill? And was it fear, or simply tiredness, the end of a long story? I would never know. That was part of the pain, the fact that her last days belonged to him and not to me. But for a few words . . .

Lenny had been wrong when he said the money was her bequest to me. It was not. My inheritance was what I held in my hands. An order for the disposition of property. "Bring the luggage with you. He wants it." Elly Cameron's last will and testament. Don't worry, Elly. He will get it. That I promise you.

Eighteen

Elly's funeral took place a week later in a large rambling cemetery somewhere near the North Circular Road in London. It was a quiet, tasteful affair. Dorothy cried throughout the service, leaning on her husband's arm. Patrick Cameron, on a flying visit, stood stony faced, thinking perhaps about business. I shed no tears. Neither did I attend the reception afterward, held at Dorothy's sister's house in Pinner. I stayed on for a while after everyone had left. The day was golden, warm, and sunny. The end of August, and already some of the trees were turning copper, their leaves beginning to fall.

For two months I did nothing. Life returned to a dull, plodding normality. There was a time — just after the funeral — when I thought I was being followed. A man with dark hair and a variety of leather jackets seemed to keep crossing my path. One evening on my way home from work I recognized him standing beside me on a rush-hour platform just as the train was pulling in, and I had to force myself back into the crowd to get away from him. Another time, he — or someone very like him — accompanied me to Kew Gardens for the day. I contemplated digging a few holes to give him some kind of satisfaction, but in the end I just lay on the grass and watched the sun arch its way over the sky. By the time I got home he was gone. And by mid-October he seemed to have faded away altogether. If anyone replaced him, he or she was much better at their job, because I never spotted them.

Term came and dragged on — another bunch of acned, eager faces waiting for London to explode in their laps, a fireworks display of life, sex, and drugs. They found me boring, I could tell.

I heard from no one. No letters with American stamps, no phone calls, no formal or informal visitors. It was as if it had never happened.

Winter came early, crisp and cold, with the weatherman forecasting a white Christmas. On the last Saturday in November I took a train to Dover and then the hovercraft to Calais. It was a miserable day, wet and gray, and the crossing made me travel sick. From Calais to Paris, where Gem fussed and grumbled over me, told me I was looking dreadful, wasted and sick. She force-fed me broth and vitamins and asked me all kinds of searching questions, to which I lied. That night in the spare room I lay awake waiting for the house to sleep. Then, in the darkness, I dragged the chair to the cupboard and pushed my hand into the cave at the back. The bag was covered in dust. The balls felt heavier than I recalled. I sat cradling them in my lap: my inheritance, to do with as I liked. I packed them at the bottom of my holdall, covering them with a couple of bottles of wine and a hideous silk scarf that Gem had forced upon me. Braving the storm of her displeasure, I cut a long weekend short and went home the next day, arriving back in Dover on the last boat. In the customs hall, no one stopped me. Back in my castle, I locked the balls in the bottom drawer of a new filing cabinet. Unless there was another sack of Carthage, no one would find them.

Then I waited a little longer. It had become almost a kind of pleasure, the anticipation, like gratification deferred. I knew, you see, exactly what I was going to do. I had known it for months, ever since that first night when I lay curled and uncomfortable on a mattress half disemboweled, the bedroom door barricaded shut with the remains of a bookcase. To overcome my fear, I had set my imagination to work on revenge. The idea was perfected over an age of sleepless nights, shaped and polished until it shone. It was with me always, hovering in the back of my mind in lecture halls and seminars, perched on my shoulder as I sat amid walls of books in the London Library: comfort and warmth through the coming of winter. I fed on it like placenta, until I was ready for the birth.

Step-by-step preparations were made. At the beginning of December I rang Blackwell's in Oxford to check on an overseas account they had in the name of Dr. L. Ascherson, resident of New York City. I was a close friend, I said, due to travel to the States in a couple of weeks, and I wondered if there were any books he had ordered that I could pick up and take by hand. Save them the time and expense of postage. The young man treated my request as if it were a reasonably normal one. He came back ten minutes later to say yes, and could I confirm the address? In front of me sat a Blackwell's invoice, which I'd discovered in one of the volumes borrowed from Lenny's library on that last New York afternoon. I read out Lenny's address, typed neatly at the top:

P.O. Box 743, New York City 10022. The very same. Yes, Dr. Ascherson did have a request in for a couple of books: a new biography of Napoleon, translated from the French, and Clerkenwell's major study of the dissolution of the monasteries. But neither book was available yet. Publication dates were not until January. That would be too late for me. Yes, indeed it would. Never mind. I thanked him warmly for his trouble.

A week later I had to go to Oxford for a two-day conference. On the Saturday afternoon I made a trip to Blackwell's, where I bought a large number of books, for which I paid cash. I separated out two of the bigger volumes, a recent biography of Oliver Cromwell and a glossy tome on the Carolingian churches, and asked the girl at the desk if she would wrap them for airmail. I held the package in my lap all the way home on the train. Just feeling the weight of it gave me pleasure. Step by step . . .

Term ended and Christmas came, gray rather than white. I spent it alone. The twenty-fifth, Christ's birthday and the four-month anniversary of Elly's funeral. A very special day. I woke early, anticipation prizing my eyelids open while it was still dark. After checking that the door was still firmly bolted from the night before, I took a leisurely bath and a good breakfast. Then I rang Gem to avoid her ringing me. I sounded, she said, much better. Happy almost. I wished her *Joyeux Noël,* then took the phone off the hook. In the bedroom near my desk, I put on the radio, loud. The announcer was full of good cheer, introducing a concert of carols to be followed by a recording of Handel's *Messiah.* Music while you work. I arranged my tools on the desk. To one side the twenty leather juggling balls. To the other the package of Blackwell's books, a sharp new Stanley knife, and a pair of plastic gloves, my Christmas presents to myself.

I put on the gloves and began cutting through the leather skins, lifting out the inner plastic bags one by one, harvesting the crop, pure and fertile. Then I turned my attention to the books. They were wrapped in a padded bag, well stapled. Gently I removed the staples from one end: the surgeon removing stitches, intent on making the wound as neat as possible. I pulled out the books. They were plump and heavy, joined together by a rubber band and a Blackwell's compliment slip. Putting aside the picture book, I began with the biography. On the radio the opening chords of *Messiah* blasted into the room. It took me to the celebration of Christ's birth to disembowel Oliver Cromwell. "Rejoice, rejoice greatly, rejoice, O daughter of Zion." I worked slowly and with pleasure, leaving the flyleaves and the title pages with their dedication to Anne, "without whom this book would not have been possible" (thank you, Anne), then cutting into every page a large rectangular hole; marking it with a ruler, and gouging along the line with the Stanley knife. Precise and painstaking. There was a lot to say about Oliver Cromwell, a life's work, eight hundred pages including the index, and their removal made a deep and satisfying grave. "Then shall be brought to pass the saying, that death shall be swallowed up in victory." Oliver and *Messiah* finished, I started work on the Carolingians. By the time the second grave was dug, I was sweating lightly, and a man on the radio was reading Dickens.

Next came the packing. I had known the books would be too small to take all the cocaine. But the bags were tightly packed, and with pushing and persistence I managed to get three into Oliver and four into the Carolingians. It was enough. I didn't want to be greedy. The drugs weighed less than the words, but not so much as anyone would notice. I closed up the books and secured them with their Blackwell's label and rubber band. Cromwell's face regarded me with a cold, unforgiving stare. Lenny would have approved: a man of will and substance. I put both books in their bag and stapled it closed, using, as far as possible, the original holes. It looked, I thought, a very academic package.

Then I sat down with a pile of old newspapers and magazines and began cutting out words: enough words to write two letters. It took a long time. At some point during the afternoon the radio played the National Anthem, and Her Majesty told me of the pleasures of grandchildren and the Commonwealth, with rounded vowels like pebbles in her mouth. There followed more carols and another concert, and eventually I finished. There was one last task.

I took the rest of the plastic bags into the kitchen and poured the contents into the sink. I did this carelessly, deliberately without ceremony. Then I turned on the hot tap. The mound of white powder disappeared slowly down the plughole, all two hundred thousand dollars' worth. Outside it was dark. The wind rattled the windowpanes, and the central heating grumbled its way warmer. I opened a bottle of wine saved from my trip to Paris and toasted myself.

Merry Christmas, Marla, and goodwill on earth to all men. Except for one, that is. Then I took a sleeping pill and went to bed.

During the night of January 4 it snowed. I woke to feel its haunting stillness, muffling the city sounds. I got up, packed the books into the faithful canvas bag, and called a cab. Outside it was bitter cold. We crawled along gritted roads to Paddington, where trains to Oxford were running late. At midday I caught the 11:05, clutching a cheap day return in my gloved hand. The journey was dazzling, miles of white fields shimmering under a winter sun. The city center still had its Christmas decorations up, and the streets had turned to slush under the feet of an army of bargain hunters in the New Year sales. I pushed my way through them to the main post office, where I stood patiently in line. The man took the Blackwell's parcel without comment, weighed it, then counted me £8.45p of stamps. I moistened them on the little piece of sponge provided — I would not be identified by my saliva — then stuck them on, with as much care and symmetry as my gloved hand would allow. On the customs declaration form, I wrote the word BOOKS in childlike capitals with my left hand. I handed him the package and watched it disappear into a sack behind him. If there was a moment of glory, I expect that was it. From another queue nearer the door I posted the letters. Special delivery. Guaranteed to arrive within four days. It was pension day, and the place was packed. If the woman had time to read the addresses she certainly didn't seem interested. Head of the Drug Enforcement Agency in Washington and the Chief of Police for the City of New York. Both had names as well as titles. Names I had checked through international telephone calls made from my office. You couldn't be too careful. Which was why both envelopes had been typed on a machine from the Geography Department.

It was midafternoon. I stood outside and wondered what to do next. I felt suddenly numb, as if all the anticipated triumph and pleasure had been used up in the waiting, and now there was just the anticlimax of it all; the beginning of the rest of my life. I walked through the town and down to the river. From pavement to earth. On the ground, the snow had frozen into a thin layer of ice, which cracked and crunched under my feet. The backs were deserted, no one mad or sad enough to brave the cold. I began walking. And as I walked I thought of Elly. For the first time in many months. Not since the cemetery, when I had banished all memory of her for fear of the pain it would cause. Instead I had fed on hatred, and the promise of revenge, and that had been enough for me. But now all that was over, I opened up and let her in.

At first it hurt so much I couldn't bear it. The sight of her, the memory of her tearstained face in a darkened hotel room on that last afternoon, all hope and optimism splintered and gone. But then the picture changed: another Elly in another climate, sitting in the California sunshine, smiling and sure. From there I traveled further back, back beyond the time of Lenny to the years when she was exclusively mine. And as I thought of her in that crisp, clear winter's afternoon, I realized I was feeling something else, something as well as the grief, something that soothed and quietened. There was, inside me, almost a sense of her again. The images were familiar ones. This was the Elly I had cultivated over two years' absence: a deliberate attempt to construct a companion out of memory, a way of living without her. I had, during that time, almost acclimatized myself to memory rather than reality. Maybe, just maybe, I could do the same again. In which case she would always be there for me, at least through a past if not a future. It was better than nothing. Because without her what was there left?

I imagined her walking with me along the path, head down against the wind, hands clutched under her armpits for warmth, scuffing ice and leaves with the tips of her boots. She hated the cold. Always had done, even when we first met: would do anything to avoid hockey practice on a winter's day.

"You should wear more clothes," I said under my breath. "No wonder you're freezing."

I heard her groan softly, wind in the trees. "God, you sound just like my mother."

"I know. That's why I said it."

Above, a blackbird burst out of the tree and took off over the fields. I stopped to watch him go, lazy winged, a speck of black against the gray snow sky.

"Wouldn't you have liked to go to Oxford?" she said suddenly. "We came here once, remember? On a school outing. I was sick on the coach. You spent the whole time mooning around the cloisters like some female Rupert Brooke. In anyone else it would have looked like affectation. With you it just felt like destiny."

"I remember doing it." I did. "You were right. It was affectation."

"Poseur." She laughed, but the sound was whipped away by the wind. The cold bit into my face. "Come on," I said, turning back along the path. "We'll freeze to death out here. Let's go back to the central heating."

And so I took her hand and led her back through the streets of Oxford to the station. And she sat next to me all the way home.

Epilogue

Summer in the city. The students are long gone and I am adrift on an ocean of time. I have not been well. It was such a long winter. I forsook scholarship for current affairs and spent my life scouring back copies of New York newspapers. It was late May when I came across the following short piece in the *New York Post.*

Customs officers investigating a package of books containing two kilos of cocaine sent from England have uncovered a chain of murder and mystery. The books were addressed to Dr. Lenny Ascherson, a New York businessman reported missing from his Westchester home two months ago. Subsequent investigation led the authorities to connect Ascherson with a headless, fingerless corpse found on a Manhattan building site, and further forensic tests confirmed identification. Ascherson is suspected of having run a large-scale drug ring between South America, the United States, and Europe. His brutal murder is the last in a long line of recent underworld killings.

Poor Lenny. Those sculptured fingers and sleek cheekbones. Such poetic revenge. The image haunts me still. I suppose it was not quite the triumph I had been looking for. So many versions of the truth. Who killed him? Was it Tyler or J.T.? It hardly matters. I have tried explaining that to Elly, but I'm not sure she understands. We don't spend much time with each other now. I'm having trouble sleeping again. I put my flat on the market. It didn't seem safe anymore, too many noises in the night. I spend so little time there anyway. I work every day in the London Library, burying myself in the past. But there are shadows there too, and people's footsteps echo so on the metal floors.

I have been offered a year's teaching post in Dublin. The head of my department is very keen for me to take it. He has shown unexpected interest in me recently, hinted that I had been overworking and maybe I should see a doctor. I think there may have been a few complaints. Of course there is nothing really wrong with me. Except perhaps an overactive imagination. And that will fade with time. I might take the Dublin post. There is a girl in the records department at work. She is small and dark and laughs a lot. Reminds me of Elly. Sometimes I find excuses to go and talk to her. Dublin would be good for me. Don't misunderstand me. I am not dodging the issue. And I'm not sorry for what I did. He deserved to die. That's what I think. It's just I need a change of scenery. Somewhere people don't know me. And I do so like that rush you get when you first arrive at an airport, bound for wherever it is you are going. Don't you?

About the Author

SARAH DUNANT has written seven novels, including the *New York Times* bestseller *The Birth of Venus*, and edited two books of essays. She has worked widely in print, television, and radio, and until recently hosted the leading BBC Radio arts program, *Night Waves*. Now a full-time writer, she is working on her next historical novel, under contract with Random House and set in Renaissance Venice. Dunant has two children and lives in London and Florence.

We hope you have enjoyed this Large Print book. Other Thorndike, Wheeler, or Chivers Press Large Print books are available at your library or directly from the publishers.

For more information about current and upcoming titles, please call or write, without obligation, to:

Publisher
Thorndike Press
295 Kennedy Memorial Drive
Waterville, ME 04901
Tel. (800) 223-1244

Or visit our Web site at:

www.gale.com/thorndike
www.gale.com/wheeler

OR

Chivers Large Print
published by BBC Audiobooks Ltd
St James House, The Square
Lower Bristol Road
Bath BA2 3BH
England
Tel. +44(0)800 136919
email: bbcaudiobooks@bbc.co.uk
www.bbcaudiobooks.co.uk

All our Large Print titles are designed for easy reading, and all our books are made to last.

5	6	7	8	9	10
15	16	17	18	19	20
25	26	27	28	29	30
35	36	37	38	39	40
45	46	47	48	49	50
			58		